TEN FACTS ABOUT GARVIE SMITH

1. Lazy, rude, golden-hearted, aggravating, economical with the truth, kind (to those who deserve it).

2. Highest IQ ever recorded at Marsh Academy.

3. Lowest grades.

4. Best mates with Felix (cat burglar), Smudge (stupidest boy at school and proud of it), Alex (who's been selling something he shouldn't).

5. Wouldn't dream of telling his mother he loves her. Besides, she wants to move back to Barbados, and what's the point of that?

6. Smokes, mainly tobacco.

7. Liked by girls.

8. Hated by the police, teachers, other boring adults.

9. Exceptionally good at maths.

10. Scared of dogs.

A GARVIE SMITH MYSTERY

HEY, SHERLOCK!

SIMON MASON

David Fickling Books

31 Beaumont Street
Oxford OX1 2NP, UK

Hey, Sherlock! A Garvie Smith Mystery
is a
DAVID FICKLING BOOK

First published in Great Britain in 2019 by
David Fickling Books,
31 Beaumont Street,
Oxford, OX1 2NP

Text © Simon Mason, 2019

978-1-78845-065-2

1 3 5 7 9 10 8 6 4 2

Papers used by David Fickling Books are from well-
managed forests and other responsible sources.

MIX
Paper from
responsible sources
FSC® C018072

DAVID FICKLING BOOKS Reg. No. 8340307

A CIP catalogue record for this book is
available from the British Library.

Typeset in 11¾/16 pt Sabon by Falcon Oast Graphic Art Ltd.
Printed and bound in Great Britain by Clays Ltd, Elcograf S.p.A.

For Gwilym and Eleri

And in memory of Joe Nicholas (1951–2019)

1

It was a wet and windy August night. A storm was coming. Rain from the east began to fall in ragged bursts out of swirling cloud. There was a low groan of thunder, a sudden fracture of lightning, and the deserted downtown streets jumped with water. The long, low suburbs of Five Mile and Limekilns blurred under the downpour.

Up at Froggett, trees in the landscaped gardens of the elegant villas swung sluggishly in the wind. Froggett was the most expensive postcode in the city, a leafy enclave of tasteful old homes surrounded by woodland. None of the houses had numbers. They had names – 'Meadowsweet', 'The Rectory', 'Field View'. It gave them personalities, standing at ease with a sort of plush modesty behind pink brick walls or copper beech hedges in grounds laid out with ponds and lawns, tennis courts and terraces. Now, in the storm, rain-mist boiled in their immaculate gardens, their ponds crackled and fizzed, their exotic trees clashed their boughs.

It was midnight. In the living room of one of these houses – 'Four Winds', a late Victorian villa in biscuit-coloured brick, all gables and chimneys –

Dr Roecastle sat alone working on her notes. She was a senior surgeon at City Hospital, a slender middle-aged woman with dark hair in a feminine cut and a narrow face that never relaxed. From time to time she sipped herbal tea with a look of careful concentration.

The living room was a direct expression of her personal style. It was decorated entirely in monochrome: a white rug on the black japanned floor, a glossy black table on the rug, two sharply geometrical black-and-white sofas and a number of chairs receding towards the black glazed fireplace in the end wall, above which hung a huge silkscreen print of a black triangle against a brilliant white background.

Hearing thunder, she glanced towards the streaming window as it flared suddenly with the shocking exposure of lightning. Irritated, she looked at her watch. Eleven minutes past twelve. At that moment, cocking her head, she picked out a different sound among the clatter of the storm – the muted opening and closing of the front door, and she pushed aside her laptop and sat there, waiting severely.

Her sixteen-year-old daughter appeared, advanced slowly into the room, head down, and stood there, dripping.

'I don't call this ten o'clock at the latest,' her mother said after a moment. 'Do you?'

Amy Roecastle said nothing. She had a beautiful, unruly face – blue eyes, heavy eyebrows, a wide, crisp mouth – and she stood there, soaked, in black bondage trousers, German-issue army jacket and drenched woollen hat pulled down over her forehead, staring at the floor, saying nothing while her mother talked. She was very still. Occasionally she trembled. Water dripped from her sleeves onto the white rug.

'We had an agreement,' her mother said. 'Which you have broken. What's the reason?'

Her daughter remained silent. Blank-faced.

'There is no reason, of course,' Dr Roecastle said, watching Amy carefully. 'I don't know why I ask. Thoughtlessness is the reason. Selfishness. A complete disregard for anyone else.' She thought she saw her daughter briefly smile. 'Are you drunk?' she asked sharply.

Still Amy said nothing. Rain drummed against the windows, but the silence inside the room was very silent.

Her mother got to her feet. 'I'm going into the kitchen to get another cup of tea. You're going to wait here and think about your behaviour. And when you're ready, you're going to come in and explain yourself to me.'

Amy spoke. 'All right,' she said.

Dr Roecastle scrutinized her daughter for a moment, then turned and left the room. On her way, she stopped at the front door to put on the nighttime alarm, then went on to the kitchen.

There was a bang of thunder and almost

immediately another flare of lightning, and for a moment she thought she heard a cry somewhere, and muffled shouting, then a gust of rain clattered against the windows and the sound was lost. Sitting at the kitchen table, she pulled her collar round her throat and shivered.

She made her tea. Several minutes passed.

'I'm waiting,' she called out.

Waiting, she brooded. All summer Amy's behaviour had been intolerable and, reviewing the situation now, she felt all the force of righteous anger inside her. Frowning as she picked a speck off the rim of her cup, she rehearsed what she was going to say.

After a while, she called out again, more loudly, 'Amy! I said I'm waiting!'

At last, exasperated, she got up and went back into the living room.

Her daughter was no longer there. Just a wet patch on the white rug where she had been standing.

Dr Roecastle strode out of the room into the hall and stood at the bottom of the stairs.

'Amy!'

No answer. Only the rain trying to crack the windowpanes.

'Amy!' she shouted once more. 'I'm not chasing after you. I can wait as long as necessary. You *will* come down and explain yourself.'

A long rip of thunder reverberated round the house, and in the quiet aftermath Dr Roecastle heard the wind-bent trees shudder and moan. There was no sound anywhere in the house, but again she thought she heard a cry outside, immediately swept away by the crashing of the storm. She looked at her watch. It was half past twelve.

She went back into the living room and sat down at her laptop to wait.

2

Branches whipped Amy's face, and she slipped and fell with a cry, and got up wet, and staggered on again through the roaring trees. Rain blinded her. She ducked and skidded along the path as the storm boomed and crashed around her like a surging sea.

From time to time she paused, panting, to look behind her anxiously, wiping her eyes with a muddy sleeve and squinting through the darkness, before hurrying on again, drenched and shivering. Twice she cried out at shadows flung towards her by the wind. Thunder made a noise like cliff faces breaking apart; she fell again, hauled herself up and stumbled on.

She was already deep in the woods. In the heaving darkness she stopped and looked behind her. Her house was lost to view; there was nothing but the chaotic darkness of the wood. A sudden noise nearby made her spin round, looking frantically from side to side. Through the trees ahead there was a gap of moonlight flickering with rain, and she shielded her eyes and peered towards it. There was something there. What was it? Was it . . . a van? A van parked in the middle of the wood?

She stood in the shadows, dripping. Then one of the shadows lurched forward and grabbed hold of her.

3

As arranged, Smudge's brother picked them up in his Ford Transit at the corner of Pollard Way, a little after 6.00 a.m. He was a dark-haired man with a distracted face, and he said nothing, just glanced round once, as Garvie and Smudge settled in the back among the tools. The other men in the front said nothing either. One was a baby-faced giant with corkscrew hair and a missing front tooth. His name was Tar. The other was a pale Welshman called Butter. All three wore dust-caked boots, baggy sweat pants and hooded tops crusted and stained like the clothing of victims of violent crime.

It was a shiny, tranquil morning after the storm, nauseatingly early. All along Town Road it looked as if the tide had just gone out, leaving behind the naked city exposed to daylight: puddled pavements, flooded parking lots and glittering streaked windows of empty showrooms. They drove east into the rising sun, a second van following, towards the dual carriageway. On the radio were sports results, jingles and a news report on a riot in Market Square the night before: extensive damage to property, a fatal shooting, an injured policeman and a police horse with a broken leg.

Smudge paid it no attention. He was seventeen and had just passed his driving test. He lovingly patted the armrest of his seat and said, 'What I like about the Custom is the rear air suspension. Don't you? Like gliding.'

He grinned. He was a morning person.

Garvie said nothing. He was not.

'Though to be fair,' Smudge added after a moment, 'I like it all. Adaptive cruise control, parking distance sensors. Auto high beam.'

Butter turned in the front seat. 'Intelligent all-wheel drive.'

'Rain-sensing wipers,' Tar said, also turning. 'Everyone loves a rain-sensing wiper.'

They all looked at Garvie.

Butter said to Smudge, 'Doesn't say much, does he? This genius friend of yours.'

'Vans not really his thing,' Smudge said apologetically.

Tar said, 'What's your thing then, brainbox?'

Garvie looked at him. 'Listening to van lovers talk,' he said. 'Luckily.'

There was banter in the van. It washed over Garvie like the radio, which twittered on with other news stories. Two people critically injured in a collision on the ring road. An arson attack on an office block. Further delays to the police enquiry into money-laundering at the Imperium casino: they still hadn't traced the principal 'smurf' – the runner who had been colluding with the club to exchange dirty money for gambling chips.

On the ring road they hit the early morning commuter traffic and went slowly in convoy as far as the Battery Hill exit, then picked up speed climbing the shallow hill towards Froggett Woods.

'Well,' Smudge said, peering out of the window, 'it's another great day for fencing.'

Garvie reflected on this. It was a fresh, sunny morning in August, that much was true. It was also his ninth straight day of working for Smudge's brother, of weekend overtime, early morning starts, jolting rides and chit-chats about vans. And, of course, *fencing*. Two months ago he had been at school; now he was in the world of work. He wasn't sure about this world yet. It got up too early for his liking.

The van went slowly now along a single-track lane, rocking slightly, between high green banks frilly with hedge parsley, the houses a rumour of roof tops and gables beyond hedges and walls. Turning by an ornamental bus shelter with a thatched roof into a recess, it pulled up in front of the gates of 'Four Winds', home of Dr Roecastle FRCS. Before Smudge's brother could speak into the entrance intercom, the automatic gates trundled open, and both vans accelerated up the long sweep of driveway towards the house.

A silence descended, a moment of contemplation

of the day's fencing ahead. And into this silence, Garvie said calmly:

'Something's wrong.'

Smudge looked at him blankly.

'It's a non-sequential term,' Garvie said.

'What is?'

'You know what she's like. The woman whose house this is.'

'Yeah. Bit uptight. So?'

'Always ready for us when we get here. All the blinds up. Door open. Waiting for us with our instructions.'

'Yeah. So?'

'Every day so far she's asked who we were before she buzzed us through. Today she didn't ask. Just opened the gates straightaway. Non-sequential term. It breaks the sequence.'

After he finished speaking there was a moment's silence, then, except for Smudge, they all broke out laughing.

They drove up the rise until the house came into view, and then Smudge said, 'Oh, look, the blinds are still down.'

Now they fell silent, looking up at the house as they drove slowly along the front and parked. It was true. All the blinds in all the windows were still down.

Dr Roecastle was not waiting at the door.

Everything was still and quiet.

There was a moment of awkward silence. Butter

11

said, 'Come on, man. It's not exactly hardcore. What do you want us to do, call emergency?'

'No need,' Garvie said. 'If it's bad enough, she'll have done that already. She's that sort of woman.'

Even as he spoke, a squad car came into view round the drive behind them.

Getting out of the vans, the men stood there warily, watching it approach. They were not the natural friends of law enforcement; Smudge's brother was just coming off the back of a charge – or, as he preferred, 'mistake' – about stolen property. The car came at speed up to the house and stopped, and a policeman got out. He was a small, trim, bearded man of about thirty wearing a correct-looking uniform and bulletproof turban, and he carefully adjusted both before setting out towards the house. As he went, he glanced over at the eight men standing awkwardly by their vans in their sloppy sweat pants and creosote-smeared hooded tops – and stopped in surprise, staring at Garvie.

'What are you doing here?' he asked.

'The fencing.'

For a moment Inspector Singh's mouth remained open, but it seemed that he could find nothing else to say, and at last he collected himself, gave a curt nod and made his way to the front door, which was abruptly opened as he approached by Dr Roecastle, still wearing her clothes from the night before, who said in a critical voice high-pitched with emotion, 'At last!'

She showed him into the house and shut the door behind them, and all the men outside turned as one to stare at Garvie, who was smoking quietly, looking at his boots.

4

In the black-and-white living room Dr Roecastle sat on one sofa and Detective Inspector Singh of City Squad sat on another with his recorder.

'So,' he said, in his usual careful manner, 'tell me what has happened.'

She told him her daughter had disappeared.

Speaking with emotion, much of which was anger and irritation, she described Amy coming in after midnight, their conversation, and how she'd waited for Amy to continue it.

'At first I didn't realize she'd left,' she said. 'I'd just put the alarm on, I would have heard her if she'd deactivated it, so I searched here for an hour before it became clear. How she left the house I don't know. Then I waited for her to return for two more hours before calling the police. I haven't been to bed at all.'

'And, understandably, you are now very anxious,' Singh said.

'I'm furious. I'm extremely busy and I frankly don't have time for this.' She looked at him critically. 'And now that I've reported her missing, I'd like to know what happens next please.'

Singh outlined standard procedures. A risk

analysis would be run and the police would coordinate with other services to develop the appropriate strategy; local support would synchronize with national networks. Dr Roecastle did not appear to be listening.

He moved on to practical details. Could Dr Roecastle remember what Amy had been wearing when she left the house? Could she provide him with a recent photograph?

Abruptly, Dr Roecastle raised a hand to silence him. Getting up, she went to the door and looked out into the hall before returning to her seat.

'I have workmen on the premises,' she said, 'not all of them well-behaved, and I have to keep an eye on them when they come in for a toilet break. There are valuable artworks in the hall. Please go on.'

She listened to him with a distracted air while he asked about Amy's movements the night before.

'She spent the evening in town with a friend,' she said. 'When she got in, frankly I thought she was drunk.'

'She's sixteen, you said?'

'Seventeen next February. She's at Alleyn's studying for her A levels.'

'She's very young to be drinking in town, isn't she?'

'I can tell you don't have children of your own,' she said drily.

He hesitated, then went on, 'Who was the friend she was with?'

'Sophie Brighouse. A friend from Alleyn's. She lives at Battery Hill. She's the same age as Amy. Of course, they can both look much older when they want to. Suddenly they think they're adults.'

'Do you know where they went?'

'Sophie will be able to tell you. You'll want to talk to her, I assume.'

He nodded. 'I'll go there on my way back to the station.' He thought for a moment. 'Has anything happened recently to prompt Amy to leave? Trouble at school? An argument with a boyfriend?'

'She doesn't date.'

'An argument with you?'

'She argues with me all the time. Little things.'

He thought about that. 'Has she left home before?' he asked.

Tight-lipped, Dr Roecastle said, 'In February she disappeared for three days.'

'What happened?'

'We didn't involve the police, we conducted our own enquiries. We were worried, of course. Searched everywhere. And in the end we found her checked into a hotel in town. Where she'd run up a not inconsiderable bill for room service. My daughter thinks she's a rebel, Inspector, wearing all these goth-punk clothes, flirting with unsuitable boys, smoking weed at her exclusive school, protesting against politicians, but at heart she's like any teenager. Thoughtless. Thinking only of herself. She's discovered alcohol. The summer's been an absolute nightmare. I'm a single parent, I have a senior position at the hospital, and it's not possible for me to monitor her all the time. Because it's still the holidays I'd allowed her to go out on the understanding that she would be back by ten o'clock at the latest. She wasn't. Of course, I've been too liberal with her, I know that. She has her own credit card. We're not poor. She's extremely privileged, but she's abused my trust. She did it before; now she's doing it again.'

Singh considered all this. 'What was happening in February?' he asked after a while.

Dr Roecastle's nostrils flared. 'That's when my marriage was falling apart.'

Singh nodded sympathetically. 'And Amy's father lives elsewhere now?'

'He does.'

'Could she have gone to him last night?'

'Amy's relationship with her father is even worse than with me. They don't talk. Besides, neither of us knows where he is. He's a mathematician; he conducts research into string theory. The last I heard he was in California. Typically, he's not around to give me support now. No. I warned Amy that if she ever did anything like this again I would not hesitate to involve the police, and I've been as good as my word. You could do worse than begin your search with the smart city hotels.'

Singh nodded. 'Thank you for being so frank. We'll check the hotels, of course.' He paused. 'Is there anything else that might be relevant?'

'I think I've said all that needs to be said. I'm handing this over to you.'

He got to his feet. 'May I look upstairs?'

'Why?'

'I'd like to see Amy's room.'

Dr Roecastle shrugged and led him out of the living room into the entrance hall.

'Oh, one other thing,' Singh said as they went. 'Did anything else unusual happen last night?'

'Unusual?'

'Anything out of the ordinary.'

She stopped to think at the foot of the stairs, and Singh waited, glancing round the hallway. Like the living room, it had been redesigned along artistic lines, the original dark panelling of the nineteenth century replaced by modern features in glass, pale wood and chrome. Now sunshine flooded in through sash windows, brightening the whitewashed walls and illuminating the artworks which rested on plinths in front of them, tubular shapes in glossy scarlet ceramic vaguely resembling sex toys. It was less like a room than a gallery, in fact – the result, Singh thought, of a firm, even rigid, mind. The only thing out of place was a Doc Martens shopping bag – buff-coloured, thick black lettering – dumped on its side at the end of a table. Otherwise, it was almost mathematically perfect.

'Now you mention it,' Dr Roecastle said, 'by a strange coincidence there was another disappearance last night.'

'Really?'

'Our guard dog, Rex. A Dobermann. He sleeps in the outhouse. He was chained up last night as usual, but this morning he's gone.'

'Might Amy have taken him with her?'

She looked at him with scorn. 'I doubt the Astoria or the Hilton allows pets. No. In any case, Amy's always been frightened of the dog. He's a bit of a brute, in truth. The chain is old and worn; I expect it broke. Perhaps the storm agitated him and he pulled against it. Still.' She reflected for a moment. 'It is a coincidence. Two disappearances on one night.'

She proceeded up the stairs, Singh following with a frown.

As he went, he checked his watch – 08:00. Amy Roecastle had been missing for seven and a half hours.

5

In the garden, above the rise and out of sight, Smudge's brother stepped across to give Garvie an earful.

'*Something's wrong?* I'll tell you what's wrong. Your fucking useless bit of fence.'

The garden of 'Four Winds' was an extensive affair half an acre in size, rising beyond the stone-flagged patio up three levels of trimmed lawn to a picturesque fringe of shrubbery. The new fence, half finished, would be just as extensive, a graceful, encircling stockade, disappearing at points above the rise, threading its way through the edge of wood-land. Classic featherboard in red cedar, comprising twenty-nine taper-sawn pales per 2.4 metre section on 150 mm traditional cured gravelboard, with 2.70 metre inter-posts capped with custom ball-and-collar finials. Not insignificant. Not cheap either.

The section along the side of the lane had been erected by Tar and his team, the section from the gate to the pond by Butter's team, and the section between pond and shrubbery, furthest away from the house, by Smudge's brother, with Smudge and Garvie's help. All of these sections stood complete, trim and upright – except for Garvie's single 2.4 metre span, in the middle of Smudge's brother's section, which had somehow collapsed.

'Three days,' Smudge's brother said. 'That's how long you were working on it.'

Garvie said nothing.

'Well?'

Garvie said, 'Two days, four hours, fifty minutes.'

Smudge's brother stared at him. 'Two days, four hours and fifty minutes of complete fucking uselessness.'

Garvie took a drag on his cigarette and blew out smoke. 'It was standing last night,' he said.

'You understand they're meant to last longer than a day, don't you? We don't do pop-up fencing, you know that, right?' Smudge's brother walked around the fallen panel while Garvie finished his cigarette. 'How many times did I tell you about the depth of the post holes? What did I tell you about the ballast? Did you even use a string line?'

Garvie gazed down the garden to the shrubbery, where Smudge had stopped working and was looking at him anxiously. He lifted a hand and waved.

'Well, Wonder Brain?' Smudge's brother said. 'What's the news?'

'Remind me what a string line is.'

Smudge's brother went a little apeshit, and Garvie lit another Benson & Hedges, and waited until the noise stopped. When he looked again, Smudge's brother had gone back down the lawn, where he was

21

talking to Tar and Butter. Garvie sighed. Without looking at his fallen panel, he walked across it, stepped over the remains of the previous wire fence at the perimeter of the garden, and stood there for a moment, smoking. Ahead of him, to his left, was rough pasture. To his right was woodland, a thick black tangle of birch and sycamore. A footpath, coming up from the direction of the road, curved at the fence where he stood and ran away between pasture and wood into the distance.

It was peaceful, the birds in the trees sounded pleased with themselves, and Garvie stood there envying them. As he turned to go back into the garden his attention was caught by something on the fallen panel of fence. He bent down and removed from a nail head a long scrap of black fabric.

Like the rooms downstairs, Amy's bedroom was beautifully decorated. Unlike them, it was chaotically messy. Alternative lifestyle and music magazines were scattered across the floor. The wardrobe doors were open, and clothes had spilled out onto the floor, where they lay in heaps, punk and goth-wear, mainly black, combat gear, T-shirts, belts with silver studs, aggressive-looking shoes and lace-up boots.

Singh stepped through the mess, looking round alertly.

Little details struck him: on a high wooden shelf above the bed, a row of tiny hand-painted papier-mâché models of people in strange poses; on the

22

desk, still lit by the anglepoise lamp, a half-finished picture of a woman in war paint; next to it a school exercise book open at an advanced maths problem. The impression of an artistic, clever, rebellious person.

For a moment he hesitated by some flowers in a jug on the mantelpiece. They looked out of place, thin and dirty, not the usual immaculate bouquet from a shop.

He went to the window and looked out across the garden below, then stood again in the room, looking around. Something in the wardrobe caught his eye, and he went over to it, pulling on his latex gloves.

After a moment he called Dr Roecastle in.

'Is this the jacket she was wearing last night?' he asked.

Stuffed into the back of the wardrobe's top shelf was a short olive-green jacket, still soaked through.

Dr Roecastle peered at it. 'Yes, I think so.' She frowned. 'Though I don't know why she would have taken it off before going out again. The rain was torrential.'

'Does she have another coat?'

'She hates coats. I didn't even know she had this one. She has a budget with which to buy her own clothes.' She gestured around the room. 'You can see for yourself what the result is.'

They went out onto the landing.

Singh said, 'The bedroom is now an area of police interest. It will be sealed so that Forensics can carry out their work. Please avoid going into it.'

'Another inconvenience.'

'And now I'd like to look in the garden, if I may.'

'Really? Why?'

'Her bedroom window is unlatched. Does your alarm monitor only the ground floor?'

'Yes.'

'I assume your daughter knew that when she climbed out.'

Leaving Dr Roecastle there, he went down the stairs and out of the front door round to the patio at the back of the house. There, he saw immediately the clear impression of footsteps visible in the flower bed directly below Amy's bedroom window. The soil was still wet from the rain the night before. Mud footprints led across the patio onto the grass, and Singh followed them up the rise, bending occasionally in his usual methodical way to examine marks on the ground, watched warily all the way by the men doing the fencing.

Only one of the fencers did not stop work to watch him. But it was towards his length of collapsed fence that Singh made his careful way.

As he reached it, Smudge's brother reluctantly went over and Singh immediately began to question him.

'All this fencing is new?'

'Yeah.'

'All of it erected before last night?'

'Yeah.'

'Including this panel?'

'Yeah.'

'Did you notice anything different this morning?'

'Yeah.'

'Well? What?'

Smudge's brother finally took his cigarette out of his mouth and pointed it diffidently at the fallen panel. 'It'd fallen down.'

Both men looked at Garvie, who had continued all this time with his back to the policeman, whistling quietly to himself.

'Anything else?' Singh asked Smudge's brother. 'As you arrived this morning, for instance, did—'

Without turning round, Garvie said, 'Probably it fell down when she climbed over it.'

Smudge's brother frowned and opened his mouth.

Singh said, 'Why would she have climbed over?'

'To get to the other side.'

'What's on the other side?'

'The path.'

Smudge's brother looked in bewilderment from one to the other. 'Listen—' he began anxiously.

'You can see the worn line in the grass as well as I can,' Garvie said to Singh, who looked back across the lawn.

'So you think she came this way often? Why?'

''Cause it's quiet. 'Cause it's better than having the bother of going through that securitized gate down there. 'Cause it's where she was heading.'

Singh nodded. He looked across the fallen panel at the dark woodland, dense and faintly steaming beyond. As soon as he saw it, he felt a sensation of foreboding.

'Where does the path go?' he asked.

Smudge's brother said, 'I don't know.'

Garvie said, 'Somewhere she wanted to get to. She must have been pissed off to find someone had put a fence up here. Especially,' he added, 'such a sturdy one.'

Singh reflected on this. 'Your post holes aren't deep enough,' he said at last.

Garvie shrugged. He looked at Smudge's brother, who was furiously smoking a Marlboro as he looked from one to the other. 'Anyway,' Garvie went on, 'I can't stop to help you, I've got to get on, mate. We're all busting a gut to get a job done here.'

Singh gave him a look, nodded briefly and moved off. Smudge's brother, who had remained in an attitude of confusion all this time, gave Garvie a long and hostile stare, then went the other way. And Garvie stopped work, leaned against the one upright fence post and lit up another Benson & Hedges.

He was joined a few moments later by Smudge. Together, they watched Singh intercepted at the bottom of the lawn by Dr Roecastle.

She seemed to be giving him a hard time.

'Posh girl gone missing then,' Smudge said, as they watched.

'Not before flattening my fence.'

'I think your post holes could have been deeper.'

'Don't start.'

They watched Singh take out a notebook and make a note.

'Couldn't help overhearing on my toilet break,' Smudge said. 'She took the dog. Bit of a monster, seems like. Went off to one of them funny hotels that cater for pets.'

'Is that right?'

'That's the rumour. Could be something else.'

'Got any ideas?'

'I'm toying with terrorism. It's an angle. Posh girls go for terrorists. What do you think?'

'I'd keep working on it.'

Smudge looked at him. 'Hey, Sherlock. You really ought to give plod a hand. You know, like last time.'

'Not sure he'd appreciate that, Smudge.'

'What I'm saying is, he needs it. With these coppers it's always one step forward one step back. Or sideways,' he added after a moment's reflection. 'One minute they've worked it out, next minute they've lost their bicycle clips.'

Garvie looked at his piece of fallen fence and sighed.

'Tell you what,' Smudge said, 'I'll give you a hand getting it back up, then you can show me those things in the house you told me about. You know the ones I mean.' He winked.

Garvie sighed. 'They're not actually sex toys, Smudge. You know that, right? They're art. Sculpture.'

'I just want a look,' Smudge said in an injured voice.

'OK. Later. But no touching. And you'll have to keep your voice down. We don't want that woman on our backs.'

'You don't have to worry about that, mate. I'm good with people.'

'You're not good with her. Trust me.'

Down by the driveway Dr Roecastle said something sharply, turned abruptly with a gesture of impatience and marched into the house, leaving Singh to walk thoughtfully back to his car. Garvie stubbed out his Benson & Hedges and looked up at the shimmering blue sky. It was, unfortunately, a glorious day for fencing. Smudge handed him a hammer and they got to work.

6

*Location: large, comfortable kitchen, farmhouse-
style.*
Aspect of interviewer: calm, neat, careful.
Aspect of interviewee: blonde, nervous, defiant.
*Aspect of interviewee's mother: face carved out of
wax.*

DI SINGH: Thank you both for agreeing to talk to me
at such short notice. You know why I'm here?

SOPHIE BRIGHOUSE: You say Amy's gone missing.

DI SINGH: I'm afraid that's the case.

SOPHIE BRIGHOUSE: But I don't understand what that's
got to do with me.

DI SINGH: I'd just like to ask you some questions about
last night.

SOPHIE BRIGHOUSE: But nothing happened last night.

DI SINGH: You went into town?

SOPHIE BRIGHOUSE: Market Square. We didn't stay
there long. We had a drink in Chi-Chi, on the
corner of Well Street, and then we went over
to The Wicker and got in at Wild Mouse, the
underground place. We weren't there that long.
An hour, an hour and a half. They started

playing all that psychedelic stuff so we left and came home. That was it.

DI SINGH: And how did you get home?

SOPHIE BRIGHOUSE: Cab. We always get cabs – that's part of the deal. Amy got out at hers, and I came on here.

DI SINGH: And what time did Amy get out?

SOPHIE BRIGHOUSE: Around midnight. Just before.

DI SINGH: That's late to be getting home, isn't it? How old are you, Sophie? Sixteen?

SOPHIE BRIGHOUSE: I've got my own key so it's not a problem. I'm allowed out twice a week so long as my grades don't drop.

MRS BRIGHOUSE: [*drily*] This is an arrangement that's currently under review, Inspector.

DI SINGH: You didn't go to the rave that was taking place in The Wicker?

SOPHIE BRIGHOUSE: Of course not.

DI SINGH: You weren't in Market Square during the riot?

SOPHIE BRIGHOUSE: No.

DI SINGH: OK. Did you meet anyone at Chi-Chi or Wild Mouse?

SOPHIE BRIGHOUSE: No. I mean, we talked to some guys, but we didn't know them or anything.

DI SINGH: You don't know who they were?

SOPHIE BRIGHOUSE: [*shakes her head*] Just guys.

DI SINGH: Did Amy talk to anyone on the phone?

SOPHIE BRIGHOUSE: Not that I remember.

DI SINGH: How much alcohol did you both drink?

SOPHIE BRIGHOUSE: [*hesitates*]

MRS BRIGHOUSE: Sophie. The inspector needs to know exactly what happened.

SOPHIE BRIGHOUSE: We had a margarita at Chi-Chi. They were *so* expensive. At Wild Mouse we just had water.

DI SINGH: Was Amy inebriated?

SOPHIE BRIGHOUSE: No way. Neither of us was.

DI SINGH: Did she take any illegal substances?

SOPHIE BRIGHOUSE: Of course not. We're not stupid.

DI SINGH: So, at the end of the evening, would you describe her as sober?

SOPHIE BRIGHOUSE: Completely.

DI SINGH: Was she behaving normally?

SOPHIE BRIGHOUSE: Of course.

DI SINGH: Did anything happen during the evening to upset her?

SOPHIE BRIGHOUSE: Nothing.

DI SINGH: Are you sure?

SOPHIE BRIGHOUSE: Nothing happened. That's why . . .

DI SINGH: That's why what?

SOPHIE BRIGHOUSE: [*pause*] That's why all these questions are pointless.

DI SINGH: [*pause*] OK. Just a few more things now. After the taxi dropped her off, did you see her again that night?

SOPHIE BRIGHOUSE: No.

DI SINGH: [*pause*] Did you speak to her?

SOPHIE BRIGHOUSE: Why would I speak to her?

DI SINGH: Did you?

SOPHIE BRIGHOUSE: Course not.

DI SINGH: OK. Can you answer some more general questions about Amy now? What sort of girl is she, would you say?

SOPHIE BRIGHOUSE: Well, she's really, really smart. You know her dad has, like, two brains, and her mum's this top surgeon, well, she's like them. But she's really cool too. I mean, she's completely her own person. And she's loyal. If you're her friend, she'll stick with you, no matter what.

DI SINGH: OK, that's interesting. Is there anything particular that's been on Amy's mind recently?

SOPHIE BRIGHOUSE: Not really.

DI SINGH: Anything you can think of will be helpful.

SOPHIE BRIGHOUSE: Well. [*pause*] She's in a bit of an angry phase.

DI SINGH: Angry? About what?

SOPHIE BRIGHOUSE: She argues with her mum.

DI SINGH: Anything else?

SOPHIE BRIGHOUSE: Not really. But she's got this whole guerrilla girl thing going. Like, you know, protest.

DI SINGH: What does she protest against?

SOPHIE BRIGHOUSE: Injustice, poverty, repression, stuff like that.

DI SINGH: I see. [*makes notes*] Has anything in particular upset her? Her mother said Amy was distressed by her divorce.

SOPHIE BRIGHOUSE: Frankly, I think she's glad her dad's

out of the picture. He's a bit of a nut. He went abroad, I think.

DI SINGH: What about Amy's friends? Does she have many?

SOPHIE BRIGHOUSE: Everyone likes Amy.

DI SINGH: What about boyfriends?

SOPHIE BRIGHOUSE: Boys especially like Amy. Boys are, like, queuing up. She doesn't date, though.

DI SINGH: No one she's close to?

SOPHIE BRIGHOUSE: No.

DI SINGH: OK. Just before I go, let me ask again if you can think of anything – anything at all – that might have upset Amy last night. It needn't be an obvious thing. Something she might have seen or overheard. Something that might have come up in your conversations.

SOPHIE BRIGHOUSE: I've told you. Nothing happened. It was a completely normal evening.

DI SINGH: Thank you then, Sophie. I'll give your mother my contact details in case you remember anything else later.

Sophie Brighouse got up quickly from the kitchen table and hesitated with her hands on the back of the chair. In the light from the kitchen window she was quite startlingly blonde, with small features, creased mauve eyes and pale lashes. Her eyes were full of tears. She bit her pale pink bottom lip.

'You're going to find her, right?' She had a lisp.

Singh said, 'That's our aim.'

'I mean, she's going to be all right?'

Singh made no response, and Sophie turned and went across the room with rapid, self-conscious steps.

Singh turned to her mother sat at the end of the table. 'Before I go, can I ask if you share your daughter's view of Amy Roecastle?'

Mrs Brighouse was one of those people who always pause before they speak. She kept her heavy-lidded eyes on Singh while she pursed her lips slowly. 'Yes, I think so,' she said at last. 'Amy's a bright girl. A bit wayward at the moment. I will say one thing, though.'

'What's that?'

'I've always thought she's a girl who has her secrets. Although they're all a bit like that at her age.'

Singh nodded, made a note. 'And what's your opinion of her mother?'

Mrs Brighouse blinked slowly, paused. 'I think she's an appalling woman,' she said at last.

Singh did no more than raise an eyebrow. 'And what is her relationship like with her daughter?'

'It's her relationship with her daughter that I'm thinking of.'

He walked across the lane outside Cross Keys House, looking around. A typical village scene: a row of cottages, a post office, a bus stop and the Royal Oak pub, all picturesque, quiet and deserted. Beyond the pub was the entrance to a path into woodland.

It came to him at once.

Stopping abruptly in the middle of the lane, he turned and retraced his steps to the Brighouses' home and banged on the front door.

Mrs Brighouse opened it and looked at him in surprise.

'The path,' Singh said, 'next to the pub over there. Where does it go?'

This time she didn't pause. 'Through the woods,' she said, 'all the way to Amy's house.'

Singh said, 'Please call down your daughter. I have some more questions for her.'

Location: large, comfortable kitchen, farmhouse-style.
Aspect of interviewer: tense, controlled, assertive.
Aspect of interviewee: blonde, weeping.
Aspect of interviewee's mother: face in resting mode of disapproval.

DI SINGH: So. She called you. She told you she was coming over.

SOPHIE BRIGHOUSE: [*weeping*] She told me not to tell anyone.

DI SINGH: This is important, Sophie. You should not have kept it secret. What time was it?

SOPHIE BRIGHOUSE: Half past twelve. I was already in bed.

DI SINGH: What were her exact words?

SOPHIE BRIGHOUSE: She said, 'I'm coming over.' I was,

like, 'What? *Now?* What's going on?' I mean, it was totally out of the blue. I'd only just left her at hers. But she wouldn't tell me any more. She just said, 'No one must know this, Soph. *No one.*' And then she rang off. I didn't know what to do. I waited for her. I went downstairs and hung around the back door. But she never came. I kept calling her but she never answered. I assumed she'd changed her mind. About two o'clock I went back to bed.

DI SINGH: Where was she calling from? Inside or outside?

SOPHIE BRIGHOUSE: Inside.

DI SINGH: What did she sound like, her tone of voice? Was she upset?

SOPHIE BRIGHOUSE: No, but . . . there was something odd about the way she talked, something . . . [*beginning to weep again*] She sounded like she was trying not to panic. [*sobbing*] And that was the last time I heard her!

DI SINGH: I understand how painful this is for you, Sophie, but it was really important you told me this. The more information we have now, the better our chance of finding Amy. Now, someone from our tech team will come to collect your phone. We will need to examine it.

SOPHIE BRIGHOUSE: OK.

DI SINGH: [*pause*] You've told me that nothing happened during the evening to alarm her. Nothing at all. Yet no sooner has she left you

36

than she calls you in a panic. How can we explain this?

SOPHIE BRIGHOUSE: I don't know. I really don't. I don't understand it at all.

DI SINGH: OK. I have no further questions. But, Sophie, if anything occurs to you after I've gone, anything at all, please get in touch straightaway.

At the front door Singh said to Mrs Brighouse, 'I'm grateful to your daughter for her honesty. In the end.'

She looked at him in her heavy-lidded way. 'I'll ask you now what my daughter asked you earlier. Will you find her?'

It was Singh's turn to pause before answering. 'I have every confidence,' he said carefully.

'Oh dear,' she said after a moment. 'That sounds ominous.'

He made no response but turned, crossed the lane, entered the footpath by the side of the pub and walked into the woods, glancing at his watch.

It was 10:30. Amy Roecastle had been missing for ten hours.

7

Garvie and Smudge stood together in the elegant hallway of 'Four Winds'. Smudge was looking at a bright red tubular object on a plinth, and Garvie was looking at the shopping bag on the table.

'Know what? It's nothing like a sex toy.'

'Keep your voice down, Smudge.'

'Sex toys don't have ends like that. What would you do with an end like that? An end on a sex toy is like—'

'Give it a rest, all right. She might be about.'

Smudge moved across the hall to another piece. He pushed his face up close and scowled.

'Back off, Smudge. You can just look at it. You don't have to smell it.'

'This one here,' Smudge said, tapping the ceramic shape with a stubby finger, 'this one is more like a sex toy. Now, with an end like that, if you were fit enough, you could—'

There were rapid footsteps in the living room, and Dr Roecastle appeared at speed through the doorway with a fierce expression, clearly keen to shout at someone.

Smudge put his hands behind his back and stepped

away from the sculpture. 'You're welcome,' he said pre-emptively.

Dr Roecastle avoided looking at him. She said to Garvie, 'I've told you before, that sculpture is valuable.'

Garvie looked at it. 'Why?'

That seemed to catch her off-guard. She closed her mouth to think. 'It's an Emily LeClerk,' she said. 'One of her early pieces. Now, listen to me—'

'Late,' he said.

That caught her off-guard too. 'Pardon?'

'Done 2008. LeClerk was born in 1951. Makes her fifty-seven. I call that late.'

She stared at him for a moment. 'Are you telling me that you know this piece?'

He shrugged. 'I've read the label.'

She was suddenly angry. 'I will not have workmen coming into my house picking up the art. I shall inform your line manager.'

For a moment they stood there facing each other, radiating hostility. Then Smudge the peacemaker stepped forward.

'By the way, I just wanted to say, on behalf of the boys, about your daughter . . . We're sorry.'

She glared at him. 'You needn't concern yourselves about it,' she said indignantly. 'Or indeed talk about it, thank you.'

Smudge nodded understandingly. 'No, but I know you'll be suffering, right? Maybe it's just a terrorist hook-up in that hotel of hers. But I been thinking.

Could be kidnap. Brainwashing. Or, you know, a flit with some gangster, who's got her pregnant maybe. I mean, let's face it, you don't even know if she's dead or alive. Or, you know, in-between.'

Garvie said in a low, warning voice: 'Smudge.'

Ignoring him, Smudge went on. 'I'm just saying to the lady. You're lucky you've got Garv here.'

'*Smudge!*'

'Can't trust the police – you know that, I know that. But Garv now, he like totally sorted the Chloe thing, and the thing with the Gimp. All right, he arsed it up for that copper, but the cases got well solved. He can help.'

'*Help?*'

'Yeah. He's like one of them bloodhounds. And he's really, really good at maths.'

'Are you seriously—'

'Yeah, top set and everything.'

Garvie took hold of Smudge's arm, not lightly. 'Thanks, Smudge. Appreciate it, mate. Let's go.'

'Yeah, but. I was just—'

'Forget it, she's not listening.'

Dr Roecastle gave a twitch. '*Not listening?* This is my daughter we're talking about. What could you possibly tell me I don't already know?'

Garvie shrugged. 'Doesn't matter.'

'What? Tell me.'

'All right.' He turned to face her. 'You ought to be a lot more scared than you are.'

Dr Roecastle's eyes bulged; for a moment she was

speechless. 'On the contrary,' she said at last, 'I could be a lot angrier.'

'Why?'

'Because I've a very good idea what's happened. Without a thought for anyone else, she's just decided to storm off.'

'Why?'

'Because of some little thing. As usual.'

'Like what?'

'I don't know.'

'Like the shoes?'

She hesitated, frowned.

He nodded towards the table by the living-room door where the shopping bag still lay. 'What's in the Doc Martens bag?'

'A type of boot. Lace-up. The sort of thing a thug wears.'

'Which you were insisting she took back to the shop, right? Ongoing argument for the last three days.'

She stared at him angrily. 'Have you been eavesdropping?'

'I got eyes. I been here all week. She must have bought them at the weekend, right? Give her a clothes allowance, do you? Monday, the boots were in their box, in the bag on that table; you must have put them out for her to take back to the shop. Tuesday, the box was gone, the empty bag in the bin; obviously she'd taken them back up to her room. Wednesday, the day she did a bunk, they were back on the table, in

41

the box, in the bag, this time with a post-it stuck to it, DO IT NOW in really angry writing. If you want a bit of maths, it's a periodic sequence with oscillation. 1, -1, 1, -1. Going nowhere. Someone's bound to throw a fit, storm off.'

For a moment she could only look at him blankly.

'Well,' she said finally. 'There we are then.'

He shook his head. 'Doesn't explain it.'

'Doesn't explain what?'

'Doesn't explain why she was so terrified.'

An awkward silence grew in the room.

'What on earth makes you think she was terrified?' Dr Roecastle said at last.

'Why else would she take the dog?'

She stood there for a moment without moving or speaking, or, apparently, breathing. Her face was white with fury and alarm. Then she turned at last and swept away to the safety of the kitchen.

In the hall there was a moment's silence. Smudge said regretfully, 'Got to work on your people skills, to be honest, Garv.'

Garvie said nothing.

'We could chat about it.'

No reaction.

'Garv? Don't let it get to you, mate. We'll talk it all out, it'll be OK.'

But Garvie seemed to have instantly forgotten what had just happened. He stood staring at the shopping bag on the table, frowning. Smudge opened his mouth, hesitated, looked all around the hall, as if he might find something else to say hanging on the wall somewhere; and when he'd finished doing that he found that Garvie had gone. He really was a strange boy. No people skills at all.

Sighing sadly to himself, Smudge went back to the sex toys for another look.

8

Garvie went back up to his stretch of fencing. Smudge's brother shouted something to him, and Garvie waved a hand, nodding politely, stepped over his fallen panel and continued onto the path beyond. Lighting up, he stood there a moment, breathing out smoke, admiring the country scene, the sunlit green pasture to his left, the placid green trees on his right.

It had been very different for Amy last night. He thought about that.

Dark, unstable, ferociously wet. The pasture would have been a rough screen of racing shadows, the flattening marsh grasses obscured by the driving rain, the trees a heaving mass of blackness. She'd had the dog with her too, complicating things, slipping and sliding about.

What had she been up to? What was she scared of? Something bad. Bad enough to make her take the dog for protection.

He went down the path. Thirty metres on, poking at the edge of the path with the toe of his boot, he noted some streaks of kicked-up earth, still damp in the shadow of the woods. Further on, a skid mark.

He proceeded, smoking.

Another thirty metres and he stopped again. Here, where the path curved to the left, there was a break in the thorny undergrowth at the side, almost invisible. A narrow animal track disappearing into the trees. And on some brambles just inside the tree line, another scrap of black fabric.

He frowned. Again he imagined the chaos of the woods last night, rain lashing down, branches clashing, drenched blackness shaking the packed trees.

Why had she left the path?

He threw away his cigarette butt and pushed his way into the undergrowth. It was hot among the trees, steamy, still wet underfoot from the rain. He slithered as he went, bending and twisting, parting low thorny stems, stepping over trailing creepers. Birds called around him. After a while the track became more distinct. He went along it warily, glancing about him, checking the ground. There were scratch-marks here and there that could have been made by a large dog's paws scrabbling for purchase, deep prints in the mud churned up by running feet.

Why had she been running?

He went on through the tangled vegetation. The track forked; he hesitated, found more footprints, and went on again, following them, off the path now, deeper into undergrowth.

Gradually he began to feel afraid.

She'd run through the trees, then she'd run off the path into the thicket. Why?

He pushed his way through it carefully. Everything was quiet. All he could hear was the noise of his own shallow breathing. These signs – scraps of fabric, footprints that may have been hers, branches she may have broken – were all that Amy had left behind. But he began to have the feeling that he was not alone. As if something was there with him, now, in the woods. As if his fear was slowly leading him to it.

He stopped and looked around him, and listened, and went on again.

The first sign was a faint noise at the edge of the silence, unreal. Gradually it became real. A low hum, a buzzing.

There was a screen of alder ahead of him. Cautiously he went towards it. The buzzing grew louder. Through the shadows he saw movement. Innumerable flies seething in a cloud, settling in clumps on a darker shape humped in the under-growth. Fat shiny bluebottles in a swarm. Garvie put his hand over his mouth and went closer, slowly, moving among the flies that rose around him, step-ping through the thicket towards the spot, and found at last, lying there on the ground, legs splayed out, head twisted back, the body of the Dobermann.

He found a clearing nearby, a grass patch surrounded by birch trees narrowing at one end into a broad mud track for vehicles, and walked round it until he found a convenient stump, and sat on it, thinking.

It was bright there after the damp darkness of the trees and he lifted his face to the sun and breathed the warm air.

The dead dog was called Rex: its name was on a medallion attached to its collar. It was big animal, heavy-looking; its body had already begun to swell in the heat. Its head was twisted at an angle from its shoulders as if wrenched round violently, and its lips were curled back from its powerful jaws in a fixed snarl.

For a while Garvie thought about the dog. It was a monster, like Smudge had said. Then he thought about the sort of a person who might kill such a dog.

At last he got up and began to make his way through the wood to the path.

Singh was walking briskly along the path from Sophie's house towards 'Four Winds'. The wood stood tall around him, beech trees in full leaf, blocking out the sun. As he went, he called the station and arranged for a member of the tech team to pick up Sophie's phone. He also put through a call to a local volunteer group to organize a sweep of the woods. He looked at his watch again. He had to return to the Police Centre as soon as possible to deliver his preliminary report.

He was anxious. He knew now that, for reasons still unknown, Amy had set off in the storm for Sophie's house. She hadn't got there. Increasingly he feared she had been in some sort of danger. He peered into the crowded trees at the side of the path, and his heart sank, thinking of them heaving in the rain and wind.

He walked on. The path bent down over a shallow stream and rose again. Dusty shafts of sunlight filtered through the leaf canopy and dissolved in the shadows. He looked at his watch and increased his pace as the path rose up the hill. At the top of the crest it flattened and broadened, the trees shrank back, and he emerged into sunlight with the pasture on one side of him. Ahead of him he saw the gables of 'Four Winds', and he accelerated again. He walked on for another hundred metres or so, and then a boy stepped out of the bushes just ahead of him and stood in the lane wiping his hands.

Singh came to a stop. 'Garvie! What are you doing here?'

The boy turned and frowned. 'Just taking a break.'

'Isn't this a long way from the house?'

'Compared to what?'

The boy stared expressionlessly at Singh with those unblinking blue eyes, and Singh felt again his strangeness.

Garvie said, 'Been talking to one of her friends?'

'Yes, Sophie Brighouse. How do you know?'

'Where else would she be headed at midnight in the middle of a storm?'

'OK, but—'

'But she didn't get there.'

Singh paused. 'No, she didn't. How do you—'

Garvie parted the branches at the side of the path. 'Something in here you need to see.' He glanced back at him.

'What?' Singh said.

Garvie said, 'Hope you're not bothered by flies.'

'Flies?'

But Garvie had turned away, and Singh followed him into the trees.

9

An hour later, downtown in the Police Centre, Singh handed his preliminary report to the chief.

The chief was a narrow man with a narrow expression and a thin-lipped mouth that looked as if it didn't get much use, and he sat behind the gleaming, bare desk in his office, listening impassively.

When Singh had finished, he thought for a moment before speaking.

'She left the house voluntarily?'

'It seems so.'

'Then the likeliest outcome is that she will return as soon as she's calmed down.'

'But her behaviour—'

'Is entirely consistent with a certain sort of teenager. Acting on impulse. Heightening the drama.'

'But the dog—'

'Has no bearing on the case until we establish that she took it with her. We don't even know the cause of its death yet.' He fixed Singh with his gaze. 'Have you ascertained the whereabouts of the girl's father?'

'No, sir, not yet. He's on sabbatical and his university doesn't know where he is. He's an eccentric,

50

apparently. They think he's flown to California to stay with someone working in the same field. I've been making enquiries there.'

'And the hotels?'

'Nothing, sir.'

The chief continued to look at him.

'Sir,' Singh added, 'I have a feeling that we need to make progress very quickly.'

'Is there evidence that a crime has been committed?'

'No definite evidence.'

'Then there can be no justification for extra resources. We're stretched thin as it is, with Bob's investigation into the Imperium, and now the murder during the riot in Market Square.' He paused. 'But keep me informed. As it happens, I know Elena Roecastle slightly. She needs to be carefully managed until her daughter returns.'

He made a minimal gesture and Singh took his leave.

At the far side of the open-plan area there was a coffee machine and television, and Singh paused to watch it.

On the over-bright screen a policeman was being interviewed about the riot in Market Square the night before. His name appeared in unnecessarily colourful lettering alongside his shimmering head: Detective Inspector Bob Dowell. He was a bald man with a wide face generously spread around a squashed nose, crumpled mouth and small, watchful eyes, like an ex-boxer, which in fact he was; and on his left arm, in the manner of a man bravely casual about such things, he was wearing a sling.

In answer to the interviewer, he described what had happened. An illegal rave in a disused warehouse at the end of The Wicker had got out of hand. Early in the evening fighting broke out inside, and at ten o'clock the police were called in. Panic-stricken people streamed out of the building across the canal and railway tracks into Market Square, where Inspector Dowell, off-duty, was relaxing in a bar. There were running battles between rival groups of partygoers throwing stones and bottles, and the police, mounted and armed with night sticks. Shots were fired.

Dowell said modestly that he had done no more than any officer in his position would have done: directed his colleagues, assisted the wounded and, finally, helped to bring the situation under control. In the course of these efforts, he had been hit in the arm by a stray bullet. But, as he reminded viewers, another man – named as Joel Watkins from Tick Hill, a dispatch rider – had been killed. It was not yet known what he had been doing in the square. Uncorroborated witness statements, as contradictory as usual, put him variously fighting the police, fleeing the fighting, sitting quietly at a café with a man wearing a beanie with the HEAT logo on it, and lying drunk in the gutter.

The investigation into his death, presumed accidental, had been placed under Inspector Dowell's direction, and he would be tireless in his efforts to bring the perpetrator to justice. Swirly mobile-phone footage of the riot began to play – Dowell visible in black leather jacket stalwart among panicking men and women, baton-wielding policemen towering above their rearing mounts – and Singh turned away and continued towards the staircase.

Before he reached it, however, the stair doors opened and Bob Dowell himself appeared. No longer in uniform, he was wearing blue jeans, white T-shirt and a single-breasted black leather blazer. When he saw Singh he stopped and took off his Ray-Bans, and gave him a thin smile.

They were not friends.

Singh spoke first. 'How is your arm?'

Dowell displayed his sling with another smile. 'Caught one for the boys,' he said in his growling Scots.

'And you're looking after the case yourself? As well as the Imperium investigation?'

'Leading from the front, Raminder. There's no other way. And how about you? Found that missing teenager yet?'

Singh hesitated. 'Not yet.'

'You'll be wanting some more manpower.'

'I've just been talking to the chief about that.'

'Has a crime been committed?'

Singh said nothing.

'Then you won't get it,' Dowell said. 'A shame. I know how hard it is working on your own.'

He slipped his shades back on, and went, stocky and bandy-legged, towards the chief's office, raising a hand in farewell without looking back, and Singh went up the stairs to his own office above.

His office had been a storeroom previously, a cramped, windowless space with marks on the walls of multiple shelves now removed and a partial desk installed in the small space away from the door. It was all that could be found for him, apparently, after his recent rehabilitation. Sitting there, he gave himself briefly to meditation. He thought about rehabilitation. He reflected on the paths of fate, so obscure and difficult to follow, and on people, both young and old, who lose their way – who go missing. As a Sikh, he believed in the notion of karma, that our actions are our fate, that we travel slowly towards a higher purpose, without understanding how.

He was the youngest DI in the city, the result of his discipline and diligence – and, some would say, lack of humour – but his professional ambitions had been frustrated by the mismanagement of two recent cases, in puzzling circumstances. After the failures of the Chloe Dow and Imperium investigation in May he had been, for the first time in his career, formally reprimanded; during the Pyotor Gimpel case the following month he had actually been suspended. Oddly, both cases had been successfully concluded. He thought about this. Faults he could acknowledge as his own, successes too. But the disruptions in his karma, he believed, were strangely linked to another person – a sixteen-year-old boy called Garvie Smith, who had interfered in both investigations. Now he had turned up again. It seemed uncanny.

He did not believe in the uncanny. He believed in truth, or revelation, however difficult. He gave himself a little shake. Philosophizing would not help him find Amy Roecastle. The first seventy-two hours were crucial. After that, the chances of a missing person returning safely diminished rapidly.

He thought about Amy setting out from home the night before, taking the dog with her, heading for Sophie's house. What urgency, what fear, could have driven her out in the storm – and into the woods?

He looked at his watch. Without assistance, there was so much he had to do himself – to make contact with Forensics and the Missing Persons Bureau, make a start on identifying witnesses from Chi-Chi and Wild Mouse, organize the sweep of the woods. Too much. But he would do it. He lifted his phone and called Len Johnson, Chief Pathologist.

It was 14:30. Amy Roecastle had been missing for fourteen hours.

10

The summer afternoon ripened and faded. At 'Four Winds' the fencers completed their day's tasks, put their tools back in their vans and drove home, leaving the shadows to creep slowly across the empty garden. Dr Roecastle sat in her living room with a cup of herbal tea, uselessly alternating between anger and indignation. Detective Singh turned on the overhead light and worked on in his makeshift office in the Police Centre. And at Flat 12, Eastwick Gardens, Garvie Smith and his mother, his uncle Len and aunt Maxie and their infant son Bojo ate their dinner. Scrambled fish and pumpkin fritters. Aromas of cinnamon and frying butter hung like a veil of spice in the steam: the smell of faraway Barbados, where Garvie's mother had grown up.

It was a small flat, drab in layout but bright in furnishing, with one room for cooking and living, two bedrooms and a bathroom without a bath, situated on the top floor of a six-storey apartment block backed onto the ring road, just across from the car plant.

Uncle Len put out his plate for just a little more. Aunt Maxie frowned, and he said, in all innocence, that if he didn't make use of the remaining scrambled fish he might just waste away. There seemed no danger of that. At one hundred and thirteen kilos, Len Johnson was the solidest thing in the room, not excluding the sofa. He was chief pathologist of the city police, an expansive, relaxed man who carried his authority with an air of ease.

He modestly suggested another rum punch, to go with the scrambled fish.

Outside the Forensics labs Aunt Maxie was in charge and, after her, Bojo, three years old, a tyrant of satiny skin and enormous dimples. Uncle Len didn't mind; he liked it. With a fresh rum punch in his fist, he turned his goodwill on his sister.

'Have you lost weight? What've you done with your hair? I don't know why, but you're looking good.'

It was true. Whatever the reason, Garvie's mother seemed to have got younger. She was a broad, handsome woman with smooth black skin, a pretty mouth and a firm gaze. Her hair was newly braided and she was wearing a kaftan in bright orange and green.

Uncle Len winked at his nephew sitting opposite him. 'Eh, Garvie?'

Garvie made no response. His mother was his mother. She had a loud voice, an over-developed sense of good behaviour and an irritating ability to detect bullshit. It was true, there had been changes recently, but they didn't have anything to do with her looks.

New arrangements were in place now that Garvie had left school. They had a deal: he was paying her rent; she was treating him like an adult. She'd bought him a real-leather wallet, to put his first wages in, and because, as she put it, 'Everyone needs to be given something once in a while'. He understood. From now on she would be giving him the occasional gift, not providing for him. She didn't quiz him any more about what he was doing, or nag him, or inspect his bedroom, or get on his case about personal hygiene. But she didn't always cook for him either. And, unexpectedly, she'd started doing stuff on her own, going out more herself, to the movies or for drinks with colleagues from work. It was a bit difficult getting used to.

'Doing anything this evening, Garvie?'

'No.'

'Tired after a hard day's work, eh?'

The truth was: his friends were busy. Smudge had gone with his brother to a van showroom out-of-town. Felix was helping out Tiger at Burger Heaven. Dani was working an evening shift in the back office of Imperium. The world of work: ruining their social lives.

And at that moment the doorbell went. A little look of surprise went around.

Garvie's mother spoke into the intercom. 'Yes?' she said. '*Who?* Oh, I'm sorry. Yes, come up, of course.'

A few moments later Detective Inspector Singh walked in.

'Raminder!' Uncle Len got up to greet him.

Singh stood there, looking out of place. He was still in uniform. He had come from work, he said, in the hope of finding Len there. He had a question.

'You could have called, Raminder. No need to come all the way out here.'

Singh looked shifty. 'I was in the neighbourhood,' he said. He turned to Garvie's mother. 'But I apologize. I'm interrupting.' He looked around. Exchanged a wary glance with Garvie.

'We're just finishing. Please. Have a drink. Sit down.'

Accepting a glass of water, he held it formally, almost reverentially, in front of him.

Uncle Len said, 'You never get chance to say the important things at work, Raminder, so I'll say it now. It's good to have you back after all that nonsense.'

'Thank you.'

'What's your question?'

'I was going through the forensics report from Amy Roecastle's house and couldn't find anything on the coat Amy was wearing. An army jacket.'

'Yes. German manufacture, well-made, double-lined. Heavy-duty sort of thing.'

'I have a suspicion about it.'

'What's that?'

'It's big for her. At least two sizes larger than her other clothes.'

'You think it didn't belong to her?'

'I wonder. Will your report throw any light on it?'

'Doubtful, I'm afraid. It was soaked right through. Really drenched. Most of the biology will have been damaged.'

They were all silent for a moment.

Singh said to Garvie, 'It was a surprise to see you up there today, Garvie. I hope fencing is proving interesting.'

Uncle Len turned to Garvie in surprise. 'You're working at the house of the girl who's disappeared?'

'Yeah.'

'Why didn't you say?'

'No one asked.'

Garvie's mother said, 'I know Dr Roecastle from the hospital. She's a difficult woman.'

'That's an understatement.'

She fixed her son with a suspicious look. 'You haven't been bothering her, have you, Garvie? She might be difficult but I can't help feeling sorry for her right now.'

'No need. She's sorry enough for herself.'

'I hope you're not interfering.'

Singh said cautiously, 'In fact, Garvie has been helpful.'

They were all frankly astonished.

Singh described the finding of the Roecastles' dog.

'But what were you doing in the woods in the first place?' his mother asked.

'Cigarette break.'

Frowning, Garvie's mother asked Singh about

the investigation. He admitted to both anxiety and frustration. Working on his own, progress was going to be slow. Long hours would not be enough. Without formal assistance, he needed luck. But there had been no luck so far. Since the public announcement of Amy's disappearance that morning, the police had received several sightings from members of the public – Amy on a bus with a bloody bandage round her head; Amy behaving strangely in the shopping centre in town – but none of them could be confirmed; they were the usual dramatic imaginings of people reacting to the drama of the news. What they now knew for certain was more worrying still.

He told them about the phone call Amy had made to Sophie, her midnight flight along the path, her disappearance into the thickest part of the woods.

Uncle Len interjected a comment about the dog. 'By the way, Raminder, we've got a very early indication on the death. TNI: traumatic neck injury. It's possible there was a natural cause – but equally possible that someone broke its neck. Which would have taken uncommon strength, not to say savagery.'

There were all quiet for a few moments.

'What sort of girl is Amy Roecastle?' Len asked the detective.

'If you listen to her mother, she's moody, disobedient, thoughtless and selfish.'

By chance, both men happened to glance at Garvie.

'I like the sound of her,' he retorted. He looked at Singh. 'What manpower you got?'

'Just me for the present.'

'Not being funny, but that's not enough.'

'No crime has been committed.'

'How do you know?'

His mother objected to his tone. 'Garvie!'

'It's all right, I'm going anyway. I've done my bit.' He got to his feet.

Singh said to Uncle Len, 'I'm very worried. To leave the house in the dark, at the peak of the storm, to take a dog for protection, and to go into the woods, is an act of special desperation.'

Uncle Len nodded. 'What would make her do such a thing?'

'I think perhaps she was in danger.'

'What danger?'

'I don't know. Nothing out of the ordinary happened all evening. She was sober and calm. She got home safely. She agreed to have a talk with her mother. And five minutes later she was fleeing into the woods. Why? I don't know yet.'

There was a silence after he said this. Into this silence, Garvie said casually, 'You don't know 'cause you're not thinking.'

'*Garvie!*'

'Not thinking about what?' Uncle Len said crossly.

'About real things.'

'What do you mean? Like what?'

'Like her jacket.'

There was a silence.

Uncle Len said, 'I just said. There's almost no chance of any useful information from the jacket, it's soaked through.'

'Don't you see? That *is* the information!'

And he went into his bedroom and shut the door.

He was irritable and he knew it. Half past eight. Early. All his friends were busy; he didn't feel like going out anyway. He didn't feel like doing anything, in fact. For a few minutes he stood there uncertainly. On the floor was one of his old school textbooks, *Mathematical Analysis*, and he picked it up and flicked through the pages. Arithmetic and geometric sequences. He dropped it again, and lay down on his bed, face to face with the ceiling. From the living room he could hear the continuing muted voices of his mother and Singh, probably still talking about Amy Roecastle, why she'd left, what she'd done next.

A series of events with gaps in it.

A sequence containing unknown terms.

After a while he took out his phone and called Abdul. Abdul drove a cab out of the rank on Bulwarks Lane, a beautiful, uncomplicated man. When he first came over from Morocco he had been befriended by Garvie's mother, and remained joyously grateful to the family.

'Abdul, mate. Garvie.'

Abdul's goodwill seemed to radiate out of the phone. 'My Garvie man, how is?'

'Is good, thanks. Got a question for you.'

'For you, Garvie, is *plaisir*.'

'Does your cab log times of passengers' journeys?'

'*Bien sûr*. Is *obligatoire*. I have machine.'

'Good. Don't suppose you took a girl up to Froggett last night, did you? House called 'Four Winds'. About midnight.'

'*Non*. Was not I.'

'Could you ask around, find out which cabbie did?'

'For sure.'

'I need the exact time they dropped her off.'

'I comprehend. I will ask now, quick, quick.'

'Cheers, Abdul.'

He rang off and lay there, staring at the ceiling.

11

Six storeys below his bedroom, at the entrance to Eastwick Gardens, Garvie's mother said goodbye to Raminder Singh.

'I feel I should apologize for my son's attitude,' she said. 'Not just for now, but for all those other times as well.'

He shook his head. 'No need. How old is he?'

'Sixteen. Going on seven.'

'His attitude is his own.' He paused. 'When I was his age . . .' he began, and then his phone rang. 'Excuse me.'

He did not recognize the number.

'Hello?' he said. 'Detective Inspector Raminder Singh.'

A refined voice said, 'This is Jane Brighouse, Sophie's mother. I know it's late, but I wonder if you could come over. My daughter has thought of something else she wants to say.'

Singh said to Garvie's mother, 'I must go.' He hesitated. 'Please don't worry about your son on my account.'

'You're very generous. I'm afraid he hasn't found his way yet.'

65

'He's on his way. He just doesn't realize it.'

He turned, a little stiffly, as if he felt he'd been too informal, and walked quickly to his beige-coloured Skoda Fabia, and Garvie's mother went back inside the building.

In the kitchen of Cross Keys House, they sat around the table. Sophie had evidently been crying again; her face looked spongy and swollen. But she held Singh's gaze when he asked her what she wanted to say to him.

'I don't honestly know if it's anything. But you said get in touch anyway.'

'Yes, please.'

She took a breath. 'There's this guy's been hanging round. I've only just thought of it.'

'What guy?'

'I've only seen him a few times. I don't think he's from Froggett. He looks sort of east city to me. Older. Like twenty, twenty-five. He drives this old white van.'

'What do you mean, "hanging around"?'

'We were joking that he was Amy's stalker. We'd turn round and he'd be there, across the road or under the trees. I saw him in front of Amy's house. And we saw his van a couple of times parked at the side of Rustlings Lane, on the other side of the woods. He was sitting in it, smoking, not looking as if he was doing anything, just hanging about. Of course,' she added, 'it might be nothing.'

'Why do you say "*Amy's* stalker"?'

'It was definitely her he was looking at.'

'I see. What did she think about it?'

'She's not the nervous type, she just laughed it off. I didn't think it was serious either. But now I don't know.'

Singh thought. 'How often have you seen him?'

'Just now and then.'

'When did you first notice him?'

'Maybe two or three months ago.'

'What sort of van does he drive?'

Sophie frowned. 'Well. It's white. And it's old. I don't know anything about vans.'

'And you've seen it parked where?'

'Round about. Sometimes on the road in front of Amy's house.'

'Have you seen him in the woods?'

'No. But a few days ago I saw someone on the path at the back of 'Four Winds'. I think it could have been him. I was in Amy's bedroom, and I called her over, but when she got there he'd gone.'

'What was doing?'

'Just looking up at the house. That was the odd thing. Like I could *feel* him staring. He looked . . . nervous. He was sort of moving his head from side to side, you know the way people do to relieve the tension in their necks, but he kept his eyes on the house all the time.'

'OK.' He made notes. 'Anything else?'

Sophie shook her head and Singh turned off his recorder. 'Thank you, Sophie. This is very helpful.'

'Do you think it's important?'

'I don't know. It might be. Would you be able to provide a police artist with a description of this man, do you think?'

She nodded.

'Good. I know it's late, but if it's all right with you I'd like to get someone to come over immediately. I'm sure you understand that in the case of disappearances we want to make progress as quickly as possible.'

She nodded again.

He turned to Sophie's mother. 'In the meantime, can you let me have the names of as many of your neighbours as you know? I'll want to ask them too about this man and his van.'

Sophie had begun to cry once more; she left the room with her mother, and for a moment Singh sat there alone. Obvious conclusions were often too easy, but the possibility that Amy had a stalker was a new and alarming development.

He put through a call to the station to organize the police artist.

So the first day of Amy's disappearance ended. 22:00. She had been missing for twenty-one and half hours.

12

The second day of Amy's disappearance was another great day for fencing, warm but fresh after a second heavy downpour during the night. In the middle of the morning Smudge and Garvie took a cigarette break, and stood looking across Garvie's panel, still lying on the ground, at the woods beyond. They were being swept by a volunteer force of neighbours and friends marshalled by Singh. From time to time they heard shouts among the trees.

'This girl gone missing,' Smudge said thoughtfully. 'What's she look like, do you think?'

'If she's out there she's probably still damp.'

'No, but, I mean, you know, looks-wise.'

'Oh. Just your type, Smudge.'

'Really? Why d'you think that?'

'One hundred per cent probability. All girls are just your type.'

Smudge nodded. 'That's true. Weird, when you think about it.' He cleaned his ear for a while.

'Interesting, though,' Garvie said.

'I think I'm just made for love.'

'No, not that.' Garvie gestured towards the woods. 'All this.'

'Oh. Yeah. They're after someone already. Did you hear? Plod's put out a picture of some guy they want to interview. "Seen in the vicinity". And, hey, you'll never guess what.'

Garvie looked at him. Thought about it. 'He drives a van,' he said after a moment.

Smudge's face fell. 'You've spoiled it. And vans aren't even your thing.'

'I could get interested in vans, Smudge.'

Smudge frowned. 'Could you?'

'If I had a genuine expert telling me about them.'

Smudge looked modest.

'I hear they're good over rough ground,' Garvie said. 'Dirt tracks through woods, that sort of thing.'

Smudge lit up, but before he could share some of his encyclopaedic knowledge about tyre traction, rear air suspension and the like, his brother appeared to remind them that there was a fence needed putting up this year.

'Never mind, Smudge. Laters.'

Garvie gazed for a moment longer at the woods, then bent to the gravelboard and resumed work.

Not far away, out of sight in the woods, a dozen people were moving slowly in a line through the undergrowth, head down. They were wearing hiking gear, hi-viz jackets, and most of them carried poles. One or two had brought their dogs, which moved between them energetically. From time to time one of the searchers called out, and Singh went over so they could show him what they'd found. They had begun the sweep at 05:30, just after daybreak, and they were getting tired. All they'd found so far were a few scraps of black material caught on briars and the usual items of litter.

The overnight rain had been unfortunate. Footprints and other marks in the earth had been obliterated. And progress remained painfully slow. The artist's impression of 'Amy's stalker', the man in the van, had so far led mainly to calls from cranks, all of which had to be carefully sifted. Singh glanced at his watch, sighed, and moved off again with the rest of the search party, making their laborious way towards Battery Hill.

It was late in the afternoon before he returned to his office at the Police Centre. More responses to the artist's impression of the suspect had come in and he went through them methodically. The drawing had shown a lean-faced young man with overhanging eyebrows and dark hair, but the respondents had paid little attention to this. The man they had seen was sometimes young and dark, sometimes young and blond, sometimes middle-aged; one caller remembered distinctly that he had a patch over one eye. They were slightly more consistent about the van, which had been described in the suspicious vehicle notice as 'white' and 'old'. Several Froggett residents claimed to have seen it parked in the neighbourhood, up on the pavement alongside the main road, or in

Rustlings Lane, beyond the woods. One elderly lady – a dog-walker – said she had seen it rocking violently from side to side on the verge one night, though it had driven off before she was close enough to find out what was happening.

A friend at MID – the motor insurance database – had provided Singh with a list of local owners of white vans, and he began now to work his way methodically through it. He focused on those in the right age bracket, then everyone else within a twenty-mile radius, concentrating first on the east city districts: Limekilns, Five Mile and Strawberry Hill.

It was slow-going. The light panels overhead burned evenly as if time did not pass, though outside, across the wasteland of parking lots and old brick warehouses and glass-plated skyscrapers, sunshine dimmed, shadows lengthened and daylight failed at last. By ten o'clock contact had been made with most of the people on the list, without result. There were three owners left, all of them older men: a decorator in Brickfields who had been finishing a job in Froggett; a window-cleaner from Tick Hill; and a middle-aged odd-job man called PJ, an eccentric apparently, who lived in a converted garage in Halton Woods, further off. None of them fitted the physical description of the 'stalker'.

Fearing he would be too tired later, Singh got up and stood in the corner of the room to say his evening prayers. Eyes closed, under his breath he recited lines from the *rehras sahib* – 'Where is that door of yours, and where is that home, in which you sit and take care of all?' – and then his phone rang.

It was the switchboard. There was a Dr Roecastle on the line, wanting to speak to him urgently.

Singh glanced at his watch. 'Put her through.'

Dr Roecastle came on, her voice clear but unsteady. 'There's a man in the garden.'

'Now?'

'A few minutes ago.'

'Tell me what you saw.'

Her voice was over-loud, as if she was holding the phone tightly against her mouth. 'A man on the lawn,' she said, 'near the outhouse.'

'What was he doing?'

'Looking up at the house. At Amy's window.'

'Is he still there?'

'I don't know.'

'I will come now,' Singh said, and rang off.

13

As his car drew up, she opened the door to him, but he went past her round the side of the house onto the lawn. It was dark and colourless in the garden, a sunken pool of shadow pressed round by cut-out shapes of trees and bushes in heavy black silhouette. Somewhere in the invisible woods beyond, a bird sang, tranquil and lonely. Singh went across the grass, scanning this way and that, to the gap in the fence and looked down the lane. He went down the slope to the outhouse, then returned to the main house.

Dr Roecastle said, 'Has he gone?'

'There is no one there,' he replied. 'But the outhouse has been broken into.'

They sat in the black-and-white lounge. Singh took out his recorder and put it on the table between them. 'Tell me what you saw.'

ELENA ROECASTLE: A man in the garden.

DI SINGH: Can you describe him?

ELENA ROECASTLE: It was too dark. I saw his outline framed by the doorway into the outhouse. He was very still, as if he was concentrating.

DI SINGH: Young or old?

ELENA ROECASTLE: Young, I think. In his twenties.

DI SINGH: Why do you think he was in the garden?

ELENA ROECASTLE: I don't know. I got the impression he wanted something. And that it was [*pause*] something to do with Amy. I don't know why I thought that. But he was looking up at her window. As if, whoever he was, he had some sort of . . . intention. He seemed . . . menacing. It was the way he stared. He was moving about a bit, rolling his shoulders, as if he was preparing to . . . do something. It has shaken me. I'm frightened.

DI SINGH: Did he attempt to get into the house?

ELENA ROECASTLE: No. He moved away, up the lawn.

DI SINGH: Towards the broken fence panel where the path is?

ELENA ROECASTLE: Yes. After that I didn't see him again. I phoned you.

Singh put away his recorder.

'It's possible this is a coincidence,' he said. 'It might be an opportunist, someone who has taken advantage of that fence panel being down to come in and see if there was anything worth taking. But it is also possible,' he added, 'that there is a connection with Amy's disappearance. We can't rule that out. We will need Forensics to look more closely at the outhouse.'

Sitting upright on her chair, Dr Roecastle stared

at him, white-faced. The event had changed her attitude towards her daughter's disappearance, he could tell at once. Irritable and dismissive only the day before, she was now in the grip of her worst fears.

'She's not in a hotel, is she?' she said at last, her voice fragile, unstable.

Singh said carefully, 'Not as far as we can tell. We've rung round, but so far there has been no evidence to support this view.'

'Is there any trace of her? Her credit card?'

'There's been no activity on her card.'

There was a longer pause.

'She took Rex, didn't she? She took him because she was frightened.'

Singh hesitated. 'There is that possibility.'

'Is she in danger?'

Singh said carefully, 'We must avoid jumping to conclusions. But of course we must also consider all the possibilities.' He hesitated. 'There have been further developments since I last spoke to you, in fact.'

'What developments?' she said quickly.

'Concerning Rex.' He described what they had found.

She got to her feet and began to pace up and down in agitation. 'I don't understand. You think that someone's *killed* him?'

'I'm afraid it's possible.'

'In other words' – her voice quavered – 'it's also possible that someone has attacked Amy.'

He said nothing.

She sat down and stood up again.

'I told you how irresponsible she is,' she said. 'Now you tell me this. She's *vulnerable*. She's only sixteen!'

Singh said nothing. He saw how agitated she was becoming.

She faced him. 'I assume you now have more resources. Do you?'

He began to explain, and she interrupted him.

'So what's being done?'

He told her about the partial sweep of the woods carried out by volunteers. 'And we have been following other leads,' he said.

'What leads?'

Singh took a breath. As carefully as he could, he began to explain about the white van, and the man described by Sophie.

'A stalker?' Dr Roecastle cried.

'It's not yet clear.'

'The man who attacked her?'

'We can't yet be certain that she has been attacked.'

'The same man in the garden tonight.'

Singh reluctantly acknowledged the possibility.

She looked dazed, sickened. 'A man has attacked my daughter,' she said hesitatingly, as if gingerly trying out this new reality. 'Perhaps taken her somewhere in his van. Is keeping her. A man has attacked and abducted my daughter and is keeping her somewhere, *using* her.' She put her knuckles in her mouth while Singh watched her anxiously. 'Who is he?' she asked suddenly.

'We don't yet know.'

'Surely you can trace him through the sightings of his van?'

Singh began to explain about the notorious unreliability of witness descriptions. The type, size, make and even colour of the van were still unclear.

She interrupted him. 'I assume you have databases you can search through. Surely you've been doing that.' Her voice was shrill.

'We have not yet completed the research.'

'Why not?'

'It takes time.'

She became emotional. 'This stalker, this attacker, this man from east city or wherever. He's not going to wait for you to find out who he is. What else are you doing?'

Singh told her that a suspicious vehicle alert had been posted on various sites, and that he had already checked many of the local van owners, but Dr Roecastle was not impressed. She was incredulous.

'Your plan is to wait until he comes forward to help you with your enquiries? Suspicious vehicle notice! My sixteen-year-old daughter has been abducted, and your response is to sit back and—'

The rising tide of her voice stopped at once when Singh's phone rang. She looked at him in sudden fear.

'Excuse me,' he said. Getting up, he went out into the hallway. Dr Roecastle heard only, 'When did this happen?' and then, 'Where is he now?' and after that only a general murmuring. Soon he returned to the living room.

'I'm afraid I must leave you,' he said.

Dr Roecastle's mouth bent slowly. 'Why?' she said. 'What's happened?'

Singh hesitated. 'One of our officers has apprehended a young man. He is the owner of a white van, and he says he has something to tell us about Amy.'

He said no more, but left her sitting upright, rigid, on her seat, and went out to his car and headed back to the city.

14

On his way through the monitoring station for Interview Room 2, Singh paused to look at the bank of screens in the wall. From nine different fixed angles they patiently showed the room beyond, a regular windowless space whitewashed into anonymity, empty apart from a grey metal table and two metal chairs. On one of the chairs, sitting at an awkward angle to the table, was a young man, good-looking, wiry, wearing a maroon hooded top and red baseball cap. His face was lean, his brows overhanging, his hair dark. Altogether, his features were a striking match to those in the police artist's picture.

He was obviously nervous, full of sinewy, irritable energy. As he sat there he rocked from side to side, bobbing his head and rubbing his face with his hand. He kept picking up and putting down again a packet of tobacco. He seemed to be talking to himself. Singh glanced at his watch: 23:00. He watched the young man for a while longer, then composed himself, tucking a cardboard folder under his arm, and moved off towards a door at the end with a red light above it.

Aspect of interviewer: neat, careful, calm.

Aspect of interviewee: unkempt, flaky, ill-looking.

DI SINGH: Would you confirm your name for me please?

DAMON WALSH: Damon Ryan Walsh.

DI SINGH: And you are twenty-four years old, and you live at 47 Beeston Place, Brickfields.

DAMON WALSH: That's it.

DI SINGH: I'm afraid this is a no-smoking area, Damon.

DAMON WALSH: [*putting away tobacco*]

DI SINGH: Thank you. [*reading file*] Now, you were stopped this evening at the junction of Wyedale Road and Town Road. Erratic driving.

DAMON WALSH: Yeah, it's a crap corner, innit, you can't see the lights, they're sort of hidden, and I wasn't doing nothing, 'cept—

DI SINGH: And the traffic officer of course noticed your van, and asked if you'd seen the suspicious vehicle notice, and also mentioned the missing teenager Amy Roecastle; and it says here that you appeared to be, quote, agitated and evasive, unquote, so he asked you to accompany him here—

DAMON WALSH: Yeah, well, first thing is. Didn't see no notice. Wasn't looking for it. Bazza told me. Down O'Malley's, early doors. He said you been up there, ain't you, Froggett way, in the van and that, and I said yeah but not like suspicious or nothing, and he said they pull you in now, mate, you won't even get to sit on your own arse at the hearing they'll have you inside before you can piss yourself, know what I mean?

DI SINGH: [*reading from the file*] I . . . think so. Yes, it says here you just finished your licence period, and you're worried, I take it, about another enquiry so soon.

DAMON WALSH: My problem, right, it's always the same, my problem is, no one listens. People get the wrong idea. I get mixed up in stuff I don't have nothing to do with, and it's me who gets the blame. Just 'cause it's me, and they see my record, and—

DI SINGH: I understand, Damon. I mean only that you are naturally anxious to avoid misunderstandings. Now. Before we start. You mention your record. You've volunteered in your statement here that when you were fifteen you were placed on a Young Offender programme.

DAMON WALSH: Never hid it.

DI SINGH: And, more recently, our records show you served a three-month custodial sentence for possession of cannabis.

DAMON WALSH: What am I meant to say? It was bad inside. You don't know. No one knows till they done it. I done my stretch and got good behaviour and everything, *and* I done my three months under licence. I'm never going back. I done all the talking and listening and that. I know what people think. I got issues, right. I know that. One day at a time, that's what they say to me. I believe it. I want to get a job, and—

DI SINGH: OK. Now, Damon, back to this evening. We think you might be able to help us in our enquiries because you have a van that matches the description in our notice, and you've been driving it up at Froggett, and you say you have something to tell us about Amy Roecastle.

DAMON WALSH: That's it. I been up there, in the van. Though to be fair, sometimes I think it's not going to make it, up that hill. There's something wrong with it, I think. Bought it off a mate. Not finished paying for it yet, and that's not my fault either, but I got the money for it upfront, so it's all legit. If it helps me get a job—

DI SINGH: I take it you brought the papers for it, by the way.

DAMON WALSH: No one said nothing about bringing papers. No one said—

DI SINGH: It's OK, Damon. But before you go tonight you must arrange with the duty officer to bring them in tomorrow. Now, to come back to what you were saying. You've been driving your van up at Froggett.

DAMON WALSH: Yeah.

DI SINGH: Why?

DAMON WALSH: What do you mean?

DI SINGH: I mean, why up at Froggett?

DAMON WALSH: 'Cause of Amy, course.

DI SINGH: Amy Roecastle?

DAMON WALSH: Yeah.

DI SINGH: And how do you know Amy Roecastle?

DAMON WALSH: What do you mean? She's my babe.

DI SINGH: [*long pause*] You're telling me you're in a relationship with Amy Roecastle?

DAMON WALSH: Yeah. Course.

DI SINGH: So far as I am aware she is not in any relationship.

DAMON WALSH: We have to keep it quiet 'cause her mother's a bit mental.

DI SINGH: Amy's friend Sophie Brighouse knows nothing about this relationship either.

DAMON WALSH: The blonde chick? Amy didn't want her to find out. Bit of a blabbermouth.

DI SINGH: Damon, I have to tell you, I find it hard to believe this.

DAMON WALSH: Yeah, figures. 'Cause it's me, innit? Same old, same old. Gets on my tits.

DI SINGH: Let me put it this way. How can I corroborate what you're saying?

DAMON WALSH: What d'you mean?

DI SINGH: Can you prove it to me?

DAMON WALSH: Yeah, course.

[*silence*]

DI SINGH: Tell me something about her room, for instance.

DAMON WALSH: Never been in the house.

DI SINGH: What does she wear when you meet her?

DAMON WALSH: I'm not good at noticing stuff like that.

DI SINGH: What do you know about her? Tell me something. How many brothers and sisters does she have? What school does she go to? What does she like?

DAMON WALSH: Stop it, you're doing my head in.

DI SINGH: I'm sorry. This won't do.

DAMON WALSH: I gave her flowers. She liked them.

DI SINGH: [*pause*] What?

DAMON WALSH: The other day. Don't know nothing about flowers, got them out of a garden, to be honest. But Amy liked them. Said she was going to put them in a vase and that.

DI SINGH: OK. I've seen those flowers. They are in a vase. Tell me more about Amy then.

DAMON WALSH: Well, usually there's quite a bit of hanging about waiting for her. Sitting in the van and that. Hanging about in those woods. She wants me to keep out of sight till the coast's clear. Fucking pain, to be honest, 'scuse me.

DI SINGH: Damon, how long have you been in this relationship with Amy?

DAMON WALSH: Don't remember. Must have been May sometime.

DI SINGH: And how did you meet?

DAMON WALSH: At O'Malley's, I think it was. Yeah. Seen her standing there giving me the eye. After that, I don't know, she's calling me up and stuff. Saw her at a gig in town one time.

Anyway, we got it together. And that's why I'm telling you all this, through no fault of my own. Do my bit for my babe.

DI SINGH: I see. How often do you see Amy?

DAMON WALSH: Two, three times a week maybe.

DI SINGH: Where do you meet her?

DAMON WALSH: Wherever I've parked the van. Or outside her house. On the path at the back, sometimes.

DI SINGH: And what do you and Amy do?

DAMON WALSH: Well. It's not all what you think. There's quite a bit of that, of course. Might go a for a ride. Go into town. She loves those places down The Wicker. I haven't got money for that, though, usually. Might just sit and talk in the van. She likes to talk. You know, save the world and that. Yeah. And other stuff. [*hastily*] Don't matter about that, though.

DI SINGH: What other stuff?

DAMON WALSH: Forget I said it.

DI SINGH: What other stuff, Damon?

DAMON WALSH: [*pause*] She helps me.

DI SINGH: What do you mean?

DAMON WALSH: [*silence*]

DI SINGH: Damon!

DAMON WALSH: [*shouting*] I'm not very good with books! [*silence*] All right? Just not my thing.

DI SINGH: [*pause*] She's teaching you to read?

DAMON WALSH: I told you, I want to get a job.

DI SINGH: OK. Two weeks ago, your van was seen by

a neighbour parked outside the gates of Amy's house, rocking violently from side to side.

DAMON WALSH: Yeah? Well, there wasn't nothing violent about it. We were just getting it on, I expect. Listen, I know what you think about me, same as everyone. I know I got issues. But I didn't even have any idea about her going off till Bazza told me. That's the truth.

DI SINGH: Did you meet her on the night of Wednesday the 8th of August? The night she went missing.

DAMON WALSH: [*scratching head*] What time?

DI SINGH: Between midnight and two o'clock in the morning. In the woods at the back of her house.

DAMON WALSH: Course not. What would she be doing out there? It was pissing it down.

DI SINGH: Did you meet her that evening somewhere else, at some other time?

DAMON WALSH: No.

DI SINGH: Are you sure?

DAMON WALSH: Course.

DI SINGH: [*pause*] Do you know why she's gone missing, Damon?

DAMON WALSH: No.

DI SINGH: When did you hear that she had gone missing?

DAMON WALSH: Yesterday. They were talking about it in O'Malley's. Bazza said . . . well, it don't matter what Bazza said. Couldn't believe it. She'll be all right, though. I know Amy. She's my babe.

DI SINGH: Do you know where she might be?

DAMON WALSH: No idea. It's a weird one, innit? California?

DI SINGH: Why do you say that? To visit her father?

DAMON WALSH: Don't know anything about him. Just remember her talking about it one time. I love to hear her talk.

DI SINGH: OK, Damon. So you didn't see her on Wednesday night.

DAMON WALSH: No.

DI SINGH: What were you doing on Wednesday?

DAMON WALSH: Why do you want to know that?

DI SINGH: That's when Amy went missing.

DAMON WALSH: Yeah, but I told you, I don't know nothing about it.

DI SINGH: Just tell me what you did.

DAMON WALSH: Wednesday? I got to think. I don't remember things too well. Oh yeah, I was down there by the station in town.

DI SINGH: What were you doing?

DAMON WALSH: Nothing. Just with a friend.

DI SINGH: Were you there all evening?

DAMON WALSH: Yeah.

DI SINGH: So you must have been aware of the riot in Market Square.

DAMON WALSH: No. Well, not really.

DI SINGH: You'd left already?

DAMON WALSH: Well, I hadn't left. I mean, I saw what was going on, and I left afterwards.

DI SINGH: Were you at the rave?

DAMON WALSH: No. No way. Saw what was happening and went home. I didn't hang about or anything.

DI SINGH: You didn't see Amy or her friend Sophie?

DAMON WALSH: No.

DI SINGH: [*pause*]

DAMON WALSH: That it then? Can I go now?

DI SINGH: Do you have anything else to add?

DAMON WALSH: I want it written down.

DI SINGH: What?

DAMON WALSH: Not my fault. All this you've been saying, me driving up there, and hanging about, and Amy being my babe. Whatever's happened, it's not my fault. I want it written down proper, what I'm saying, that it's not, see?

DI SINGH: OK. Noted. I'll take you to the duty officer now. And if we need to talk again we can get in touch with you on the contacts you've already given, yes?

DAMON WALSH: No problem, mate. Thing is, I just want to help. That's why I come in. Cheers.

It was another half an hour before Singh left the Police Centre. Nearly midnight. Under a dark, smooth sky, he drove slowly out to the ring road, and eastwards towards Dandelion Hill, where he lived.

He was thinking about Damon Walsh, about all young people lost to their karma. In truth, Damon wasn't so much younger than he was. And there had been times in his life when he too had been lost; he thought of his boyhood in Lahore fifteen years earlier. Some people go missing, like Amy Roecastle, because they disappear suddenly and strangely. Some, like Garvie Smith, just seem to lose their way. Others, like Damon, live with a disturbed karma, lost to themselves; perhaps they are the least fortunate. But how will they all be found again?

How will I be found? he thought suddenly.

He brought his thoughts back to Amy Roecastle spending her third night away from home. If Damon had told the truth, she was a girl of surprises and secrets. But he didn't know if Damon was telling the truth. Not once had he expressed anxiety about Amy's whereabouts. Singh would have to see him again, the next day.

The night sky was dark blue haze as he drove slowly into Dandelion Hill, thinking these things.

It was midnight on Friday the 10th of August, the second day after Amy's disappearance, and she'd been missing for just under forty-eight hours.

15

Friday nights at Eastwick Gardens were usually family affairs. Not this Friday. Garvie's mother was going out. She disappeared into her room at seven o'clock to get ready, leaving Garvie with Uncle Len, who had called round to pick up Aunt Maxie's handbag, left there the night before.

Garvie was lying supine on the sofa, eyes shut, as his uncle passed by.

'So,' he said without opening his eyes, 'has your man solved it yet?'

Uncle Len halted and grunted disapprovingly. 'You know the constraints he's working under. They won't give him any resources. But he's a fine detective, he works all hours. He's making good progress.'

'For example?'

Uncle Len frowned at his nephew. 'He spent the morning sweeping the woods with a volunteer force he'd organized.'

'Result?'

'He was unlucky with the downpour the previous night. We have some black threads, which could be from Amy's trousers. Otherwise, it was mainly rubbish.'

'What rubbish?'

'The usual.'

'What usual?'

His uncle looked at him lying there, and felt the familiar irritation. But he remained calm.

'It's surprising what rubbish finds its way into a wood. A tooth mug. Deflated football. Shoe-care kit. A car radio, wrapped in a plastic bag. A bathing costume, can you believe it? All sorts of things.'

Garvie made no response and his uncle moved away towards the door.

Garvie said, 'What shoe-care kit?'

Uncle Len hesitated. 'Usual sort of shoe-care kit. You know, the sort of complimentary thing they sometimes slip into the shoe-box.'

'What brand?'

'I don't remember, Garvie.'

'What colour?'

His uncle sighed. 'Buff, I think. Thick black lettering.' He stared at his nephew lying there so unmoving, eyes still closed. 'Why?'

But Garvie said no more, nor made any move-ment, and, shaking his head, Uncle Len turned and left the apartment.

At eight o'clock his mother came into the living room wearing a knee-length dress with a stripy black flower pattern on a white background, and white buckled high-heeled ankle-length boots. Round her throat she had a looping silver necklace and matching loops in her ears, and her straightened hair was done in a short, puffy bob, side-parted and streaked with henna-coloured dye. Her burgundy lipstick matched her toenail polish.

'Well?'

Garvie opened his eyes. They showed his astonishment, an attitude he tried otherwise not to show. He sat up.

'Oscars cast party then, is it?'

'Night out with the girls from work. Who knows who we'll meet? A cocktail or two, and maybe a dance in town.'

'Really?'

'Why not? You think I can't dance?'

'No, it's just . . . What about tea?'

'You'll have to get tea yourself.'

Something about his mother dressing up to go out was unsettling.

'Aren't you going out, Garvie? It's Friday night.'

No comment.

'Your friends all busy again?'

Nothing to say.

But she was still looking at him.

'What?' he said.

'I was meaning to talk to you. Dr Roecastle asked me about you at work this morning.'

Garvie got off the sofa and headed for his room.

'Garvie!'

He turned. 'You know she's psycho, right? I can't help it if it's her nature to make all these unreasonable complaints.'

'As it happens, she wasn't complaining. Yes, I know. I was shocked. She asked me if it was true you helped the police in their investigations into those murders.'

'What did you say?'

'I said she ought to ask Inspector Singh.'

He looked at her. 'What else? You said something else, didn't you?'

'I told her you were rude, difficult and interfering, and as smart as all hell when you want to be. And at the end of the day you're my boy and anyone with a problem with you has a problem with me. OK?'

He thought about that for a while.

'What do you mean, "difficult"?'

'Don't fight me, Garvie. All that's done. I can't tell you what to do, and I damn well can't tell her what to do. So as far as I'm concerned her daughter's disappearance is nothing to do with me. It's just, I can't help feeling sorry for her.'

'That's where you're going wrong.'

'You think she doesn't deserve my sympathy.'

'She doesn't need any help thinking about herself. First she was pissed off. Then she'll be alarmed. Pretty soon now she'll be hysterical.'

'Well, I hope she can stay positive. And I think Raminder will find her daughter soon.'

'He doesn't have enough help.'

'He's a good detective.'

'Debatable.'

'I don't know what you've got against him. He's bright, resourceful, hard-working. Everyone says so.'

'Uptight. Got no sense of humour. Misses things. I bet they all say that too.'

'I don't believe it.'

'You should. He missed the fact she stood outside in the rain for half an hour before she went into her house.'

He didn't wait for her reaction, just went into his room and shut the door; and shortly afterwards he heard her leave.

Now it was midnight. Garvie lay on his bed. Hands behind his head, unblinking, staring up at the ceiling. Police sirens in the distance, fading away and washing back again.

Abdul had called earlier to tell him that the cabbie dropped Amy off outside her house at eleven forty. According to Dr Roecastle, her daughter got into the house at eleven minutes past twelve. The walk up the drive took a couple of minutes at most. So, after the taxi dropped her off, she stood outside in torrential rain for half an hour.

That was interesting.

An unknown term in a series of events.

He thought about sequences, the way they worked. Like the Fibonacci series, one of the simplest. $F_n = F_n\text{-}1 + F_n\text{-}2$. In other words, each new number in the sequence is the sum of the previous two numbers: 1, 1, 2, 3, 5, 8, 13, 21, 34, 55, 89 . . . F_n increases exponentially, each increase bigger than the one before. Ordinary, but alarming. Like little things suddenly piling up without warning. Tiny risks leaping out of control. Danger, one minute so small you hardly notice it, the next minute off the scale.

An unknown term in a series of events about to spiral out of control. Half an hour in the pouring rain, talking to someone who had given her his coat to wear. Talking about what? Unknown. But ten minutes afterwards she was running for her life through the woods.

Interesting.

One o'clock came and went. Two o'clock. He heard his mother come in quietly and go to bed. He lay there, unblinking, listening to the silence, thinking about sequences.

16

Saturday morning Singh was at his desk, as usual. The duty officer called him just after ten o'clock to let him know that Damon Walsh had not returned with his vehicle registration papers.

At once Singh had a bad feeling.

'Have you contacted him?'

The officer on duty hesitated. 'The phone number he gave in his paperwork is unobtainable.'

'What about the address?'

'He's not known there. We've tried it.'

Singh sat there quietly, staring at the blank wall of his makeshift office.

'Next of kin?'

'None. All we've got's a contact in the database from his prior conviction – someone called Paul Tanner.'

'Who's he?'

'A baker at one of the supermarkets in Strawberry Hill.'

'Address?'

The duty officer gave it to him. 'Out in the sticks. Near Tick Hill. By the way,' he added, 'a Dr Roecastle has called for you. Twice already.'

Singh didn't say anything to that. He put down the phone and left the room.

Along the northern stretch of ring road, between the white high-rise of the hospital and the cramped low-rise of Tick Hill, was a turn-off signposted only *Childswell Garden Centre*. A narrow road ran uphill between fences for a hundred metres or so, then forked. There, Singh turned onto an even narrower road, no more than a track. On either side the brambly scrub was thick and green, and he jolted slowly onward for a quarter of a mile until the track petered out in a small gravelled clearing in front of a new bungalow built of brick and wooden panels.

He got out and stood in the breeze. Traffic on the ring road buzzed like distant surf. A ploughed field rose from the back of the house and climbed towards a copse of trees on the horizon. In the oaks surrounding the bungalow pigeons rattled their wings and cleared their throats. So close to the city, but so rural, it seemed a forgotten spot of peace. Straightening his turban, Singh breathed in the sweet air and felt a rare moment of calm. He walked through a pretty garden to the front door, and knocked.

The fenced-in lawn curved round the back of the building. There was a barbecue cabin and an awning under which Singh could see fitness equipment. The grass was strewn with toys and building materials.

A small woman with a baby on her arm answered the door and stood rocking it gently while he talked.

'He's in bed,' she said. 'He does nights.'

'I apologize,' Singh said. 'It won't take long. He's not in trouble,' he added. 'We're simply hoping he can help us with an enquiry.'

He followed her down a passageway to a bright living room, and waited there among more toys until a man appeared. He was in his middle thirties, with dark hair cut army-style and a wide-open pleasant face, heavy stubble, thick above his upper lip, dark against pale skin.

Singh stood. 'I'm sorry to have disturbed you, Mr Tanner.'

'It's all right. I can't always get to sleep straight-away. Takes a while to wind down after the shift. I get so stiff working the ovens.'

He winced as he sat down. He swallowed a para-cetamol, and a small boy ran in and he grabbed him, mussed his hair until he squealed with laughter, and set him on his feet again.

'All right, now go and keep your mother company. I've got to talk to this gentleman here.'

The boy ran off, laughing.

Singh said, 'This is a nice spot.'

'We're lucky. I've done most of the work myself. Couldn't afford it otherwise.'

Singh smiled. 'I just want to ask you a few questions about a young man you might know.'

'Who's that?'

'Damon Walsh.'

At once Paul sighed. 'What's he done now?'

'We don't know he's done anything yet. We're trying to locate him. A girl has gone missing. It's possible Damon may know something about it.'

Paul considered this, rubbing stubble with his hand. 'Poor Damon.'

'Why do you say that?'

'He can't seem to stay out of trouble.'

Singh took out his notebook. 'OK. Tell me about him,' he said. 'How do you know him? From the supermarket?'

Paul shook his head. 'Can't imagine Damon holding down a job. No.' He paused. 'Is this off the record? I know that you have to be careful about data these days.'

Singh hesitated only a moment. 'It's OK,' he said. 'Damon has already volunteered the information that he spent some time in custody and on the youth offender programme.'

'OK. That's where I know him from, the Y.O. Back in the day I was a social worker. Made redundant with the cuts. But, anyway, a lot of the job was liaising with the police – a guy called Bob Dowell was my contact there – and one of the things I did was help supervise sports and leisure on the programme.' He smiled. 'I miss it, to be honest. Thing about young offenders is, they don't get the same support as most people. They make mistakes and there's no one to help them out. They need someone to put an arm round their shoulder, have a quiet word with them.'

Paul knew little about Damon's background. He'd heard of an older half-brother somewhere but didn't think they were in touch. He had the impression his parents gave up on him early on. After that, there were minders and mentors, foster parents, unofficial 'guardians'. Everyone on the programme had to have a sponsor to look after their interests.

'None of them took to Damon long-term, though.'

'Why?'

Damon had been difficult at school, an anxious child. He was easily led into trouble, at first petty burglary, later drugs. When he was fourteen he'd been convicted of possession of an illegal substance with intent to supply.

'Typical Damon. He tried to sell some pills to a plain-clothes policeman. The guy said he was so friendly and hopeful he almost bought them.'

'What was he like on the programme?'

'What you see with Damon is what you get. He's flaky, chaotic, thoughtless, massively unreliable, easily tempted. Nervous, very nervous. But he's an innocent, really. Sweet, even. He just falls into one thing after another. I liked him. I've seen him a couple of times since he got off the programme. He was the worst footballer I ever coached. No co ordination at all.'

Singh made notes. 'You said you've met him since the programme?'

'Yeah. Last time was quite recent. He wanted some advice, he said.'

'About what?'

'He was thinking of buying a van. But he didn't have any money.'

Singh wrote again.

'You say there's a girl involved,' Paul said. 'Doesn't surprise me. He's always been popular with the girls. Good-looking, I know. But he appeals to their protective side, I think. They want to save him from himself. Of course, he's a mother's worst nightmare.'

Singh nodded. 'Anything else?'

Paul thought. 'You know that part of his course was anger management?'

'No.'

'I think so. You could check. Damon's this real gentle guy most of the time, dopey even. Then something happens. He gets frightened for some reason and he loses it. Anyway, that's what I was told. Never saw it myself. Is any of this helpful?'

'Very helpful,' Singh said. 'Thank you. Now, do you have any idea where I might look for him?'

Paul rubbed his bristles. 'I think I've got his number. Wait. Yes, here it is.' He handed Singh his phone, and Singh shook his head. 'He gave us that already. It's no good.'

Paul snorted. 'Typical Damon again. He's probably had his contract cancelled.'

'You don't know where he might be living?'

'I've no idea. He moves around a lot.'

'OK. Never mind.'

Paul shook Singh's hand. 'Look, I know Damon

can make some stupid mistakes. But he's a good kid at heart.'

'Thank you again for your time. I hope you can sleep now. One last thing. If Damon contacts you again, please get in touch straightaway.'

Paul hesitated a moment, then nodded.

Outside the house the sun was bright, the air tart with scents of the surrounding vegetation, and Singh stood there a moment checking his phone. There were three missed calls from Dr Roecastle.

He hesitated. The only person seriously helping them with their enquiries had disappeared and Singh did not feel confident of finding him again. He would have to tell Dr Roecastle this. She would, he knew, be deeply disappointed. Her attitude towards Amy's disappearance had changed dramatically, and her anger with the police was obviously a sign of her belated, deep anxiety about her daughter.

But he was, above all, a dutiful officer. Apprehensively he got back into his car and headed again towards Froggett.

17

Saturday morning, Garvie had to put in a few hours fencing at 'Four Winds'. Weekend overtime. The custom ball-and-collar finials on his panel needed finishing. At midday he stopped and went down to the house to wash up. He'd missed Singh's visit earlier but as soon as he went inside he was faced with the result of it.

There was a noise from down the hall, a harsh, explosive sound like fat spluttering in a frying pan. Pausing at the open living-room door, he saw Dr Roecastle sitting bunched up on a sofa, head in hands, shoulders heaving, weeping bitterly.

Before he could move on, she lifted her head and stared at him, her tear-streaked face frozen in a look of agonized incomprehension.

'Wait!' she croaked at him angrily.

Garvie waited, keeping his eyes on her in case she did something unpredictable.

'They've let him go!' she blurted out in a voice crackly with mucus.

'Who?'

'The suspect.'

'What suspect?'

She was as hysterical as he had feared; she'd exploded all at once into desperation. Her face jerked when she spoke. 'A man with a criminal record. Been seen in his van in the woods. Twenty-four years old. Said he was her *boyfriend*. Asked me if I'd heard of him. Damon. Damon Walsh. No!' She looked at Garvie distraught. *'She's only sixteen.* He's been stalking her,' she went on, 'waiting for an opportunity to . . .' She swallowed, panted. 'They think he might have taken her and put her in his van, and . . .'

Garvie waited, and she went on again. 'The police had him, they actually had him in the station, and they've let him go. He's fooled them. Given them a false address, vanished. They have no idea where he is, where he's keeping Amy.' Her wild eyes were on him.

Garvie said at last, 'Why are you telling me this?'

She cleared her throat and swallowed. 'You were right, what you said before. I should have been more scared. Now I am. I'm more scared than I've ever been.'

Garvie's silence acknowledged this, but he said nothing.

'You don't like me,' she said after a moment.

'No.'

'I don't like you either.'

He nodded.

'Your mother works at my hospital.'

'I know where my mother works.'

'I talked to her yesterday. About what you did, helping with those police investigations.'

'Yeah, I know that too.'

'Your mother told me that—'

'I'm rude and difficult. Yeah, I know.'

'And interfering.'

'Only sometimes. Sometimes I can't be arsed.'

Dr Roecastle looked exhausted suddenly. Her mouth fell open.

Garvie shifted slightly in the doorway. 'Likeliest thing is, she'll come back,' he said at last.

'Listen to me,' she said in a quiet, strained voice. 'This is the third day she's been missing. *Nothing's happening.* One policeman on his own, that's it. I've been to see his chief, I've called all my friends in the media. No one's helping. All this time she could be suffering. *I'm scared. I will do anything.* Do you understand what I'm saying? Anything.' She paused and added quietly, 'I'll even ask a boy like you to help me.'

Garvie said nothing.

'Please,' she said. 'Please. If you can. Please help me.'

She turned her glistening face to his, and he looked at her impassively and she felt again all his strangeness. His blue eyes were weirdly still. It was as if he wasn't listening to her, didn't even see her.

'You think you're the only rude and difficult human being, do you?' she cried out. '*I'm* rude and difficult. And if my daughter was here she'd agree with me. But I'm her *mother*! And someone like you will never know what it means to make the mistakes

I've made or to feel the pain I feel. But,' she added bitterly, 'your mother knows.'

She held his gaze as long as she could, and looked away, blinking, as if terrified by her sudden confession.

'Forget it,' she muttered.

When she looked back he was still there.

'What do you want me to do?' he said.

They sat on the sofa.

'Why do you think this Damon's got anything to do with it?' he asked.

'Why else would he have gone into hiding now that the police are on to him?'

''Cause he doesn't have papers for his van. 'Cause he's scared about getting done for re-offending. 'Cause he can't cope with any of it. 'Cause he's off on a bender. 'Cause something else has cropped up. 'Cause no one ever listens to him anyway. Etcetera.'

Dr Roecastle pursed her lips. 'I know the sort of young man he is.'

'Oh yeah?'

'Yes. Delinquent. No qualifications, no proper job, no long-term goals. Not enough money. All sorts of problems. Drinks too much, smokes too much, no proper interests, lives in some awful place like Five Mile or Limekilns. You forget that I'm a doctor. I see people from all over the city. I know more about these men than you think.' She looked at him, at those expressionless blue eyes. Too late she said, 'Where do you live, Garvie?'

'Five Mile.'

'I see.' She looked away.

'You think I can find him because I'm like him.'

'I only want my daughter back. She's vulnerable. She thinks she knows the world, but she knows nothing.'

'Just to be clear,' Garvie said. 'I'm not doing it for you. I couldn't care less about you.'

'Do it for Amy then.'

'I'm doing it for my mother. She has to work with you.'

Dr Roecastle compressed her lips. 'I understand.'

He was silent for a moment. 'Tell me exactly what happened the night she left,' he said.

She told him. Her memory was precise, her manner harsh.

'What was she wearing?'

She told him about the jacket.

'Tell me about the hat.'

'How do you know she was wearing a hat?'

'I don't. But you said her wet stuff was dripping everywhere. "Stuff", not "jacket". More than just a jacket.'

'You're right. She was wearing one of those woollen hats. I'd forgotten.'

'Where is it now?'

'I don't know. Is it important?'

'Everything's important. I thought doctors knew

that.' He stood up. 'I'll take a look in her room now.'

'It's a crime scene,' she said. 'The police have sealed it.'

He didn't stop, or turn, as he went out of the front door. 'Yeah, which is why the window'll still be open.'

Over the years Felix had given him a lot of practical advice about what he called 'entering made easy' – the builder's ladder, the tap on the frame, the blade in the sash – he had even given Garvie a 'bag of tricks' for inconvenient locks, but Garvie didn't need any of that now.

He eased himself up on Smudge's shoulders.

'One day,' Smudge said in a strained voice, '*you're* going to do the bracing and heaving in the flower bed, and I'm going to stand on *your* shoulders.'

'Yeah,' Garvie said. 'But today's not that day.'

As he climbed up from the sill of a downstairs window to the sloping roof of the bay to a section of sturdy iron drainpipe, he wondered how often Amy had found it convenient to get back into her room that way. At the bedroom window he paused to look down. Smudge wiped his face and grinned, gave a little wave. Dr Roecastle stood behind him, looking up anxiously. Behind her, with expressions more disgusted than anxious, stood Smudge's brother and the rest of the fencing crew, also watching.

The bedroom window was still ajar, as he had

expected; and the next moment he was inside, crouching on a tall bed in his crusted boots.

He didn't have long. Dr Roecastle was too antsy. He analysed the room, mentally sorted its contents into a few key categories – furnishings, decorations, clothes, stuff – and ignored all categories over which Dr Roecastle had some influence. He went over to Amy's wardrobe and pulled open the doors.

It smelled of perfume, the source of which he found in a purple glass bottle: *Alien* by Mugler. The clothes fell into two sub-categories: 1) fancy: expensive-looking posh-girl trousers, tops, sweaters and skirts; and 2) alternative: tartan minis, ripped denim, bondage trousers, camouflage stockings, slogan T-shirts. Those in the first category looked hardly worn, those in the second, far more numerous, were messed up, creased, faded with hard use. Stuffed into a shelf was a tumbleweed of studded belts, mesh gloves, chains and steel bracelets.

No hats anywhere.

No shoe boxes either.

From outside in the garden, he heard Dr Roecastle calling already, but he tuned it out.

There was a cork board on the wall with four photographs attached to it: Amy in studded leather sitting on the grass somewhere; Amy slouching in front of the Eiffel Tower in Paris; Amy with a blonde girl in a photo-booth; Amy on her own.

He stood there, staring. He could feel his breath going in and out.

110

He took down one of the photographs and held it between his fingertips. No make-up; she didn't need it. In her ear was a black hoop. In her nose a black stud, on her third fingers matching rings, silver bands with unusual spiral patterns picked out in black. Her eyes were blue, her eyebrows heavy, her hair dyed black. Lips parted, she was smiling slightly at the camera.

Now he was holding his breath.

Her face.

He couldn't stop looking at it. He'd never seen a face like it. She looked back at him fearlessly. A girl who didn't do fear.

But she'd been frightened that night, frightened enough to go out into the storm, frightened enough to take the dog with her.

He peered closer. All those studs and hoops, all that rebel-leather designer wear. In-your-face clothes for show-offs. But the expression on her face was different, guarded. Was she playing a part? There was just a glint of something hidden in her eyes. She seemed to hold his gaze, and ask him what he was up to, and suggest it wasn't much. A mischievous challenge. *You can't find me.*

He thought about that, the wit of it: a flashy photograph giving nothing away. He put it in his pocket, and went on round the room pulling open drawers and cupboards, looking in boxes and files, sifting through piles of stuff scattered on the floor. He could almost hear her laughing at him as he worked. A smart girl with secrets.

He found nothing.

Dr Roecastle called out again, and he ignored her.

There was a vase of flowers on the desk – miserable, wilting things. Not from a shop. He stood for a moment staring at them. He'd seen flowers like that before and he instantly remembered where: in the garden of Dr Roecastle's neighbour.

That was interesting.

He bent over the desk. There was a piece of artwork, looking like nothing very much to him. It was odd how arty people just couldn't draw. Next to it was a school book open at a maths problem. It caught his eye. Sequences again. Two parts to the questions.

Part one. Suppose $a_n = 1 + (1/8)^n$. Answer the following questions:

What is the fourth term in the sequence? Amy had answered $\frac{4097}{4096}$.

Is the sequence 'convergent' or 'divergent'? Amy had answered 'convergent'.

What is the limit? Amy had answered '1'.

Three questions in the first part answered correctly. She was smart, really smart.

But she'd left the second part unfinished.

He gave it his attention. It was something he'd literally never seen before, a question concerning the 'definition of the limit of a sequence', in which λ is the limit, ε is an arbitrary value, and N is the point at which the difference between the term and the limit is less than ε.

$|a_n - \lambda| < \varepsilon$ for all $n \geq N$. If $\varepsilon = \frac{1}{5000}$ what is N?

Find the missing number in a sequence.

Amy had begun the problem but abandoned her workings. Garvie stared. From outside came Dr Roecastle's twitterings, but again he ignored them, gazing steadily at the problem, zoning out everything else. He went into the space of numbers and patterns, the beautiful labyrinths of mathematical logic.

After two minutes he took up Amy's pen again and wrote 5.

With Dr Roecastle calling continuously now, he went round the room a last time collecting things – a lipstick, a necklace, a stocking, a bracelet, some other stuff, and a sheet of paper from Amy's exercise book and a pencil – and exited via the window.

She was waiting for him on the lawn.

'Well?' she said. 'Did you find it?'

'Find what?'

'I don't know. What were you looking for?'

'Just nosing around.'

'Nosing around!'

'Yeah.' He looked at her critically. 'Some of those clothes. Bondage and stuff. I'm surprised you let her wear them.'

She was going to say something else, but he didn't wait for an answer, walking away across the lawn, watched again – with distaste – by Smudge's brother and the other workers, to join Smudge at the top of the rise.

'How'd you get on?'

'Good, thanks. I'm going to need your help now, though.'

'Thought you would. If it's to do with girls, ask a man who knows.'

'It's not to do with girls. It's to do with vans.'

'Oh.' Momentarily disappointed, he brightened. 'Just as good, though, really, in a way.'

Garvie nodded. 'And you're going to need these.' He gave Smudge the paper and pencil from Amy's room. 'I hope you're better at drawing than she is.'

Smudge looked doubtful. 'Is it like art?'

'No, Smudge. It's like a murder investigation.'

He looked relieved. 'That's good. 'Cause I dropped art way back.'

'Afterwards,' Garvie said, 'we've got stuff to do in town. We better get going.'

Garvie glanced at his watch. Just after midday. 'Sixty hours,' he said.

'What?'

'That's how long she's been missing. Too long. Pretty soon we're all going to be looking for a dead person.'

18

Saturday afternoon found them back in Five Mile, getting busy. First Garvie put out some calls. Smudge helped. He was pleased to help. He took credit, in fact, for Dr Roecastle asking for Garvie's assistance. Good with people.

'By the way, who we looking for? The girl?'

'Not yet. Van driver, name of Damon.'

Smudge looked interested. 'What sort of van?'

'Don't know yet. But if we find him, I'll let you talk to him about intelligent all-wheel drive.'

Smudge called Tiger and Dani and some kids in Strawberry Hill. Garvie called Felix. Felix's older brother had worked with a lad in south Brickfields who'd known Damon at school but hadn't seen him for a while. Smudge went to visit Alex. It turned out Alex had run into one of Damon's friends a couple of times while he was squatting; this friend told Smudge he'd shared time with Damon on the Youth Offender programme, and passed on the rumour that he was currently sleeping in a van somewhere in Limekilns. Smudge called a couple of other guys, both currently assisting police with enquiries, and they offered the information that

Damon had been popping up in Five Mile too, here and there.

Smudge reported to Garvie. 'Nervous sort, they said he was. All right, but – you know.'

'All right but what?'

'All right, but a bit psycho.'

Damon's mate at O'Malley's, Bazza, had told Smudge he was keen to find out where Damon was as well. 'But then Bazza's a bit psycho himself,' Smudge said.

Garvie was impressed with all the information. 'Good work, Smudge.'

'People skills, innit. Question of trust. Sort of face I got.'

'I thought you called them.'

'They could sense it, I think.'

In a couple of hours they'd put together a map, a Damon Walsh zone of activity. Then they went visiting with the things Garvie had taken from Amy's room. He gave one of the necklaces to the girl who served behind the bar at O'Malley's, and a bracelet to Stanislaw Singer who ran the Strawberry Hill corner shop. Smudge left a lipstick with the girl in the place in Five Mile centre where you could cash cheques, and everywhere they said the same thing: 'If you see Damon, give him this, and tell him Garvie wants a word about Amy.'

The only solid address they turned up for Damon was in Pirrip Street, number 8b. Everyone said he'd left it suddenly a few weeks before.

'I'll take a look, anyway,' Garvie said.

'All right. Mind the dog. Heard it's a big one.'

'OK. Cheers.'

Pirrip Street was a lost street. It ran straight for a couple of hundred metres past the roadworks depot off the Town Road. Though it was so close to Marsh Academy – Garvie's old school – Garvie had never been down it before, hadn't even known it existed. There were only half a dozen habitable houses among the sooty brick tenements, the ones with a working door and at least two windows with most of the glass left in. 8b was one of these.

The door was opened a notch by a meaty woman in black leggings and blue T-shirt, who told the dog behind her to shut the fuck up and swivelled her gaze back to Garvie waiting politely on the street.

'Damon Walsh,' he said.

Her eyes narrowed as the dog continued to explode in the hall. 'What's he done now?'

'I don't know yet.'

'What are you? A *friend*?'

Through the half-opened door Garvie glimpsed the pit bull distractedly performing a range of jaw exercises behind her.

'No,' he said prudently.

She sneered at him pleasantly. 'Well, he don't rent with us no more. Gone. Disappeared. No warning, just upped and left.'

'Sorry to hear that.'

'So if you find him,' she added, 'give him a slap from me.'

She banged shut the door, there was a violent crash from inside and the dog fell abruptly silent.

Garvie leaned against the house wall. He thought about Damon, and dogs, and people skills. He thought about the woods again, where Amy had fled, the thicket, the twisted body of the Dobermann.

He thought about Amy, the cool look of her in the photograph, the shape of her mouth, the half-smile that played about it.

He took out his Benson & Hedges, tapped one out and threw it up into the corner of his mouth. He sighed and lit up, and when he looked round there was a kid about eight years old with his thumb in his mouth standing next to him. He was a grimy sort of kid with saggy short trousers and the big round face of a very disappointed middle-aged man.

The kid took out his thumb, and said, 'Shouldn't smoke.'

Garvie exhaled and flicked ash onto the pavement. 'What makes you think I smoke?'

The boy thought about that for a long time. He removed his thumb and said, 'When I smoke I get a slap.'

'You and me both,' Garvie said. 'Sometimes I get a slap when I'm not smoking.'

The kid nodded solemnly. 'I'll fight you,' he said. 'If you like.'

Garvie smoked on peaceably. 'Go on. I'm not in a fighting mood just now.'

The kid spat inexpertly on the ground. 'Pick pig's bones out of that,' he said.

Garvie nodded. 'Very well done. Wipe your chin.' He looked at the kid thoughtfully. 'Don't suppose you know someone called Damon Walsh?' he asked.

'Why? What's he done now?'

'Forget it,' Garvie said. 'I'm busy smoking.'

The kid nodded and backed away. 'I like you,' he said, put his thumb back into his mouth and disappeared down a passage.

For a while Garvie stayed where he was. At last he pulled himself off the wall, strolled to the end of the street and went down a litter-strewn footpath between wire security fences until he came to the end of Badger Lane. Round the corner was the Academy, where, until the previous month, he had spent a large part of his life, a place now consigned to his childhood. He had a peculiar feeling in his chest as he went across the end of the lane and, a moment later, found himself standing at bottom gate, looking at the familiar institutional buildings beyond.

In these last weeks of the summer holidays there was no one around. Besides, it was the weekend, Saturday afternoon. The staff car park was deserted but for one forgotten car; the school stood silent and empty, abandoned. It was empty of him. His memories were ghosts.

He was about to turn away when someone

appeared in the driveway, a diminutive lady in a severe suit walking stiffly towards the car park with two overloaded bags and a sheaf of papers under one arm. It was Miss Perkins, the much-hated principal enforcer of the Academy, Garvie's old maths teacher and particular adversary while he had been a pupil.

He should have turned and left. For some reason, as if mesmerized, he stayed. And after a moment watching Perkins struggle with her bags down the driveway, he found himself inexplicably going forward, into her line of vision, towards her in fact, and heard himself offering to help.

She looked at him with her green inhuman eyes, and he felt all the awkwardness of the situation he had put himself into.

'Smith,' she said at last.

'Good memory for faces.'

'Surprising perhaps, seeing as you attended school so infrequently.'

'Working in the holidays?'

'I'm always working.' She looked at him. 'I under-stand the value of work.'

She had put down her bags, and he picked them up.

'That your car?'

She nodded, and they walked together towards it. It remained awkward.

'So, Smith,' Miss Perkins said, as they walked. 'What are you doing with yourself now?'

A variety of lies came easily to mind but he said,

'Fencing.' He stopped himself from adding 'miss' just in time.

She looked at him in silence. 'Panels or sabres?'

'Panels. Smudge's brother's business.'

She looked at him.

'Ryan Howells,' he said. 'His brother puts up fences.'

'And so now do you.'

'Yeah. Sometimes they don't stay up.'

That was something else he hadn't meant to say.

They reached her car and she loaded her bags.

'Thank you.' She was looking at him again, with great intensity, and he felt – too late – that it was time to go. But her eyes would not let him.

'Do you believe in fate, Smith?'

'What?'

'Fate, destiny. The belief that things are outside our control, that they happen just because they're meant to.'

'No.'

She nodded, didn't smile. Neither did he.

'Then you should stop acting as if you do,' she said.

Without saying goodbye, she turned from him and got into her car, and he watched her drive away.

In the evening his mother was at work. There was no one else in the flat when he got home. It was quiet, except for the endless muted drone of the ring road traffic.

Garvie lay on his bed keeping an eye on the ceiling. An hour passed.

There was a crack against the windowpane. He turned his head, but didn't move. Another crack, then his friend Felix's voice.

'Hey, Sherlock!'

He stood at the window. Felix's foxy upturned face below caught the evening sunlight.

'Coming out?'

'Where to?'

Felix shrugged. 'Old Ditch Road.'

Garvie thought about the kiddies' playground where they usually met, the miniature roundabout, the crippling swings, the shadows lengthening across the fouled grass, the drizzle coming on, the always-almost-empty vodka bottle and the finger-singeing speck of spliff passed round, the late-night visit from the community officer to move them on.

'Think I'll give it a miss tonight, Felix.'

'Busy, eh?'

'You wouldn't believe.'

He went and lay on the bed again. He looked at his watch. Seven thirty. Not long now till Amy Roecastle had been missing for seventy-two hours. He knew what that meant.

He thought about sequences. The rain, the dark, the dog, the woods, the box. He thought about the unknown rule that bound them all together, and he reflected that sometimes the unknown remains unknown.

Then his phone rang. It was the girl from O'Malley's. She'd got word from Damon: *be on supertram at eight.*

19

The free downtown tram went continuously round a circuit that took in, counter-clockwise, the cafés and restaurants of Market Square, the business district, The Wicker, the shopping mall, the railway station and the historic centre. It had a bar and restaurant carriages and was popular with visitors wanting a brief walking-pace tour of the city centre without the hassle of actually walking. Everyone else used it for convenience.

Twilight in the city, everything lit up in party colours. Garvie sat at the back of the rear car, looking out at it. He took the photograph of Amy out of his pocket and put it on the table in front of him.

The tram heaved itself over the bridge above Town Road and descended swaying towards the cathedral. It stopped at the Guildhall to let off a group of tourists, curved round to Market Square, where it stopped again at the end of pedestrianized Corngate, and moved off once more towards Exchange Street, where the business district began. People got on and off; they stood round the doors or sat with drinks at the tables talking and looking out of the windows at the city trundling by.

The tram went all round its circuit once. It was just reaching The Wicker for the second time when Damon showed up.

He sat down in a rush, wiped his mouth nervously with the back of his hand, and stared at Garvie. He had a smooth, sculpted face and overhanging brows, very black, and short dark hair stiff with neglect. His mouth was wide and oddly friendly, his eyes were large and black and pleading. He was wearing a plain maroon hooded top and grey sweat pants and canvas baseball boots slightly ripped and very dirty.

He glanced down nervously at the photograph, moved his head around.

Garvie said, 'Got it out of her room.'

'Why?'

''Cause I didn't like the one of her in Paris. It's a nice room, though, isn't it?'

'Dunno, never been inside.'

'Nice house.'

'Course. Big and that. Big old garden.'

'What do you think of the fence?'

'What fence?'

Garvie looked at him a while. 'You're hard to find.'

'Got housing issues.'

'Pirrip Street?'

'Didn't work out.'

'Not surprised. I met your landlady. And her dog.'

'Thing is, you can't trust no one.' He looked hard

at Garvie. 'You're only a kid, aren't you? Aren't you scared?'

'Why? Are you going to pull a gun on me?'

Damon bit his lip. 'What makes you think I've got a gun?'

Garvie said nothing.

'Don't like guns,' Damon added. 'Make me anxious.'

'Anxious you might get hurt? Or anxious you might kill someone?'

Damon looked sick. He said, 'Rylee in O'Malley's said you were OK, but' – he shrugged – 'I dunno. If it helps Amy . . .'

For a moment they were both silent, looking out of the window at the brilliantly lit Perspex boxes of the shopping centre going by, and the neatly stacked ribs of the multistorey car park dim in the gathering darkness. The gates of the depot next to it cranked open with a dull chain-metal groan to let in a lorry, and when the sound had faded away Garvie said, 'Where're you hanging now?'

'Here and there. Lying low.' Damon was staring glassily out of the window again, at the centre, the car park, the depot. He said quietly, 'Sometimes I just got to get away. You know? Somewhere different. I got a place. Can't always get there, but sometimcs. Place where I can forget things.' He gave a sly grin. 'Smoke the pipe of peace. Listen to the air, know what I mean?'

'Not really. Obviously you're a free spirit.'

Damon's face lit up. 'Free spirit, yeah, I like that.'

'Like to give a girl flowers.'

'Romantic, that's me.'

'Easy to get them too, out of the neighbour's flower bed at the front there.'

Damon scowled. 'She won't miss them.'

'Don't worry about it.'

'Don't want no worries. I follow my instincts, know what I mean? If I'm skint I'll doss down anywhere, it don't bother me. If I got a bit of cash I'll go down one of them clubs, play the slots at the casino, whatever. Live the moment, yeah? And when it's time to disappear . . .' He glanced at Garvie cunningly. 'You won't find me,' he said. 'I promise you that.'

'I just did,' Garvie said. 'But it's not you we're trying to find, is it?'

Damon scowled, gave a twitch. 'Whatever's happened to her, I know I'll get the blame,' he said. 'I get mixed up in stuff I don't know nothing about, see. Not my fault. But I got issues. Can't always hold my shit together. I've had dark times, man. Made mistakes. Ever been banged up?'

Garvie shook his head.

'Couldn't take it again. Serious.' He grimaced and rubbed his hair. 'If I get pulled in for this . . . Don't know what I'll do, might as well fucking top myself.' He was looking at the photograph again, and his face softened. 'Ever really loved someone?'

Garvie hesitated, and Damon looked at him.

'Ever really *trusted* someone? Like, you know, a soul mate. Put your life in their hands sort of thing.' He was acting nervous again. His hands were trembling as he looked away through the window. He gnawed his lip.

'Can't trust no one, though,' he muttered bitterly. 'Always get let down.' He looked at Garvie, breathless. 'You think you know them, then they turn on you. What's the time?'

'Nearly nine.'

'Got to go soon, so get to it. You want to ask me something about Amy?'

'No.'

He looked surprised. 'Oh.'

Garvie said, 'I want to ask you something about your van.'

He stared at Garvie a moment. 'What about it? Piece of shit, to be honest with you. I can't even get the money together.'

'Drive it up at Froggett?'

'Yeah, course. I already said that to plod.'

'Park back of the woods, on Rustlings Lane?'

'So?'

'And in the woods?'

'Don't much like trees, to be honest with you.'

'What make is it?'

'Courier. Old and that, like I said before.'

'OK.' Garvie nodded. 'Cheers.'

'Is that it?'

'Yeah.'

'You don't want to ask me nothing about Amy? I thought that's what this was all about.'

Garvie shook his head, and Damon got to his feet, uncertain. Garvie passed him the photograph of Amy. 'You might as well have this.'

Damon's face lit up. 'Cheers.'

'And this.' He handed him a card.

'What is it?'

'My number. If things get bad you can give me a bell.'

'Funny. On a funny little card and everything. I like that. Old school like me. I don't like gadgets, they make me anxious.'

'Yeah, thought they might.'

Before he went, Damon looked at him. 'Maybe Rylee was right,' he said. Then he backed away, bumped into someone, swore to himself and scrambled his way off the tram as the doors were closing. The last Garvie saw of him, he was jogging along Watt Street away from Market Square.

20

Earlier that evening Singh had been to see the chief. He was anxious, he said, about the state of the investigation. They were nearing the end of the third day of Amy's disappearance. Progress had been far too slow. He was unable to make up time on his own. He needed more resources.

Bob Dowell was called in. He stood with Singh in front of the chief's desk.

The chief said, 'Have you located the boy with the van yet?'

'No, sir.'

The chief considered this. 'Regrettable,' he murmured, 'that you didn't lock down his whereabouts before letting him go.'

Singh began to mention that there had been no grounds for holding Damon longer, but the chief put up his hand and he fell silent.

'You're right, Inspector,' the chief said. 'Not enough progress.' He indicated an iPad on his desk loaded with images of the mocked-up front pages of the Sunday morning papers. 'Our friends in the media agree with you. What would you do with more resources?'

'Sweep the woods again; the volunteer effort was inadequate. We know she was in the woods; I think there's evidence there to be found if we act quickly. Find Damon Walsh; I think he has more to tell us. And we have over a dozen sightings of Amy not pursued.'

Dowell said quickly, 'If we lose focus with Imperium now we'll never recover it.'

The chief slowly put his finger ends together, and there was silence in the office while he stared at them both.

At last he said to Dowell, 'Core Operations will move over to the Roecastle investigation.'

Dowell gave a snort. 'But, sir—'

'The girl's been missing for nearly seventy-two hours. The media are on to it. Not enough progress has been made; I don't want any more excuses. Inspector,' he said to Singh.

'Sir?'

'You have another forty-eight hours in charge. After that you'll pass the leadership to Bob, and report to him. Understood?'

Singh's face tightened a notch. 'Yes, sir.'

And, as Dowell began to talk informally to the chief of other things, he left and went back his makeshift office.

Now it was late.

He had drawn up plans of action for individual members of the Core Operations team. He had reviewed the forensic evidence. He had set up new lines of communication with partnership agencies, the Missing Persons Bureau, Children's Services, and various charities. He had spoken again to Dr Roecastle, who was in need of his constant support now. And he had reviewed the case files of Damon Walsh, which he felt held important information about Amy.

Neither of Damon's parents had had any contact with their son for several years, and had shown no interest in him now. Of the many foster parents, guardians, mentors and sponsors assigned to him over the years, only two had been contactable, and their assistance had been limited. Paul Tanner could offer him no further information. Damon's criminal records from the Young Offenders and Narcotics databases gave a picture of a likeable but unstable young man with severe anger management issues, but no clues as to his current whereabouts. Singh had even managed to talk to Damon's stepbrother, currently living abroad, but he'd had nothing to add except the fact that everyone was fed up waiting for Damon to sort himself out.

He looked at his watch. Midnight. Nearly seventy-two hours since Amy had gone missing.

Someone as unsure of himself as Damon was liable to be unpredictable. He could easily drift permanently out of view. Or for that matter, Singh thought wryly, turn up again voluntarily.

It was then that Night Reception called up to tell him he had a visitor.

'Who is it?'

'He's nervous about giving his name. A young man. He says it's about a van.'

Singh was suddenly on his feet. 'Dark hair, about six foot?'

'Yes. Scruffy-looking.'

'I'm coming down now. Please make sure he doesn't leave.'

He crossed the hall rapidly and went down the stairs two at a time. He went past the café area where the television was playing images of traffic outside the shopping mall, and was almost running by the time he arrived in the police foyer. Through the glass the receptionist silently pointed her face towards the dark-haired young man slouched head in hands in a corner seat, and Singh burst into the room, and came to a sudden stop.

Garvie looked up.

There was only one chair in Singh's room so Garvie leaned against the wall.

'I liked your other office better. I liked the interrogation room better. Prison's probably better than this. I thought you'd been rehabilitated.'

Singh ignored him. 'When they called me down I assumed you were Damon.'

'Damon's lying low.'

'How do you know that?'

'He told me this evening.'

'You've seen him? But—'

'Wait a second before you lose your blob. What do you know about vans?'

Singh was silent.

'All right. What do you know about tyre tracks of vans found in woods?'

Singh said, 'We found no tracks. The overnight rain had destroyed everything.'

Garvie put in front of Singh a piece of paper. On it were drawn two patterns. 'Smudge's own unaided work,' he said. 'Good, aren't they? Luckily, he gave up art before he forgot how to draw.'

Singh gave the drawings his attention.

Garvie said, 'This one here is the sort of tyre you find on a Courier, Damon's van. See the tread? Thirteen inch.'

'OK. So?'

'So it's the wrong van.'

Garvie pointed to the other pattern. 'This one now is your Michelin Agilis, Alpin model. Fifteen inch. From a Transit probably.' He paused. 'That's the right van.'

'What do you mean, "right van"?'

'There's a clearing in the woods at the end of a rough track. Cars couldn't get down it, but a van could. After I found the dog I sat there a while, had a squint round, saw the tracks in the mud. There was a van parked there that night. Right in the middle of the woods. She must have almost run right into it. Only it wasn't Damon's van. Some other guy's. With Michelin Agilis tyres. If you want to find out what happened to Amy, you have to find that guy.'

Singh took this in.

'How can you be sure these drawings are accurate? You said your friend made them. Did he see these tyre tracks before they were washed away?'

'No. I did. And I remember stuff.'

Singh considered this. It was true. 'But,' he said, 'we have multiple sightings from Froggett residents of *Damon's* van up there. Small white van in a state of disrepair. In other words, a Courier.'

'How many just said "white van"?'

The inspector nodded reluctantly. 'As usual, witness sightings were inconsistent, it's true.'

'There you go then. Damon was up there. But so was some other guy. You should be looking for the driver of an old white Transit with plenty of red mud on the bumpers and wheel arches.'

'Why old?'

'Newer Transits take a sixteen inch. Like Smudge's brother's Custom. This is a fifteen, like I said.'

Singh nodded. 'All right, let's think about that. A man who drives an old Ford Transit. A small trader perhaps.'

'If business is all right most of them will upgrade. Smudge told me that.'

'A small trader just scraping by then. Or a solo courier. Or someone not bothered about fancy extras or a bit of rust. Gardeners, perhaps. Clearance guys.'

He looked at Garvie. 'I didn't know you were interested in vans.'

'Couldn't care less about them. That's why it's lucky I got Smudge. He's a real van whisperer.'

'Are you sure about all this?'

'Let's pretend I am. It'll save time.'

Singh nodded. Picked up his phone.

'It's gone midnight,' Garvie said.

'It's OK. He's a friend.'

'You've got a friend?'

Singh ignored him. Instead, as the phone rang, he said softly, 'Why did you come here to tell me this?'

'You need help. You've just about run out of time.'

The phone was answered.

'Bill? Raminder here. I know you're at home. Sorry it's so late. Remember the check you ran on owners of vans? No, it was fine. I saw all of them except three. If I remember, a Brickfields decorator, a man from Tick Hill, and someone called, I think, PJ. I didn't proceed with them because at that point we went in a different direction. Now we're back again. Do you have access to the information? Thank you. Which, if any of them, has a Transit? Yes, the bigger model. Yes. I see. Thanks. No, that's good. I've got the addresses.'

He hung up.

'The decorator and this man called PJ both drive a Transit. But the decorator's is brand-new.'

'Who's this PJ?'

'He lives the other side of Froggett Woods. Camps out. An eccentric, apparently.'

'What's he do?'

Singh paused. 'That's the thing. He does odd jobs. Gardening. A bit of clearance.' He pinched his lip with his fingers, frowning. 'I missed this. I must go now. Excuse me.'

He went out of the room and down the stairs.

He said to Garvie, who had fallen in behind him, 'How will you get home?'

'You can give me a lift after we've seen PJ.'

Singh stopped. 'No, no. You're not coming with me.'

'Identify the tyre tread by yourself then?'

'Hand me your drawing.'

Garvie put it in his pocket.

Singh glanced at his watch and said without moving his lips, 'Just make sure nobody sees you.' And they turned together down the stairs to the sally port.

21

They turned off at the car plant and drove briskly uphill towards Froggett. It was pitch-dark; fields and copses around them were invisible. Clouds in the night sky were pale and wispy like the faint night-breath of the black trees.

Records had phoned through supplementary details about the man called PJ. His name was Peter James Atkins, and he was fifty years old, ex-army. He'd done a tour of Iraq in 2003 and come back a mess. Now he lived in a converted garage in the woods, a peace activist, smoker of dope, hippyish mentor to the young, working occasionally as an odd-job man, specializing in garden clearance, supplemented with stints for a dispatch company and nights at a self-storage depot on the city ring road. He was a loner. Several complaints had been made against him for harassment and loitering – one, Garvie noted, by the headteacher at Marsh Academy – but none upheld.

'One of the strangest things,' Singh said, 'is that for a time he was personal chauffeur to Nicholas Winder. You remember, Imperium's owner.'

He passed Garvie his phone. A number of photographs of PJ had come through on it. The man had a squarish jaw, deeply lined face, pierced ears and nose, and tombstone teeth. Smiling, he looked wary and frightening. His ponytail was grey and frayed. He had strong hands and tattooed knuckles. He subsisted on herbs from the woods, and roadkill.

'Mentor to the young,' Garvie said. 'What's that mean?'

'He's worked with local authorities in the past as a guardian or sponsor of vulnerable young people.'

'In the past?'

'He was debarred from further employment five years ago after a complaint of harassment by the foster mother of a girl.'

There was a moment's silence in the car.

Garvie said, 'I hope we're not too late.'

Singh speeded up.

Beyond Froggett the lanes narrowed. A few miles north of Pike Pond, they went through an old wooden gate on a dirt track winding through trees. Halton Woods. Their headlights jolted up and down tangles of undergrowth as they went slowly through streaked darkness until they reached a small dirt clearing containing a garage-like concrete building and the tattered remains of a tent. Next to the tent was an old white Ford Transit.

There was no sign of anyone around. In the evening air hung a damp singed smell.

Singh lifted his head and sniffed. 'He's been burning things,' he said.

They got out of the car and went cautiously across rutted ground. The woodland silence waited around them as if listening. Here and there the area was littered with Calor gas canisters, rolls of barbed wire, polythene sheets.

Singh stood with his back to the van while Garvie crouched down by it. 'Well?' he asked quietly.

Garvie straightened up. 'Same tyres. And reddish dirt. This is the van all right.'

Singh nodded briefly. His face was grim. 'Wait in the car.'

'No thanks.'

Singh didn't bother to argue. They went together over to the garage. Nailed up on a rough board next to the door were the dried corpses of various small animals and birds – moles, rats and pigeons – and they stood looking at their leathery remains until it was clear no one was going to answer. The door was heavily padlocked with two locks.

'Good place to keep someone,' Garvie said without expression.

Singh banged loudly on the door, sending a bird clattering out of the tree above them.

There was no response. Silence descended.

'Wait here,' Singh said in an undertone. He crept away round the side of the building following the beam of his flashlight, and when he returned a few minutes later, emerging from the darkness of the other side, the door was open, and Garvie was putting something back in his pocket.

'Just sort of came open,' he said.

Singh said nothing but gave Garvie a disapproving look as he went past him through the doorway into darkness. There was a smell, kerosene, old cigarette smoke and something else, sweetish and out of place. After a moment Singh found the light switch and they looked about in silence.

Little attempt had been made to make the place comfortable. There were a few rugs spread here and there on the rough-cast concrete floor, an old sofa and a couple of garden chairs, a folding table. In one corner was a primus stove. The breeze-block walls were unpainted, the ceiling cladding bare and grey. Stacked against one wall were dozens of bags of cement, cans of paint, brass pipes. Behind a faded orange curtain hanging at the far end they could see the corner of a mattress on the floor.

The poverty of the place made them hushed.

'What's that smell?' Singh murmured. 'Is it liquor?'

'Or perfume. I hope not *Alien* by Mugler.'

Singh gave him a puzzled look. Together they went slowly down the centre of the room, quietly looking about, stopping occasionally to pick up an empty bottle or poke at a piece of clothing. At the far end Singh reached forward and drew back the orange curtain – and they both sucked in their breath. Everywhere were the unmistakable signs of a struggle. Jagged bits of a destroyed chair were strewn across the floor. Smashed glass was scattered along the wall. A bent and broken lamp lay in a corner. The mattress itself was ripped open and partially burned, as if someone had tried to set it alight.

The smell of perfume hit them harder.

Singh talked into his radio, and went to work. He took out a tool of some sort and, crouching, began to sift carefully through the debris. He traced the trail of glass, and found the frayed flex of the lamp in a knot under the sleeping bag, and examined the dark pool of dried liquid that had formed around its edge. From time to time he put things into small clear plastic bags.

When he looked up Garvie was standing there, holding something between his fingertips. A silver ring with an unusual pattern of spirals picked out in black.

Singh took it. 'What's this?'

'Hers,' Garvie said simply and walked away.

Garvie waited by the van, smoking, while Singh sat in his car talking to Support. The woods around were blacker than ever.

At last Singh finished and they sat together in the car waiting for Forensics and backup to join them.

'One of the men will take you home,' Singh said. 'I've told your uncle where you are.'

If Garvie was concerned about this he didn't show it.

'What happens now? Manhunt?'

Singh hesitated. 'Our focus remains on finding Amy. But, yes, we urgently need to contact Atkins.'

'The media are going to love him. Hippy dropout. Dope smoker. Loiterer round schools and woods. Harasser of underage girls.'

Singh winced. 'I was too slow,' he murmured. 'Far too slow.'

Garvie ignored him. 'What happens now?'

'The case will be treated as suspected abduction. I will need to talk to Dr Roecastle as soon as Forensics and the GPR team arrive.'

'GPR?'

Singh hesitated. 'Ground-penetrating radar.'

Garvie looked at him. 'They're going to dig?'

'In these situations it is common for the body to be buried nearby. I'm sorry.'

Garvie got out of the car and walked away. In the shadow of the trees at the edge of the clearing he stopped and lit up, and stood there smoking. There would be time to think about the events that had led up to this conclusion. But not now. What came into his mind instead were random details in no known sequence he could think of: Amy Roecastle's face in the photograph with that impish expression of cleverness; the scuffed, rebel-girl clothes in her wardrobe, the maths problem in her exercise book that she had left abandoned.

The silence was broken by sudden animal squeals, and a fox barked again, nearer this time, marking a kill.

22

It hit the news. Too late for the Sunday papers, reports of the manhunt appeared on the internet throughout the morning. Breaking News flashes raised the alarm: *Police Hunt Dropout. Face of a Predator. Recluse on the Run.* By lunchtime the same picture of Peter Atkins had appeared everywhere: the bony face of a man in combat jacket with grey ponytail, gesturing blearily with a spliff across a table of empty bottles.

There were stories from his life: lurid descriptions of the breakdown after his tour of duty in Iraq; a period of peddling narcotics on a beach in Goa; minor incidents at festivals, protests and raves. Twice in the last year he had faced charges for possession of cannabis, and once for harassment, since dropped. A colleague at the delivery company where he occasionally worked called him a 'loner'. His brother, who had emigrated to Australia, said he hadn't spoken to him in fifteen years and hoped never to do so again. A resident of Froggett Woods, speaking on condition of anonymity, said he was a predatory presence in the area, often to be seen at night, unnervingly, in the lanes or the woods.

Stalker on the Run. Suspect Has 'Mental Issues'. Find Him!

Newer stories called in strident voices for his immediate capture and enforced confession, and the chief of police, in carefully neutral tones, promised approximately the same thing. The public should be reassured: huge police resources were being devoted to the hunt.

There was the unspoken assumption that, for Amy Roecastle, it was too late, however; and now that the drama of her disappearance had assumed its final and ugliest form, her picture was everywhere too, the girl of radiant possibility snuffed out by perverted desires.

The rest of Sunday disappeared in speculation and distress.

On Monday the blinds at 'Four Winds' remained down all day.

Smudge's brother and the men moved quietly about the garden, as if out of respect, digging foundations for the wooden pagoda which was to form a feature above the patio. But the only digging in Dr Roecastle's mind was being done with the help of ground-penetrating radar in a clearing in Halton Woods. Singh had been updating her every few hours. The previous evening she had identified Amy's ring, and today she had cancelled all operations and sat now on the floor of her black-and-white living room in her dressing gown, knees up to her chest, squeezing a ball of wet tissues in each fist, as if only the intense concentration of her own misery could prevent bad news reaching her about her daughter. In reality, however, she was waiting, silently, for the worst. Singh had told her that although she should not give up hope, the investigation had moved now into a different phase.

She couldn't stop herself calling him: two, three, four times an hour. He always said that there had been no new developments.

At lunchtime she took a milligram of Xanax and 20 milligrams of Inderal, and washed them down with a glass of Scotch.

By the end of the afternoon, motionless in the same position, staring with glassy eyes at nothing, she was so exhausted that when the phone rang she almost fainted as she staggered to get it.

She heard Singh say, 'Dr Roecastle?'

'Have you found her?'

'Are you OK?'

'Tell me quickly! What have you found?'

Singh hesitated. He said carefully, 'I'd like to come to see you. There have been . . . developments, but I need to see you so that we can talk face to face.'

After he rang off she held the phone for a moment, then dropped it and watched it settle on the floor. It seemed very far away from her, in a different dimension altogether. She willed it to disappear, for herself to disappear, and for the world to come to an end, but none of this happened, and she told herself to sit on the sofa to wait for Singh to arrive, to prepare herself to hear what he had to say, however terrible, but she didn't move, didn't seem able to; she stayed exactly where she was, swaying slightly from side to side in a sort of seasickness, feeling the room go in and out of focus around her, and was still there half an hour later when she heard his knock on the door.

With great effort she managed to turn to face the living-room doorway, and saw with paralysing clarity exactly what was happening. It was as if she had lived it already. As she heard the front door open and close and Singh's footsteps come down the hall, she foresaw precisely how he would appear, and precisely what he would say, and knew beyond all doubt that she would remember for the rest of her life the exact words he used to give her the news.

Then Amy walked in.

She was dirty and bedraggled, as if she'd been sleeping rough. 'What the fuck's going on?' she said. 'This fence. I thought it was only going to be at the front.'

23

She was recognizably Amy, wearing a familiar black vest and black bondage trousers, but she seemed changed, and not just because she was dirty and tired. There was a fierce expression on her face as she stood there blinking, and after a moment Dr Roecastle realized that her daughter was crying. She went hesitantly across the room, and Amy lifted up her arms and they silently caught hold of each other.

They had not moved from this position when Singh arrived five minutes later. He stood in the doorway, ignored, watching them, and at last Dr Roecastle stepped back and said to him, 'Amy's here,' and he nodded and came quietly into the room.

There would be procedures, he said, after introducing himself to Amy, investigatory debriefings, not to mention medical attention, and evaluation for post-traumatic stress and other psychological conditions, and it would be necessary to take Amy down to the station later, and of course there would be the media to deal with, but first they simply sat together on the sofas in Dr Roecastle's black-and-white living room, as if acclimatizing to the strangeness of the situation.

Singh gave the cautionary advice: 'This is probably not the time for questions.'

And Dr Roecastle said, 'But for God's sake, Amy, just tell us where you've been all this time.'

Singh watched the girl as she sat there. Dirty and tired though she was, unwashed, her long hair matted, he could see that Sophie had not lied about her friend's looks.

The girl turned her face towards her mother, and said, 'Dad's.'

Dr Roecastle gagged. 'What do you mean, "Dad's"? I thought he was in California. I thought you said you never wanted to see him again.'

'He's renting this little place in the country. He's on sabbatical from the university, and he's got this research thing he's doing there.'

'How do you even know that? You never talk to him.'

Amy gave a broken smile. '*You* never talk to him.'

Singh said, 'We will be able to go through all this at a later stage, Amy. We will need to, in fact. As I say, this may not be the right moment for questions.'

Her mother said, 'But at least tell me *why*. Why, Amy, why did you leave?'

Amy said nothing for a moment. She glanced once at Singh, and he thought she almost smiled. She sighed, looked embarrassed. 'I know it might seem like a little thing, but . . .'

She told them about the shoes.

When she had come into the house that night and had seen the shoes back in their bag, waiting on the table, something seemed to go off with a bang in her head. She closed herself off completely, couldn't even speak. The decision to leave home was taken, without forethought, as soon as her mother left the room. 'I just couldn't hack it any more.' She went upstairs, dumped her coat, and went out of the window to avoid triggering the alarm which her mother had just set.

'You went out into that rain without a coat?'

'Of course not. I took a pac-a-mac. It got shredded, though.'

Singh spoke up. 'In the woods?'

She nodded. 'At first I was going to go to Soph's, stay with her for a night, move on the next day. But . . .' She hesitated. 'The rain was much worse than I'd thought. I was going along the path and I could hardly see, and the noise was horrible. And then . . . I thought I saw someone.'

'What do you mean?'

'On the path behind me. I got scared. Not really like me, but with all the rain and the thunder . . . I ducked into the woods, along a track I know, I thought I could hide there. But somehow it was worse. I thought I could hear him following me. I panicked. I really lost it, running through the trees. I kept falling. At one point I was sure someone grabbed me, but it was just branches whipping about in the storm. Eventually I found a place to shelter, and I stayed there for, I don't know, more than an hour. And when the storm had passed and I walked back to the path it was way too late to go to Soph's.'

'So what did you do?'

'I walked over to Battery Hill and waited in that cutesy bus stop there, and caught an early bus, and hitched a bit, and got to Dad's about lunchtime.'

'What about Rex?' Dr Roecastle asked. 'Why did you take him?'

Amy looked puzzled. 'Rex? What do you mean? I wouldn't take that brute anywhere, you know that. Why, what's happened?'

'Well, he seems to have got out that night. And I'm afraid his body was found in the woods.'

'He died?'

Singh said, 'It's possible he was killed.'

'How? By another animal?'

Singh said nothing.

'Of course,' Amy said. 'He was really old.'

'That's true,' Dr Roecastle said after a moment. 'Nearly thirteen. I was forgetting that.'

Singh said, 'Wasn't your father surprised to see you when you arrived?'

Amy curled her lip. 'My dad's not surprised by anything. On account of not really caring about anything except his work. The good thing was, he doesn't read the papers so I didn't have to answer any awkward questions. In fact, he kept forgetting I was there.'

'Were you with him until today?'

'Yes.'

'Didn't you see the news? Didn't you realize there was a hunt for you?'

She hesitated. 'I didn't see anything for ages, like not till the weekend. Deliberately. I didn't want to know. When I finally realized what was going on, I was . . . embarrassed, I suppose. No, horrified. I knew I had to come back, but I stayed a day longer. I have a lot of unfinished business with my father, and I wanted to put things straight with him, but in the end, last night, we had a row, and that decided me. I caught a train this morning. By then I was feeling nervous. Well, scared. I realized how big it had all got.' She gave Singh a full, frank look. 'I guess I'm going to have to say sorry.'

Her mother said, 'Oh, Amy, I've been so worried. We just didn't know where you were. That man with the van seemed to know but the police let him go.'

'What man?'

'Damon Walsh,' Singh said.

'Damon? Damon doesn't know anything,' Amy said. 'Not about me, not about the world. Didn't he tell you that?'

'He did, in fact,' Singh said.

Her mother was looking at her aghast. 'You mean, it's *true*? You're actually having a *relationship* with this person?'

'Not any more. It's been all over with Damon for a while. He just doesn't seem to be able to accept it.'

'Amy!'

'You think I tell you everything?'

'Well, what about this other awful man, this vagrant living in the woods?'

'What other awful man?'

'The police found your ring in his hovel.'

'My ring?'

'Your spiral ring. In a den in the woods where this man—'

'I don't know what you're talking about – it's not *my* spiral ring.' She held out her hand, and on her finger was the ring.

Everything then fell into place.

'Oh, Amy!' Holding the ring in her hand, Dr Roecastle finally let herself go. 'What we've been thinking! It's all been such a nightmare!' She began to sob, and Singh stood and suggested that they get ready to go down to the station with him.

Amy went upstairs.

Singh noted the time – 17:30 on Monday the 13th of August – and went outside to make calls, and Dr Roecastle sat for a moment longer on her own in the living room, her eyes shut, her face lifted to the ceiling, her hand squeezed shut round Amy's spiral ring, just listening to the silence.

There was a noise and she opened her eyes.

He stood inside the room wearing a stained hooded top and sweat pants, watching her with that expressionless look of his, and she sat up. With as much dignity as she could manage, she said, 'She has returned.'

'I know.'

'How do you know?'

'Her bedroom window's shut.'

He said nothing else.

Irritated, but feeling herself in a position to be magnanimous, she said, 'I remain grateful for your help. Even if it was brief, and you were unsuccessful. I suppose we all jump to conclusions sometimes. I just wish the police hadn't made the ridiculous assumption that it was Amy's ring they found in that man's squat. It turns out that Amy was wearing her ring all the time.' She opened her fist and showed it to him lying on her palm.

He made no response.

More irritated still, she said, 'And, as it happens, Amy's reason for leaving was exactly what I thought. A fit of anger. About the shoes, in fact, so there you made a lucky guess.'

Again she paused, and again Garvie made absolutely no response.

'You see, our instincts aren't always wrong.'

There was silence for a few moments.

'Shoes?' he said at last.

'Yes, I just told you.'

He nodded. Thought about it. 'You should ask her what she did with the box.'

Dr Roecastle stared at him. 'What on earth do you mean?'

But he had gone.

24

The media frothed, they foamed and blared. *Amy's Back!*, *Mother's Tears of Joy*, *She Just Went for a Walk*, *Manhunt Over.*

'Couldn't care less,' Garvie said.

'Come on now,' Uncle Len said. 'Think how relieved Dr Roecastle must be.'

They sat finishing curry chicken in the kitchen at 12 Eastwick Gardens.

His mother said, 'And she didn't need your help in the end, Garvie.'

'Who said I was going to help her?'

Looking at Garvie over the top of his glasses, Uncle Len said, 'We never quite got to the bottom of what you were doing with Raminder that evening. But we'll let that pass. Her mother was right, I've got to admit it. Amy went off in a temper and came back when she felt like it. Her father corroborated everything she said. He sounds like a nut. Raminder spent hours trying to contact him, and no one knew where he was, not even his university. He didn't notice the state his daughter was in. I suppose that's what maths geniuses are like.'

They all glanced briefly at Garvie.

In the living room Uncle Len picked up a copy of the newspaper. The headline was *The Runaway's Return*. 'But this,' Len said, shaking it, 'this is what makes me really angry. They've conveniently forgotten all the things they said about that fellow PJ.'

'Did they find him?' Aunt Maxie asked.

'He's still in hospital,' Garvie's mother said.

A matter of hours before Amy's return, vigilantes had recognized the ex-hippy in a small town nearby and had taken it on themselves to express their disapproval of his lifestyle, habits, political beliefs, diet, ponytail, marijuana use and, of course, almost certain guilt. He was recovering from a broken rib and disconnected eyeball in the Ophthalmology Acute Referral Unit of City Hospital, where Detective Inspector Singh had interviewed him earlier that day.

He had looked frailer than his photographs as he lay in the hospital bed, peering warily at Singh with his one good eye. His midriff was strapped with bandages; his left arm was in a sling. As he spoke, his voice reedy and hesitant, he gestured vaguely with his right hand, a small and faded tattoo of the Buddhist symbol for peace visible on his naked forearm. He did not know and had never knowingly met Amy Roecastle; he was bewildered and frightened by the accusation that he had abducted her. On the night when she had disappeared he had been working the night shift, as usual on Wednesdays, at the Red 'n' Black self-storage centre on the ring road. He admitted driving his van into Froggett Woods on a number of occasions at night: he was a badger-spotter, a fact confirmed by a number of people who knew him. It was also true that he had lit a fire near the place where he lived in Halton Woods: he had been disposing of common household waste, the obvious remains of which had been found subsequently by the Forensics and GPR teams. The ring that had been found inside his home was his own – generally worn on the long, thin forefinger of his right hand – the spiral symbolizing the path from the outer consciousness of the ego to the inner soul of cosmic awareness. He explained it at length to Singh.

After half an hour Singh had cut short their conversation, recommending off the record that the man hire a lawyer to look into the defamatory statements made in the media, and confirming that the case against him was closed.

'A sour note,' Uncle Len said, 'to an otherwise happy ending. Amy Roecastle simply went home when she was ready.'

Garvie snorted.

Uncle Len peered at him, surprised. 'What?'

'Nothing. Doesn't matter.'

His mother watched him narrowly as he got to his feet and went without speaking into his room.

Uncle Len looked at her, and she shook her head. 'Who knows what goes on in that boy's mind.'

'You think he's disappointed it's over?'

She shrugged. 'Maybe he's just irritated the whole damn thing broke his concentration on the fencing.'

'Poor Garvie,' his uncle said.

After a moment they began to laugh together. It was the last sound Garvie heard as he closed his bedroom door, lay down on the bed and stared impassively up at the ceiling. He was thinking about Amy Roecastle. Her face in the photograph. Her mouth, lips slightly parted, her eyes too, and the point of her chin so strong and delicate; and the look on her face, secretive and teasing.

And he thought about the shoe box she'd been carrying as she ran through the wood in the pelting rain.

25

Fencing duly continued the next day without interruption. It was the hottest day of the summer, bright and glowing. In the morning there was a breeze, but by lunchtime a stiff, solid warmth filled the garden. Leaves wilted on the trees, the raw fence glared in the light. Smudge and Garvie were given the task of creosoting the finished panels while Smudge's brother and the other men worked on the pagoda. They stripped to the waist and set to.

'Funny how things turn out,' Smudge said.

'What do you mean?'

'Vans. It's like, you know, they're really important.'

'Never doubted it, Smudge.'

'And this Amy Roecastle.'

'What about her?'

'Turns out she's not bad-looking. Outstanding in the frontal lobe department, if you know what I mean.'

'Yes, Smudge, I know what you mean.'

'She looks pretty skinny from the back, then she turns round, and *wham!*'

'Yes, Smudge.'

'Like wasps' nests, mate. Ever seen a wasps' nest? The way they—'

He had no chance to develop this theme, however, because Smudge's brother decided, who knew why, to separate them. Smudge took his can of creosote down to the stretch of fence by the gates, and Garvie carried on working alone by the panels he'd put up himself.

It didn't get any cooler. The afternoon heat pressed down, expanded to fill the smallest spaces – ears, nostrils, mouths – and drove out the air. Garvie wisely paced himself, taking cigarette breaks every fifteen minutes. Twice Smudge came over to bring him up to speed with his thinking about Amy Roecastle. An airless hour passed.

Becoming aware, for a third time, of someone standing behind him, and assuming it was Smudge again, Garvie said wearily, 'No offence, Smudge, but there's no point in telling me all this stuff about skinny from behind, outstanding frontal lobes and *wham!* they take your eye out. Why don't you go find her and tell yourself?'

There was a pause.

'I can only think it's because he's shy,' Amy Roecastle said.

Garvie hesitated a moment, then turned. She stood there, one hand on her hip, in black canvas trousers and black vest. She wasn't as tall as he'd imagined from her photographs. Her hair was looser, more unruly. She seemed pale, a little pinched-looking. But that face. And that familiar look on the face, amused and knowing.

He found his voice. 'Smudge is many things. But shy is not one of them.'

'You must be the shy one then.'

He shrugged.

'Though weirdly,' she went on, 'that's not what my mother told me.'

Garvie nodded. 'I'm glad you two are back on speaking terms. And it's nice to say hello. But, you know what, I've got to get on here.' He made a vague gesture with his brush. 'Thing about a fence is, you got to give it a hundred per cent.' He turned away, dipped his brush, and began to apply the creosote.

'This the bit you put up?'

He carried on creosoting. 'Yeah. The bit you flattened.'

There was a pause, as if she was giving the fence a closer look.

'Your post holes weren't deep enough,' she said. 'I could feel it going soon as I got up on it.'

'At least you didn't hurt yourself.'

'How do you know?'

''Cause you were fit enough afterwards to run through the woods with that dog of yours.'

She hesitated. 'Quite a fantasist, aren't you?'

'Got over it yet?'

'I'm fine. Bit tired. Slight stomach upset. Nothing out of the ordinary.'

Glancing sideways as he turned back to the fence, Garvie saw that Smudge had abandoned creosoting and was standing by the gates, more or less open-mouthed, watching him.

He was aware of Amy Roecastle watching him too as he worked. After a while he heard her say, 'You're not very good at this, you know. It's not even straight. Did you use a string line?'

He carried on patiently.

She said, 'You really are a crap fencer. You should stick to breaking into girls' bedrooms.'

Garvie turned then. 'I was asked to help out, all right?'

'Were you asked to leave your bootprints on my bed?'

'Comes under the category heading Unavoidable.'

'Were you asked to steal my photograph? Comes under the category heading Rude.'

Garvie shrugged. 'I was looking for something.'

'My photograph?'

'Your beanie. Wasn't there, oddly.'

'Course it wasn't there. I don't have a beanie.'

'That's not what your mother told me.'

'You think my mother knows the first thing about me?'

He carried on creosoting, and for a while she watched him.

She said at last, 'Can I have it back then?'

'What?'

'My photograph.'

'Gave it away.'

She made a noise, half-gasp, half-laugh. 'You gave it away? Who to?'

'Damon, of course.'

He turned back to the fence and began again to creosote. There was a brief silence. When she spoke again, her voice was different, uncertain.

'I thought you didn't find Damon.'

'Let's pretend I did.'

After a while she said, in a quiet voice, 'How was he?'

'Great. You'd think he'd be bust up and broken down after you dumped him but he didn't seem to realize he'd been dumped.'

She hesitated again. 'Yeah, well. That's Damon for you.'

'You better make it clear to him. He's not very good at working stuff out.'

'How can I? He's gone missing.'

'Give him a call.'

'Don't have his number. And he never had mine. Better that way.'

For a moment they looked at each other. Then she looked past him, at the fence.

He said, 'Go for it. Cheap shots are the best.'

She said, 'You know what you should stick to?'

'Yeah. Minding my own business.'

'Numbers. You're a bit of a maths genius, aren't you?'

'How do you know?'

'Your mother told my mother, for one thing.'

He looked grim. 'That's what mothers are for. Said it yourself. For saying stuff, and pissing off their kids, and making a fuss. And for getting kids from Five Mile into trouble. Though, hey, those kids were born in trouble. They're used to it. They *like* it.'

She laughed then, and he saw how wide her mouth was, and how white her teeth, and the way her nose wrinkled like a rabbit's. 'For another,' she said, 'you left behind a clue in my room. Number five.'

He just shrugged.

'Thing is, I didn't even understand the question. And I'm meant to be good at maths. After all, my dad actually is a maths genius. You did proofs for sequence limits at Marsh?'

'Never heard of them before.'

She looked at him and pursed her lips. 'Just a lucky guess then,' she said slyly.

He said, 'Listen. We know the limit is 1. We know the value is $\frac{1}{5000}$.'

'Yeah. I got that bit.'

'So apply the definition of a_n to the definition of the limit and plug in the numbers. You worked out the fourth term in the sequence already.'

'Yeah, I remember. $\frac{4097}{4096}$.'

'Right. And the first term?'

She hesitated, but only for a moment. '$\frac{9}{8}$.'

'Right. And the second term?'

'$\frac{65}{64}$. Wait, I get it now. The limit's 1. Each term's closer by a smaller and smaller amount.'

'That's it.'

'Third and fourth terms are $\frac{513}{512}$, and $\frac{4097}{4096}$. I'd already got those. Fifth term's $\frac{32769}{32768}$.'

'Yeah. Closer to the limit by $\frac{1}{8}$, then by $\frac{1}{64}$, then $\frac{1}{512}$, then $\frac{1}{4096}$, then . . .'

'Then $\frac{1}{32768}$. The fifth term. Which is smaller than $\frac{1}{5000}$.'

'So N equals 5.'

'So bingo.'

She was looking at him now with undisguised interest.

He said, 'You'd've got it if you hadn't decided to go walkabout.' He glanced over his shoulder. 'Anyway, look. If I don't make a mess of this a bit faster I'm going to get shouted at.'

She looked at him. Smiled again. 'All right, maths boy. You better get to it. Oh, by the way.'

'What?'

'Saturday night. Party time. Place in Battery Hill. Cross Keys House, Turnpike Road. Take your mind off the fencing for a bit.'

He looked at her impassively.

'Think you might make it?'

'Maybe.'

'Got an excuse for *not* making it?'

'Could have. I could forget the address.'

'I get the feeling you're the sort of boy who doesn't forget anything.'

'I might make an exception.'

'I think you'd be making a mistake.'

'Five Mile kid with all the posh girls? What would your mother think?'

'Can we stop talking about mothers? The one

shocking thing about me going off is that my mother actually noticed. I didn't think it would register. I'm pretty sure the only reason she contacted the police was to get at me. Thing is, Dr Roecastle FRCS doesn't actually need a daughter. She's got her work.'

He watched her as she went down the lawn, something fluid, almost jokey, in the way she walked, like a cartoon fawn picking its way through cartoon scrub, fearless for all its delicacy.

Smudge materialized at his shoulder.

'Got to say I'm impressed. Never known you move so quick, Garv.'

'I didn't move at all, Smudge.'

'No, but she was over here like a ferret up a drainpipe.'

'I'm doing the fencing, Smudge. She goes for fencers, van drivers, kids from Limekilns and Five Mile. In other words, she likes to piss off her mother.'

'Sounds good. I do fencing *and* I like vans. Do you think I'm in with a shout?'

'No doubt about it, mate.'

'Did she say anything about me?'

'Yeah, she did actually.'

'What?'

'Invited you to a party Saturday.'

Smudge's face fell. 'Can't make Saturday. Still.' He grinned. 'It's the thought that counts. Say anything else about me?'

'Not that I remember. But maybe she was thinking about you.'

Smudge smiled modestly. 'You reckon? I saw her sneaking a look from time to time.'

'Only natural, you being stripped to the waist.'

Smudge took hold of some of his belly. 'Some girls like it big,' he said. 'That's what I heard. Tell you something else about girls.'

And he would have done if his brother hadn't appeared to tell them something about fencing.

On his own again, Garvie smoked a cigarette, looked at his watch, settled at last to creosoting, though his thoughts were elsewhere, with Amy Roecastle, a girl with a sharp mind and a beautiful mouth and a sense of humour, a posh girl, a rebel – and a liar.

26

Cross Keys House, a big brindle-coloured stone building, had been a farm once. It ranged in sections alongside Turnpike Road at the junction to Froggett between a row of cottages and the open countryside. At the country end a tall solid wooden gate, shut and locked now, gave on to a gravel drive, which curved round the house to the garden at the back, a declining sweep of lawn to a dry-stone wall and, beyond that, water meadows, newly mown, a pale shaved green under the dark night sky.

Mrs Brighouse had gone away and left her daughter in charge. Eighty decibels of hip-hop ripped the air as Jay-Z and Kanye West smacked the house around. About thirty kids danced barefoot on the quaking lawn with glasses of Pimm's in their hands. Some lay on the patio or in the bushes.

Amy and Sophie stood together by the marquee. Sophie was wearing an electric blue backless halter from Selfridges, and Amy was wearing a black plastic mini, fishnets and a biker top with studs. It was nearly midnight.

Sophie said, 'I haven't talked to you all evening. How are you feeling?'

She put out a hand and touched Amy's, and they exchanged a look.

'I'll be OK.'

'Not in the mood for a party?'

Amy looked around the garden and sighed. 'Don't you ever want to be *needed* by someone? I mean, really needed. Someone who thinks only you will do.' She made a gesture. 'No one here needs me. They're just the usual suspects. The guys we see all the time. The dancers and the drama set and boys from Abingford's.'

'There's a rugby team from Dylan's said they'd come. They're real party boys, apparently. And fit.'

'Not exactly out of the demographic, are they? Dylan's is like the most expensive school in the county.'

'Well, who did you want to come?'

But before Amy could answer, Sophie turned excitedly towards the house. 'Oh my God, they're here. The Dylan crew. I can hear them breaking stuff in the kitchen.'

Twenty boys carrying a mannequin lacking a leg paraded out of the back door and across the patio singing high-class smut, and began en masse to gyrate suggestively with the doll. Sophie ran towards them and was soon lost among the semi-naked bodies, leaving Amy to sip her margarita alone, looking around at everyone. She knew them all, knew everything about them. She knew their Abercrombie and Fitch, their Ralph Lauren, their Comme des Garçons

T's and trainers; she knew their excitable voices, their innocent manners, their habits, dreams and pets.

Then she saw him. He was standing on his own in the entrance to the marquee, looking as if he'd been there all evening, though he must have only just arrived. He took the cigarette out of his mouth and nodded briefly. Something about him – not just his ordinary black jeans and scuffed zip-up leather jacket, or his oddly beautiful face, or his abstracted expression – made him look so different from everyone else that a zone of exclusion seemed to have formed around him and left him on his own.

She crossed the lawn.

'You remembered the address then.'

'Yeah, well. I'm the boy who doesn't forget.'

'It's good you know who you are. In a minute someone's going to come over and ask you.'

'They done that already.'

'Well, I hope you had ID on you.'

'I told them I've got my name written in the back of my jacket. They seemed to think that was good enough.'

They stood there.

'These your friends then?' he said after a while.

'Yes. These are my friends. This is my life, right here. This is me, in fact.' She made an impatient gesture that took in the lawn, the marquee, the house, all the people in view. 'Me, me, me, multiplied I don't know how many times.'

'Forty-seven.'

She looked at him curiously. 'You counted how many people are here?'

'I just sort of noticed.'

'How weird is that?'

'You told me I should stick to numbers.'

She looked at him slyly, slantwise. 'All right, maths boy. Forty-seven people here. Party kicked off at ten o'clock. Twenty of them drink at a regular rate of a shot every twelve minutes, ten people at a rate of six shots an hour, seven people at a rate of three shots an hour, six people a double every other quarter of an hour, and four people a shot every ten minutes for the first hour, a shot every twenty minutes for the next hour, and a shot every forty minutes after that. If it takes ten shots to get drunk, how many people are still sober at one in the morning?'

'Seven.'

She thought a moment. 'Correct. The ones drinking three shots an hour.'

'But by half past everybody's drunk. Sounds about right by the look of it.'

She was looking at him curiously. 'You're a bit of a freak, aren't you?'

He just shrugged.

The boys from Dylan's had removed one of the mannequin's arms, in which was hidden a stash of weed, and people gathered around them in excitement on the patio. There was some shouting. On the lawn generalized dancing was going on unrelated to the music. Someone came out of the house carrying several bottles of expensive liquor from Sophie's mother's drinks cabinet and Amy took one.

'How about it? Want to get drunk?'

'I'm all right, thanks.'

'Mind if I do?'

He looked at her a moment. 'She's not here, you know.'

'Who?'

'Your mother. She's not here to see you piss her off.'

'Maybe I like getting drunk.'

He shrugged.

'Maybe I'm wild. Maybe you should be getting nervous.'

'I'll bear it in mind.'

She put the bottle to her lips. 'Any minute now I could get unpredictable.'

He watched her calmly as he smoked.

'That's my reputation,' she said. 'People can't work me out. Do you think you can work me out?'

'I can't even put up a fence panel. How could I work you out?'

She laughed then.

Still smoking, he looked past her towards the house and said blandly, 'Here comes your ex. Now you'll be able to ask for your photograph back.'

She turned. There was a commotion by the French windows, some pushing and shoving. The boys from Dylan's had formed a police guard around the mannequin, and a blonde girl was trying to calm people down, and out of the crowd Damon eventually emerged with his grin a little battered and came erratically towards them.

He nodded at Garvie. 'Hey.'

Garvie nodded back. 'How's it going?'

'Starting to happen, man.'

He went past him towards Amy, who stood staring at him in horror. The blood had drained from her face.

'Babe,' Damon said to her. 'Listen. It's cool. I worked it out. I know what you got to do.'

As if snapping out of a trance, Amy stepped forward and caught hold of him.

'What?' he said, but before he could say anything else she hustled him round the side of the marquee out of sight, leaving Garvie on his own, smoking thoughtfully.

The party was turning out to be more interesting than he'd thought.

After a while the blonde girl came to talk to him. She had a soft, lisping voice, and she used it on him until he actually started to feel dizzy. She was very blonde. It was fascinating how blonde she was. She didn't seem very interested in what he had to say but she had a pretty way of talking.

'You know what?' she said.

'Probably not.'

'I think she likes you. Amy.'

'Only till she finds out I know nothing about vans.'

As soon as the blonde girl had gone Damon appeared again. He was no longer smiling. He looked confused.

'Listen,' he said and fell quiet.

Garvie waited. 'Still listening,' he said after a while.

'What? Oh yeah. Listen. These people.'

'What about them?'

'Mental, innit?'

Garvie nodded. 'Yeah. Like Market Square the other night.'

'Yeah. That was bad. Like the Wild fucking West or—' He bit his tongue and scowled at Garvie. 'Told you before,' he said. 'I'm getting out till it blows over.'

'It has blown over. She came back. No one thinks you did anything.'

Damon frowned. 'Going anyway. Not sticking round to get a misjudgement slapped on. Know what I mean?'

'Not really.'

'Always me gets the blame. I been stupid, trusted people I shouldn't have trusted. Got my stash. I'm clocking out. And once I go, I told you, I'm gone, no one finds me then. Not even you.' He grinned a great grey grin, and squeezed Garvie's shoulder. 'Get what I'm saying?'

'Look the other way.'

He half turned. 'What? Oh. Yeah, that's it. You got it.' He grinned. 'Cheers, then.'

'Cheers, Damon.'

Then he was going, weaving his way stiff-legged across the lawn.

Garvie lit up another Benson & Hedges. Amy hadn't come back. It was two in the morning; time to go. The party had mellowed through several stages of numbness from Daft Punk to Kanye West to Taylor Swift and had finally stalled in a general air of dazed apathy. He picked his way across the bodies on the lawn, and went into the house, through the kitchen and down the hall towards the front door. And that was when he saw her, in a large room full of big old furniture, standing on her own in front of the television. She was watching a feature on the 24/7 news channel about the Market Square riot and its aftermath.

As he hesitated by the doorway, she looked across and he lifted a hand.

'Just off. Thanks and everything.'

She leaned down quickly and switched off the television. Something in the way she moved made him pause.

'I'm not drunk,' she said.

She came over, moving the ways drunks move, hardly at all, then all at once, and sat down suddenly on the convenient arm of a sofa.

He thought about that. 'How are you getting home?'

'Walk.' She made walking gestures with her fingers.

Garvie watched her and she watched him back.

'OK. Let's go.'

'You don't have to come with me.'

'Think of it as a favour to your mother. Seeing you don't get not-abducted again.'

'I wish you wouldn't keep mentioning my mother.'

They went together out of the house and crossed Turnpike Road, and onto the path that ran through the woods.

It was very dark among the trees, and they went slowly through the silence broken only by brief bird noise here and there and the sound of their breathing. Bits of moonlight coming through the leaves picked out the studs on her biker jacket. Her plastic mini made squeaky noises as she walked. Occasionally they bumped together on the narrow path. Once she stumbled, and he caught her round her waist and held her up, and for a moment her hair was in his face, soft and scratchy, and he put her down and they went on again without speaking.

He could feel her looking at him.

'Tell me about you,' she said at last.

'Nothing to tell.'

They went on in silence.

'Now it's your turn to ask me to tell you about me,' she said.

Garvie thought about that. He said, 'Tell me about Damon.'

'Nothing to tell,' she said at last, shortly.

'Seems to me the most interesting person around,' Garvie said. 'Mostly I like him. He's a bit on edge, of course.'

She didn't say anything to that.

'Can't always hold it together, I bet.'

She made an ambiguous noise.

'Gets mixed up with the wrong sort of people.'

'Why do you say that?'

'People let him down. He mentioned it.'

She said nothing to that either, and they went on again in silence.

'Scared of him?' Garvie asked.

She came to a dead stop. 'Why would I be scared of him?'

'Posh girls get mixed up in dangerous stuff sometimes.'

'Damon's not dangerous.'

'How do you know I'm talking about Damon?'

She bit her lip and they climbed on in silence, out of the shadows of the trees into moonlight and the open path towards her house.

Garvie spoke again. 'You're soul mates, right? You and Damon.'

'Actually, I don't want to talk about Damon any more.'

'But you had a big bust-up recently.'

She looked at him confused.

'In fact, you let him down. Big-time. He needed you and you blew him off.'

She came alive then, her voice clear and sober and outraged. '*I did not!*'

'Now that's interesting,' Garvie said. 'That's the most interesting thing you've said.'

She was almost shaking, staring at him angrily. They were standing together on the path near the back fence of 'Four Winds'. When the echo of her voice died away it was very still and quiet. Garvie could hear her breathing fiercely as she looked at him.

'Well,' he said. 'See you around.'

'You leaving me here?'

He glanced down the path. 'It's approximately fifteen seconds to your back garden. I calculate the chances of you being abducted in that time are small.'

'How am I going to get over the fence? You put it up again.'

'You did it before.'

She swayed as she looked at it. 'I'm not sure I can climb over any of it just now,' she said helplessly.

Garvie looked at her, nodded. 'You'd have a real problem if you were drunk,' he said. 'But,' he added softly, 'you're not actually drunk, are you?'

Then he was going, and Amy stood on the path alone, looking after him thoughtfully before scaling the fence and fluently vaulting over into her garden.

27

Monday was yet another great day for fencing. But not for Garvie. Smudge's brother had sacked him.

'Why?' his mother asked when she came in that evening.

Garvie shrugged. 'Something to do with fence posts. Or string lines maybe.'

He was slumped at the kitchen table. Looking at him, his mother wondered if he'd been sitting there all day. He was capable of doing absolutely nothing for long periods of time.

She went over and sat down with him. 'Garvie, do you and me need to have a talk?'

'Thought we'd finished with all that stuff.'

'I mean, do you need pepping up? Look, you're all grown up. You're out there. And what you'll find is, there're a lot of things in this world you're going to have no use for. That's natural. But you always got me, OK? You might not think it, might not always want it, but it's true. Listen, I've got some spending money you can have. Why don't you go out with your friends, have a few laughs?'

'I'm all right.'

'You sure?'

'Yeah. I'm good.'

'Up to you. Me? I'm going out.'

An hour later she was dressed for it, a different outfit this time, leopard-print trousers and a black top with big yellow bangles. While she finished getting ready he watched her. She seemed happier than he'd seen her for a long time. Younger too, somehow. She was only thirty-eight, he worked out. That was a simple sum he'd never done before. Young enough to go out, have a few drinks, have dinner, go dancing if she wanted to.

At the door she said, 'I got the late shift tomorrow, so don't wait up,' and then she was gone, and only her perfume remained.

Silence in the flat.

After half an hour or so it was broken by a call. Smudge.

'Mate. Couldn't believe it when my brother told me. How you doing?'

'You mean without fencing?'

'Yeah. Can't imagine it.'

'Well, Smudge. I'm getting through the pain, bit by bit.'

'Stick with it, man. Coming out?'

'Got stuff to do first. Give you a ding later?'

'Anytime.'

He rang off, and sat there with the phone in his hand. After a while he got up, went into his room and lay on the bed and sighed and concentrated on the ceiling.

Standing in the doorway of the black-and-white living room at 'Four Winds', wearing black combat trousers, a black long-sleeved top and an electric blue bandana, Amy Roecastle informed her mother that she was going out.

'What, now? On a Monday? It's ten o'clock.'

'One of Sophie's friends is picking me up.'

'Where are you going?'

'The new gastro out at Poplar. Just to see what it's like. One drink, that's all. Quiet.'

Dr Roecastle frowned. 'Can't it wait till the weekend?'

'I just told you, Sophie's friend is picking me up.'

Dr Roecastle stood and confronted her. 'Amy,' she said in a low voice. 'Are you telling me the truth?'

'Oh, for God's sake.'

'Where are you going? Tell me, please.'

'I just did.'

'You're not going to meet that man?'

Rolling her eyes, Amy turned and walked across the hallway and out of the house. It was a soft summer's night; the sky was the colour of blue milk, pale clouds at the horizon still luminous. Warm air in soft puffs came from the darkness beyond the garden. She walked down the driveway towards the gates until she was beyond the turn, out of sight, then, without looking back, changed direction and went quietly up the lawn through the shadows as far as the fence. Here she paused for a moment, listening, then hoisted herself up and over.

The darkness of the trees in the woods was solid. Rustlings of small creatures came out of them, and bitter smells of earth and flowers, as she went quietly down the path until she came to the bend, and, without hesitating, pushed her way into the trees, going in the pitch-dark along the narrow track, briars spooling out of the shadows and catching at her trousers, until she emerged into the clearing. There was a van parked there.

As soon as she appeared the van's headlights came on, and the engine started up, and she walked over to it and climbed in.

'OK,' she said. 'Let's do it.'

And PJ turned to her and nodded.

They drove in silence through the darkness, jolting up and down, the old van creaking and squealing, until they reached the end of the dirt track and turned onto a lane.

'How's your eye?' Amy asked. She had to shout over the noise of the engine.

PJ chewed his cheek, thought about it. 'They didn't know what they were doing,' he said at last. 'That's the best I can say.'

She looked at him. He was wearing black office-type trousers and a red short-sleeved shirt with a company logo on the breast pocket, a surgical patch over his injured eye and a red beanie tight over his big skull. He hadn't shaved in a while, and his stubble was white against his grey skin. A rat's-tail of grey hair hung down his back.

He glanced at her sideways as he drove, his broad face angular in the shadows.

'Anger,' he said, 'makes you weak. I seen it before, in the army.' He gave her a cavernous smile, and winced. 'I'm stronger than they thought,' he said.

He misjudged a gear change, and the van bucked, roaring.

'I'm sorry you got caught up in it,' she said.

'It's OK. I looked for your dog by the way, the day after, but I couldn't find it.'

'Someone else found it.'

'Handed it in?'

'It was dead.'

PJ thought about that. 'Doesn't alter anything,' he said after a while. 'You just have to stay strong. I know you will.'

'I'm nervous. Supposing . . .'

'It's OK.'

He put his hand on her leg. She gave him a look, and after a while he took it off again.

They drove downhill to the ring road and merged with the traffic, still busy at that time of night.

'Is it safe?' she asked suddenly, without looking at him.

'Oh yes,' he said. 'Just as I told you.'

Ten minutes later they exited at the car plant, and took the first turn into the business park, and drove through it until they came to the self-storage place, Red 'n' Black.

PJ looked at his watch. 'Shouldn't be long,' he said. Climbing out of the van, he went, a little stiffly, across the car park into Reception, and Amy waited. After a few moments another man, also dressed in black trousers and red shirt, came out, got into a car and drove away. Amy waited a few minutes more, then left the van and went into the building.

Everything in the lobby was red and black. Red walls, black industrial carpet, hard red sofa with black cushions. It looked like candy and smelled like a factory. There was a rack of different-sized cardboard boxes on one wall, and a large screen on another; in one corner was a cheese plant, in another a coffee-vending machine. Set in the far wall was a door to a back office; in front of it was a long desk with monitors, and behind the desk was PJ, just settling in to his night shift.

'Got what you need?'

She nodded.

He smiled at her. 'Everything's cool,' he said. He tapped a screen. 'I'll be here watching.'

She went through swing doors out of the lobby into an area with rubber flooring and ribbed aluminium walls, where flat-bed trolleys were lined up at the side of wide metal lift doors. Halfway along the wall was a keypad below a red sign – *Remember to Set Your Room Alarm Here* – and she tapped in a number and went on, through more swing doors, to a staircase and up two flights until she reached a long narrow corridor with plastic-panelled walls and grey rubber floor gleaming under the overhead strip lighting in the low ceiling, and red doors stretching both ways as far as she could see.

The intercom whined suddenly and PJ's voice said, 'Other way, Amy.'

Doubling back, she walked down the corridor to the end. Every few paces there was a padlocked red door flush in the wall. At the end she turned the corner and hesitated. She could go left or straight on, down two identical corridors.

She lifted her face and spoke to the ceiling. 'Which way?'

PJ's voice crackled again out of hidden speakers. 'Straight on. You remember.'

The place was a maze. On floors above and below her were other corridors, all brightly lit, all deserted at that time of night, a geometrical labyrinth, rat-runs in a vast laboratory. A silent, electronically controlled environment. The only sound in the whole building was the deadened squeak of her own shoes on the rubber floor.

At the end of the corridor she went through a fire door, turned again to the left, went past another turning, through another door, turned left once more and, almost immediately, turned right.

The intercom came on again briefly – 'You're there. See you later, Amy' – and went off with a click.

Walking quietly along, she took a key out of her

pocket with a tag on it labelled *W Corridor 316* and after a moment stopped at one of the red doors. She unlocked the padlock and swung the door open.

It was one of the smaller units in the building, a walk-in locker, two-metres square, plain, grey and almost completely empty. There was only one thing in it, on the floor in the corner: a cardboard shoe box with the Doc Martens logo on it.

For a moment she stood there, looking at the box, breathing deeply, as if to strengthen herself. Then, just as she was about to step inside, she heard a noise and froze. It wasn't the public address system. It was the sound of someone else's footsteps, somewhere in the empty building.

She lifted her head and called out. 'PJ?'

The intercom was silent.

'PJ, is that you?'

There was no reply, only the sound of the footsteps growing louder, coming on with a steady tread. She looked up and down the corridor. One way was a dead end; the other end was fifty metres away, already too far to reach.

She hesitated. Thirty seconds passed; they felt like five minutes. All the time the footsteps came closer.

Helplessly, she retreated into the locker. The door was useless; like all the others it locked only on the outside. Slowly she backed into the corner. Now the footsteps were in the corridor.

She had no time.

The footsteps approached the door.

She fumbled in the shoe box and stood again, arms stretched out in front of her, holding in both hands – a little shakily – a heavy, brown-metal gun. She pointed it at the open locker doorway and put her finger on the trigger.

Garvie appeared.

He nodded at the gun. 'Yeah. Good to see you too.'

28

It took a moment for her mouth to work again.

'What the fuck?' she managed brokenly.

'Yeah, I know. Do you mind putting it back in the box? Or at least pointing it away from my nose?'

She stared at him for a few seconds longer, as if still not quite sure he was real. Then at the gun in her hands, where it shook slightly, big and heavy, its snout dark and ugly. All at once she dropped it to her side.

'Thanks. That sort of thing's bad for my nerves. And I don't like that wild look people get in their eyes when they hold a gun.'

She stooped and mechanically put it back in the box, and rose again to face him, breathing hard. At last she recovered her power of joined-up talking. 'OK, I'm lost. What just happened? How did you get in? How did you get up here?' She shook her head in bewilderment. 'How did you even know where I was?'

'Keeping an eye on you, of course.'

'Why?'

'Only a matter of time before you tried to get it back.'

'You knew about the gun? How?'

He shrugged. 'It was one hypothesis. Once I knew you hadn't just stormed off over the shoes—'

'How did you know that?'

'You dropped your ring at PJ's.'

'I was wearing my ring when I got home. Ask my mother.'

'One of them, yeah. But it's part of a matching pair. You're wearing both of them in a photograph in your room. I guess your mother hadn't been paying attention.'

'All my life,' she said bitterly.

'Besides,' he said, 'I knew you'd met him in the woods that night.'

'How?'

'Van-wise, Smudge proved it to me. The boy's a genius. I thought at first you'd just happened to run into PJ. Then I realized it was him you were trying to get to.'

'But how did you know about the gun?'

'I asked myself why you ran off. From your behaviour that night I reckoned it was fear. Something had shocked you. What? Could be a number of things. So I asked myself why you'd gone to meet PJ. I knew he did nights at a self-storage place. So I thought perhaps you'd got hold of something you needed to hide, something that scared you. Needn't have been a gun. Could have been stolen property, dope. But something you really, really couldn't keep at home. You had no time to think it through. You had to grab the nearest box to put it in before your mother saw it, and head for the woods.'

'Why didn't I just dump it in the woods then?'

'Most people would have done. You're smarter than that. Dangerous stuff that gets dumped has a habit of being found. Dangerous stuff needs to be carefully hidden. I knew you'd understand that.'

'And how did you know I was going to come back for it?'

'Because you can never really hide dangerous stuff. 'Cause you worry about it. 'Cause you need it back. 'Cause someone else tells you to get it back. I just had to wait till you made your move.'

'And how did you know it was going to be tonight?'

'I didn't. I thought it was going to be last night. But I knew it was going to be as soon as possible after the party.'

She stared at him. 'You absolute freak.'

He said nothing to that.

'All right,' she said. 'What are we going to do now?'

'Think a bit.'

'About what?'

He said nothing for a few moments. 'Sequences,' he said at last. 'λ and ε and N.'

'OK,' she said. 'I guess that's your thing.'

He shook his head. 'I think, in fact, it's your thing. Let's say λ is equal to the crime.'

'What crime?' she asked quickly.

He glanced at the gun in its box. 'We don't know yet. Or at least, *I* don't. And let's say ε is a bit of deliberate confusion, like pretending to storm off.'

She said nothing.

'And let's say N is the moment when you first get past all that, and see what's what. My question is: when do we get to N?'

'I'm not telling you where I got the gun.'

'Course not. You don't even have to tell me who gave it you, standing in the rain with you outside your house that night. No. I want to know why it scares you so much.'

She thought about that. Nodded. 'All right. A number of reasons. But mainly because there's someone else after it.'

'You sure?'

'Oh yeah. He came after me in the woods that night. That's why I took that brute of a dog with me. And he nearly got me. He came out of the trees and grabbed me, but Rex went for him and I got free and made it to PJ's van. But only just.'

'Who is he?'

She faced him. 'I don't know.'

He looked closely at her and she looked back, her expression one part scared, one part defiant.

'Do you think I'm making it up?'

Garvie shook his head. 'What I think is: we should get out of here fast as we can. Now.'

'Seriously?'

'I'm always serious. It's one of my things. If *I*

could follow you here, *he* could. In fact, that's exactly what he'll do. Get the gun.'

He took her hand and half dragged her out the locker. They went along the corridor to the end, and when they got there the lights beyond them suddenly went out and everything ahead was pitch-dark.

They stood there, shocked.

'What's PJ up to?' she said.

'Not PJ,' Garvie said.

'What do you mean?'

'PJ found himself dealing with a tricky situation in the car park.'

'What situation?'

'Smudge.'

She stared at him again.

'Don't worry,' Garvie said. 'PJ was in the army. He can deal with innocents like Smudge. It was the only way I could get up here without him bothering me.'

'But,' she said, 'if PJ's out of the way, who's turned off the lights?'

Garvie said nothing.

She took out her phone.

'No signal in here,' Garvie said. 'I already checked.'

In a panic she turned and yelled to the air. 'PJ! Can you hear me?' and suddenly clamped her hand over her mouth. 'Shit,' she whispered. 'If it's some-one else doing this we don't want them to know we're here.'

Garvie said, 'They already know we're here. They're watching us right now.'

They turned to the left, away from the darkened corridor and went at speed the other way to the corner, and through a fire door, and down another corridor long and straight and narrow, and after a moment the lights ahead went off again.

Amy gave a cry.

'Doesn't matter,' Garvie said. 'It's only darkness.'

'But how do we know where to go?'

'Geometry. The building's an L shape. Corridors are parallel, longitude in the long bit, latitude in the short. I came in this way. Easy to remember. Come on.'

They ran in darkness, Garvie directing them, turning without hesitation left or right, running together down long straight stretches, and round doglegs, until they reached a long corridor with, dimly, a fire door at the end.

'The stairs are on the other side,' Garvie said. They ran hard towards the door and when they had nearly reached it they heard a click.

It was locked. Amy shook it in vain and turned to Garvie. 'He can lock doors too!'

'Electronic,' Garvie said. 'Operated from downstairs.'

She pressed her face to the reinforced glass. 'I can see the staircase. It's just there.'

'Good for the staircase.'

'We have to go back, get round the other way. Quick!'

They ran back down the dark corridor and when they got to the corner they heard a click in the darkness to their right. They swerved left down a short corridor and turned another corner. There was a door a little way in front of them and they accelerated towards it, but before they could reach it there was a third click, and they stopped, panting.

'We're trapped,' Amy said, breathless. 'He's herded us.' She looked at Garvic.

He shrugged.

'Don't just shrug. Don't you see? This door's locked. Down there the door's locked. And back there it's locked too. There's no way out. *Listen!*'

In the darkness they heard the whining of the lift rising through the building.

'He's coming,' Amy whispered. 'What do we do now?'

'Wait a bit.'

'*Wait a bit?* Don't you understand? He's coming to get us.'

In the silence they listened to the lift as it rose through the building. It shunted to a stop; for a moment there was silence, then the sound of the doors shushing open.

Then footsteps. They came out of the lift and stopped.

Amy put her fingers to her lips.

There was silence, pained and fragile, as if the whole building were holding its breath.

Then the footsteps started again, going along the corridor away from them.

'He's not sure where we are,' Amy murmured.

In the darkness they listened. The footsteps receded down the corridor, fading.

Garvie shook his head. 'He knows where we are.'

'It's a maze,' Amy whispered. 'He might not find his way to us.'

Garvie shook his head again.

After a while they heard the footsteps again, far off, but getting slowly louder.

'He's going round the same way we came in,' Amy said. 'It'll lead him here in the end. What are we going to do?'

'Wait a bit.'

'*What are you talking about, wait a bit?* Waiting a bit won't help us.'

'No. But it's nearly always the most interesting thing to do.'

The footsteps were louder now, heavy; they came faster down the corridor beyond the dogleg where they stood. They heard the click of a door unlocking and the swish of someone opening it and rapidly passing through.

'He can unlock doors too,' Amy said, groaning.

Garvie nodded. 'He must have an electronic key. That's interesting as well.'

'It's not *interesting*. It's fucking well disastrous. He's inside. He's *got* us!'

Garvie nodded. 'You're right. Let's go.'

'*Go?* Go where? Haven't you been paying attention?' She pointed at the door ahead of them. 'It's still locked.'

Garvie walked up to it and pushed it open.

Amy stared at him. 'But,' she said, 'we heard it lock.'

'It locked all right. It just wasn't shut properly. Someone must have Blu-tacked a bit of cardboard to the electronic strip.'

He carefully removed the cardboard and put it back in his pocket. 'Friend of mine who knows about this stuff said you always got to secure your exit. Electronic doors are all very well until you cut the current.'

Amy stared at him in bewilderment. 'OK. But—'

'But what?'

Her face flushed. 'But *why didn't you tell me?*'

He looked at her oddly. 'What difference would that have made?'

They went through the door and it swung shut behind them, and the lock clicked.

As Garvie paused on the other side, Amy caught hold of his arm. 'Listen,' she hissed, 'you're not making this as easy as it could be. Very smart of you to have rigged the door. But we have to go. Now. Now and very fast. He can unlock it again soon as he gets here.'

Garvie thought about that. 'Yes,' he said at last. 'But can he get through it?'

Amy thumped her forehead with the heel of her hand. 'What are you talking about now?'

Garvie took a rubber wedge out of his pocket. He put it under the door and kicked it in tight. 'Same friend,' he said. 'Good with tips. And now,' he said, 'it all depends how good he is at swedging.'

They went together down the corridor as far as the staircase.

'Wait a bit,' Garvie said at the corner.

Amy groaned. 'What, again? Really? Can't we keep running, just in case he's good at, what did you call it, swedging?'

As they looked back they saw a shadow growing on the other side of the darkened door. It grew into a silhouette that filled the whole glass panel. The door unlocked with a click and shook as he tried to open it.

Garvie said, 'Don't you think it would be useful to see his face?'

Amy stared at him, aghast. 'You planned this, didn't you? To get him here so we could see who he is. But how do you know he can't get through the door?'

'I don't. Though usually those rubber wedges are pretty good value.'

The door shook violently; the silhouette pressed itself against the glass. Then there was a moment of stillness when the man – if it was a man – stood on the other side of the door, staring at them through the glass panel so intently it was as if he could hurt them with his concentration. He rolled his shoulders.

They couldn't see his face.

Then his silhouette disappeared.

'He's gone,' Amy said with relief.

There was a sudden rush of darkness and explosion as the door burst open and a man in a balaclava and ski-mask surged through it.

Garvie said, 'OK, he's good at swedging. Running sounds like a good idea after all.'

They tore side by side down the corridor, barged their way through the swing doors and flung themselves down the steps three at a time. Above them, a few seconds later, they heard the doors crash open again, and the pounding leap of footsteps in the stairwell.

At the bottom Amy turned towards the lobby but Garvie caught hold of her hand and they ran together the other way through the loading area, following the signs down another corridor to a fire escape with a crashbar. Shoving their way through, they jumped down some concrete steps and ran across the empty car park to the edge of the dual carriageway, where traffic was still coming past with reassuring regularity, and stopped there at the side of the brightly lit road, panting.

'Fire escapes,' Garvie said. 'Always the quickest way to go public.'

Amy put her hand on his shoulder. 'Look!'

He turned back in time to see a silhouette appear

in the doorway of the fire escape at the top of the steps. For a moment the man stood there, motionless as before, staring at them, then he melted back into the building and the doorway was empty again.

29

Garvie ran.

He left Amy and ran across the car park back towards the building and round the side towards the main entrance. He ran past chained trolleys and industrial bins to the far corner. But he was too late. All he heard was the noise of an engine fading into the ring-road hum.

He went back slowly, talking on his phone, and when he reached Amy he found her standing numbly staring at the gun which she had placed carefully on the asphalt at her feet. She seemed to be in shock.

On the ground the gun was big and ugly, and they both looked at it warily as if it might leap up on its own and shoot at them.

'You OK?' Garvie asked.

She looked at him. 'Why wouldn't I be OK? It's not like we've just been chased by a maniac wanting to kill us. Oh, wait.'

'You look a bit pale.'

'Yeah, well. I feel a bit pale.'

They were standing close together, looking at each other. Without knowing how it happened, he found himself with his arms round her. He felt her hand on the back of his head, and felt her body trembling, or perhaps it was his body, and he was gazing into her eyes very big in front of his; and then her foot touched the gun and they came apart again.

'Thank you,' she said quietly. She didn't look at him. She looked at the gun. 'I'll be OK now.'

'Who was he?' Garvie said after a while.

'I don't know. That's the truth.'

'Whoever he was, he'll be back.'

'You think?'

'Oh yeah. He really wants it. You could tell.'

She nodded unhappily. 'He was desperate. He would've hurt us.'

'Yeah. But that's not the issue.'

'What's the issue?'

'The issue is: why does he want it?'

They stood in silence.

'I can't do this,' she said after a while. She gestured at the gun with the toe of her shoe. 'I don't want it any more.'

'No. Sensible.'

'I can't even touch it without feeling sick. It freaks me out.'

'Fair enough.'

'I don't know what to do. What can I do?'

He shrugged. 'Give it to someone.'

She looked at him then. 'Don't be stupid. Who could I give it to?'

Garvie didn't answer; he appeared to be studying the moon through a cloud of cigarette smoke.

'Me?' he suggested at last.

'*You?*' She looked at him, amazed. 'Why would I give it you?'

''Cause you can't keep it. You just said so. And 'cause you can't bring yourself to touch it again. And 'cause there's no one else here to take it off you. Seems to be pretty conclusive.'

'But . . . but what would you do with it?'

He took a last drag on his cigarette and dropped the butt. Shrugged again. 'Give it to someone else, probably,' he said.

Her bewilderment increased a notch. 'Who?'

He turned as a beige-coloured Skoda Fabia came into the car park and drove across the asphalt towards them.

'Here he comes now,' Garvie said.

The Fabia came all the way up to them, and Singh got out wearing a brown suit, pink shirt and tomato-coloured woollen tie, and a startling orange turban.

'Sorry to disturb you and all that,' Garvie said. 'Sounded on the phone like you were out having dinner. Didn't realize you were at a bring-and-buy sale.'

Singh ignored him. He asked Amy if she was all right, and she said she was. Moving as methodically as usual despite his civilian dress, he put on a pair of disposable gloves and put the gun in a plastic evidence bag and, when he'd done that, said quietly to Garvie, 'This is yours then? That's what you told me on the phone.'

Garvie nodded.

'I hope you can explain it.'

'Me too.'

Singh said, 'There's always a short way to do things, and a long way. It's surprising to me how many people prefer the long way. The end result is nearly always the same. So I ask you, how did it come into your possession, Garvie?'

'Give me a moment,' he said. 'Maybe it'll come to me.'

Singh sighed. 'Are you sure you choose the long way?'

Garvie said nothing.

'I'm disappointed,' Singh said.

Garvie shrugged. 'I've been disappointed all my life, mate.'

'I'll ask you one last time. How did the gun come to be in your possession?'

Garvie sighed. 'Do you know what? I think it'd be more fun if you worked it out for yourself.'

Singh's face tightened. Automatically putting his hand up to adjust his turban, he spent a few moments looking expressionlessly at his gleaming leather shoes until he was calm. Then he looked up at Garvie and said, 'Garvie Smith, I am arresting you for the illegal possession of a firearm. You do not have to say anything. But it may harm your defence if—'

'It's mine,' Amy said.

They both turned to her.

'Well,' she added, 'not mine, but, you know, in my possession.'

Singh paused, looked carefully from one to the other. 'Longer and longer,' he murmured. 'OK, Amy. I ask you the same question.'

She shook her head.

'Would it help,' Garvie interrupted, 'if I said I gave it to her?'

Singh ignored him. He sighed. 'Now we have to cut it short. Amy Roecastle, I am arresting you for the illegal possession of a firearm. You do not have to say anything. But it may harm your defence if you do not mention when questioned something which you later rely on in court. Anything you do say may be given in evidence. I'm sorry,' he added. 'Do you want to call your mother? I think it would be a good idea for her to meet us at the station.'

They moved off together to his car. Singh opened the door for her, and she got into the back, and he got in himself and started the engine.

There was a tap on the window, and he wound it down.

'What is it now, Garvie?'

'Don't suppose there's any chance of a lift into Five Mile is there?'

Without replying, Singh wound the window up, and pulled away, and Garvie watched it go.

His phone rang.

'Smudge. Cheers, mate, you were perfect. Where is he now? I thought he'd've shaken you off already.'

Smudge said, 'That's the thing, Garv. I did what

you said and got a little fire started, and I ran in shouting and stuff, but he wasn't there.'

'Not there?'

'Not at the desk like you said he'd be. Couldn't see him anywhere. I just hung about a bit and went home.'

'Very interesting, Smudge. Good work. I owe you.'

'Laters.'

He stood in the car park for a moment, thinking, then set out for Eastwick Gardens.

To Garvie's surprise his mother was home already. She'd changed into her dressing gown and was standing flat-footed in her slippers at the kitchen sink drinking a glass of water, and she watched him narrowly as he crossed the room.

'Thought you'd still be out,' he said.

'And I thought you'd still be in. So we're both mistaken.' Her tone was short and heavy.

'Yeah.'

She was looking at him mistrustfully, but she didn't say anything, and after a moment's awkward silence he said goodnight and went into his room.

In the kitchen he heard her bang down her empty glass and go off into her own room.

He lay down on the bed and concentrated on the ceiling.

Downtown, Amy Roecastle was getting out of Singh's car and walking with him through the sally port into the Police Centre and along the corridor to the interview rooms. Garvie pictured her. She was in his mind so vividly he could feel his breathing speeding up. He remembered exactly what she was wearing. Black combat trousers with overlong black canvas belt. Black long-sleeved top. Electric blue bandana, bright and dishevelled against the ivory skin of her throat. He remembered the way she spoke to him, posh accent and sharp tone, and the way her mouth moved, the way her eyes looked at him. He remembered the way her hair swung across her face as she ran.

He remembered the way she held the gun in both hands, pointing it at him.

He remembered the way she felt in his arms, light, delicate, almost fragile, the bird-fluttering of her body.

Then he imagined her sitting in the interview room, tonight or tomorrow, Singh's patient questions, her defiant answers. She was taking the long way round, but she'd reach the same place in the end. He wondered how long it would be before she confessed who it was who gave her the gun.

30

Location: Interview Room 1, Cornwallis Police Centre, East Wing.

Aspect of interviewer: neatly uniformed, careful, professional.

Aspect of interviewee: exhausted.

Aspect of interviewee's mother: firm-faced, defensive behind sunglasses, shocked.

Aspect of interviewee's lawyer: concerned, watchful.

DI SINGH: It is Tuesday the 21st of August, 12:00 p.m. With me are Amy Roecastle, and her mother Dr Elena Roecastle, and the solicitor Diane Rebuk. Amy, this is your third interview now, after you talked this morning with Detective Inspector Dowell. Before I ask you questions myself, some of which I know you will be anticipating, I need to give you news of some recent developments. Our ballistics department has been at work, and I have to inform you that the gun in your possession last night has been identified as the one used to kill Joel Watkins in Market Square on Wednesday the 8th of August, and that this is now a murder investigation.

AMY ROECASTLE: [*silence*]

DR ROECASTLE: I don't understand. I . . . What are you saying? Are you saying *you think Amy has killed somebody?*

DI SINGH: On the night of the 8th of August there was a disturbance in Market Square. The police had forcibly evicted partygoers from a rave that was taking place in a disused warehouse in The Wicker. People fled into Market Square, where fighting with the police took place. At approximately 22:30 gunshots were fired; a few people were injured, and one man, Joel Watkins, suffered several bullet wounds that proved fatal. I know that Inspector Dowell has already asked you this question, but it is more urgent and important than ever, Amy, to know who gave you the gun.

AMY ROECASTLE: [*shakes her head*]

DI SINGH: Amy, I think you arc an intelligent girl and I know you want to do the right thing.

AMY ROECASTLE: [*shakes her head*]

DI SINGH: And I know that Inspector Dowell has already made you aware of the possibility that without your cooperation we may need to proceed with charges against you.

DR ROECASTLE: Charges? What charges?

DI SINGH: Amy, listen to me now. It is worse, always worse, to try to protect someone with lies. Worse for the person you are trying to protect. I know this, I have seen it many times. Don't make that mistake.

AMY ROECASTLE: [*silent*]

DI SINGH: The only way to protect them, if they are innocent, is to tell the truth.

AMY ROECASTLE: You say that, but . . . [*silent*]

DI SINGH: It's true. Unless you tell the truth they will always be vulnerable to other people's falsehoods. So often they end up punished for what they did not do. I think you know this too. They get mixed up with things they know nothing about, and are punished while the guilty go free. Don't let that happen to the person you are trying to protect.

AMY ROECASTLE: [*long pause, speaking at last in a quiet voice*] All right. Damon gave it to me.

DR ROECASTLE: Damon Walsh? That delinquent in the van?

DI SINGH: Thank you, Amy. I appreciate you being honest with me. That was the most difficult question. All the others now are details. So. Tell me. When did he give it to you?

AMY ROECASTLE: That night. I'd been out with Sophie, I told you already. The taxi dropped me off at the turn and went on with Soph, and I was walking down to our gates, and suddenly Damon was there.

DI SINGH: What time was this?

AMY ROECASTLE: About quarter to midnight. I'd just got out of the taxi and it started tipping down with rain. He'd been in the bus shelter outside the gates, waiting for me. He was all sort of shaky, and he had this strange expression on his face, and he came out of the shelter fast and said, 'This isn't what it looks like', and gave me the gun. And I took it.

DR ROECASTLE: Amy! I can't believe it. What were you thinking of?

DI SINGH: Go on, Amy. What else did he say?

AMY ROECASTLE: Nothing sensible. Just babble. He was very scared. I could see something bad had happened. Something really terrible. He was so frightened. He wanted me to trust him. That was the most important thing. Don't let me down, he kept saying. Please don't let me down.

DR ROECASTLE: Amy, I just can't sit here and listen to this. *Why* did you take the gun from him? I don't understand.

AMY ROECASTLE: Of course you don't understand. I took the gun *because he needed me to*.

DI SINGH: 'This isn't what it looks like'. What did he mean by that?

AMY ROECASTLE: That he wasn't guilty. That he hadn't done it, whatever it was. That it wasn't his gun, that somehow it had ended up with him. That he was terrified people were going to blame him anyway. All that.

DI SINGH: Did you believe him?

AMY ROECASTLE: Yes. Damon wouldn't kill anyone.

DI SINGH: So why did Damon have the gun?

AMY ROECASTLE: I don't know. [*pause*] Someone must have given it to him.

DI SINGH: Who?

AMY ROECASTLE: I don't know.

DI SINGH: What happened after you took the gun?

AMY ROECASTLE: I was trying to hold it together, but I was scared. Straightaway I had the impression that someone else was after it. Just the way Damon kept looking round, as if someone had been following him. It freaked me out. The rain coming down made everything worse. Thunder going off, lightning. Damon gave me his jacket but it was soaked through in a few minutes. I didn't know what to do. I had to get the gun away from Damon, but I knew I couldn't keep it in the house. Luckily, I thought of PJ.

DR ROECASTLE: PJ! That strange man in the woods? My God. I thought you didn't know him.

AMY ROECASTLE: I'd met him a few times.

DR ROECASTLE: What do you mean? He's fifty years old! Where did you meet him?

AMY ROECASTLE: Bars, mainly. Anyway, I remembered he worked nights in a storage place. And he was an absolute life-saver. He came straight out to meet me, didn't ask why, didn't even ask what was in the box.

DI SINGH: You met him by arrangement in the clearing in the woods?

AMY ROECASTLE: Yes. I was so frightened I took the dog, which hates me. The storm was bad, getting worse, the noise was deafening. I nearly lost my way pushing through the trees. And when I was nearly there someone came out of the shadows and grabbed me, and I panicked and dropped the chain and Rex got loose and I could hear him snapping and snarling as if he was fighting with someone, and I just got to my feet and ran.

DR ROECASTLE: Amy, all this is so strange and frightening, I hardly believe it.

DI SINGH: Take your time, Amy. [*pause*] This man who attacked you. Do you know who he is?

AMY ROECASTLE: No.

DI SINGH: Do you think he's the same man who chased you in Red 'n' Black?

AMY ROECASTLE: Yes.

DI SINGH: Why do you think that?

AMY ROECASTLE: He was so desperate to get the gun.

DI SINGH: Why is that?

AMY ROECASTLE: I don't know.

DI SINGH: Tell me what happened after you reached PJ's van that night.

AMY ROECASTLE: PJ drove me to Red 'n' Black, and I put the box in a lockup. When PJ's shift ended I went back to his place and slept for a bit, and then I hitched to Dad's.

DI SINGH: I see. And when did you learn that there had been a murder?

AMY ROECASTLE: Early next morning. We were listening to PJ's radio.

DI SINGH: But you made no attempt to contact the police.

AMY ROECASTLE: [*pause*] No. I know Damon's flaky. He's a mess. But he would never kill someone.

DI SINGH: Did you know Joel Watkins, the man who was murdered?

AMY ROECASTLE: Not at all.

DI SINGH: Did Damon know him?

AMY ROECASTLE: I don't think so. He never once mentioned his name to me. Listen. Please. Damon's not a murderer. He's not. He gets mixed up in stuff by mistake. I told you, someone must have given him the gun.

DR ROECASTLE: May I interrupt, Inspector, to ask where this Damon is? The last I heard, he was at large. I'm assuming you've found him by now.

DI SINGH: A moment, please. Amy, would you describe Damon as a nervous person?

AMY ROECASTLE: [*pause*] Everyone knows Damon's had issues.

DI SINGH: Are you aware that when he was younger he was obliged to take an anger management course?

DR ROECASTLE: Inspector, will you please tell me where Damon Walsh is now?

DI SINGH: Amy, I put it to you that Damon Walsh is a nervous and unstable character with anger management issues liable to panic or to lash out if he feels threatened.

DIANE REBUK: I have to intervene. You're leading my client.

AMY ROECASTLE: It's all right. Yes, he's nervous. It's piti-
ful how nervous he is. Yes, he's unstable. That's
why he's the person most at risk here. He's so
frightened now, who knows what he might do
to himself. Ask Garvie. When he met him on
that tram, Damon talked about killing himself.

DR ROECASTLE: Garvie Smith? The boy doing the
fencing? He didn't tell me he'd found him.

DI SINGH: You think Damon is a suicide risk?

AMY ROECASTLE: I do.

DR ROECASTLE: Please, Inspector. Tell me. Is Damon
Walsh in custody now?

DI SINGH: He is not. His whereabouts are unknown.
[*brief silence*] I must tell both of you, very
clearly, that Damon Walsh is now a suspect in
this murder enquiry. If he tries to get in touch
with you, Amy, you must contact us immediately, do you understand? This is the law, but
it is also for your own safety. And I would ask
you now to re-evaluate your opinion of him. I
would not want you to be any more vulnerable
than you already are.

AMY ROECASTLE: Am I going to be charged?

DI SINGH: Not at present. After the various procedures
for fingerprints, DNA, photographs and so on,
you will be free to go home. But I recommend
you discuss legal protection for all eventualities
with Ms Rebuk. Now, I'm afraid I have to go
into another meeting. Do you have any other
questions?

DR ROECASTLE: I wish also to know about the complaints procedure.

DI SINGH: Amy?

AMY ROECASTLE: No.

DI SINGH: Thank you. This interview is at an end.

31

It was five thirty in the afternoon before DI Singh finally reached his office. He was tired. The interview with Amy Roecastle had been followed by his meeting with the chief, lengthy briefings with Dowell and his team, an hour-long news conference and further consultations with Forensics, Homicide and Youth Services.

Now he sat quietly at the empty desk.

The investigation into the disappearance of Amy Roecastle wasn't over; it had become part of the larger investigation into the murder of Joel Watkins, in which he was now Detective Inspector Dowell's deputy. It was his opportunity, as made clear to him by Dowell and the chief, to atone for previous mistakes, namely his mismanagement of the case and, in particular, his failure to apprehend Damon Walsh, now exposed as Joel Watkins' likely killer. He had been asked for – and he had given – assurances that he would not let further lapses of judgement undermine police efforts.

He had a job to do, but he was not yet sure how to proceed. First, he reflected on various difficulties.

He thought about the fact that he had been given

access to Dowell's investigative findings on a limited need-to-know basis only. It did not surprise him that he was not trusted, though he resented it.

He thought about Amy Roecastle. He did not believe that she had told him the whole truth yet. There was more she could tell him, he was sure, about Damon Walsh, but it would be difficult to win her trust. Young people could be so stubborn, so sure of themselves, so fiercely protective. He knew: he had been one himself, a proudly disobedient student in Lahore. Only later, during police training, had he accepted his need for stricter personal discipline.

Finally he thought about Garvie Smith, the archetype of disobedience, the disrupter of other people's karmas, finder-out of other people's secrets.

For twenty minutes he sat perfectly still, staring at his desk, thinking hard. And finally he decided how to proceed.

He picked up the phone and called Len Johnson.

32

At six o'clock in the evening Garvie Smith was still in bed from the night before.

Since he'd been laid off by Smudge's brother there was no urgent reason to get out of bed. At all. Ever.

Therefore he had stayed in bed all day. His mother was still out on her shift. He lay there unblinking, looking at the ceiling, thinking about mathematical sequences. In particular, recurring terms. Pascal's triangle, for instance. The triangle is an infinite symmetric number pyramid, each number the sum of the two numbers immediately above it, starting with 1 at the apex. The strange thing is that the number 3003 keeps cropping up. An event unexpectedly repeating itself. Like the same character making a sudden reappearance. You think you won't see them again, then suddenly there they are – like PJ, for instance, picking Amy up in the woods on the night of the 8th, and picking her up in the woods again on the night of the 20th.

Someone buzzed the intercom downstairs. Garvie ignored it. A few moments later someone rang the doorbell of the flat. He ignored that too. He only took notice when he heard a key in the lock and the door opening and footsteps coming in.

He got out of bed in his shorts and T-shirt and padded into the living room and there found Detective Inspector Singh in full uniform and Uncle Len in business suit and tie, looking like the Head of Police Forensics. Which, of course, he was.

He looked from one to the other. 'She's not here,' he said.

They looked at him severely.

'It's not your mother we want,' Uncle Len said.

Garvie crossed his hands in front of him. 'I do not have to say anything. It may harm my defence if I do not mention when questioned something which I later rely on in court. Anything I do say may be—'

Uncle Len said, 'Will you stop your fooling? Raminder isn't here to arrest you. He wants to talk to you.'

Garvie said nothing. He waited. Singh cleared his throat nervously.

Uncle Len said to him, 'Do you want me to stay? You know what a devil he can be.'

'No, no. I can manage.'

Uncle Len nodded. He said to Garvie, 'We've discussed this with your mother already. There's no need to tell her about it.'

'What makes you think I tell my mother things?'

Frowning, his uncle left the flat, and Garvie and Singh stood in silence, looking at each other.

Singh shifted his weight awkwardly and cleared his throat. 'I'm not quite sure how to put this.'

'Would it help if I went back to bed and you wake me up when you've worked it out?'

'There are some questions I'd like to ask you.'

'An interrogation? Down the station?'

'Off the record.'

'In other words,' Garvie said, 'you're asking for my help. Which means breaking police protocol. Which isn't something you'd do.'

There was a long pause. 'Probably it's the only way to stop you interfering,' Singh said. He did not smile.

'Is that a joke?'

'It is.'

'Didn't think you did humour, to be honest.'

'I don't.'

'I'd wait till you've had more practice.'

Both remained expressionless.

Singh said, 'You said before, I needed help. You're right. There are difficulties I need to solve, questions I cannot answer, and yet I must.'

Garvie nodded. 'Yeah, you want to know if Damon killed Joel.'

Singh stared.

'Could have been him,' Garvie added. 'After all, he had the gun.'

'How do you know that?'

'It's not hard. When I asked Amy if she'd let Damon down she got such a nark on it was obvious she'd helped him out big-time. By taking a hot gun off him, for instance. Must have been him she stood with for half an hour in the rain before she went into the house.'

Singh nodded. 'But how do you know that gun was the murder weapon?'

'He was desperate to get rid of it just an hour after Watkins was shot? Timing works. And Damon was in Market Square during the riot, he mentioned it to me. Like 'the Wild West' he said. Easy for him to drive up to Froggett by the time she got back. He would have parked the van out of sight somewhere, waited in that bus shelter, probably, while the rain came down.'

'Yes, that's what she told me, in fact. And, yes, it is the murder weapon. But even if he was in Market Square, Amy is sure someone gave it to him after the shooting.'

'Equally possible he was the shooter.'

'Yes.'

They looked at each other.

Garvie said, 'Now it's your turn. Can't help you if you're going to keep stuff back.'

They sat at the kitchen table and Singh began. The investigation into the murder of Joel Watkins had so far assumed that Watkins was an innocent bystander caught in crossfire between rival gangs during the riot that happened after the police stormed the warehouse where the rave was taking place. A reasonable assumption. Two other guns retrieved from the scene belonged to members of rival criminal gangs. Watkins had no link whatsoever with either.

Garvie took this in in his usual expressionless fashion. 'What else do you know about Watkins?'

Singh summarized. Joel Watkins, twenty-six years old at the time of his murder, seemed like a regular person. He moved jobs frequently, apparently out of choice; generally his employers made no complaints about him. He lived alone in a little flat in Tick Hill and never missed a rent payment. There was no reason for anyone to kill him.

His photograph, which Singh slid across to Garvie, showed a man about six foot four, with a powerful build, soft, bland features, thick, drooping moustache, and dark brown hair cut very short and already receding. He looked as if he worked out: his neck was thick, his shoulders bunched with muscle.

'What sort of jobs?' Garvie asked.

Security, mainly. He'd been a bouncer at the club Chi-Chi, doorman at Imperium casino until he was let go a few days before his death, a night-watch guard at the shopping mall downtown before that. Occasionally – and recently – he'd driven dispatch. He'd worked for short periods in construction.

'What was he doing in the square that night?'

Unknown. All the investigation had to go on were some contradictory witness statements.

Garvie said, 'Yeah, I remember the report on the radio. Someone saw him fleeing the fighting, and chatting in the Ballyhoo bar to a guy in a HEAT beanie, and fighting the police, and lying drunk in a gutter. All at the same time.'

CCTV was no help. There had been approximately a thousand people in Market Square, all panicking. It had proved impossible to ascertain Watkins' movements before the moment when his unconscious body had been found in an alley off the square and taken to City Hospital, where, after multiple attempts to resuscitate him, he died of perioperative shock. He had suffered three apparently wild gunshots, in the thigh, abdomen and forearm.

Garvie looked again at the photograph. Watkins stared back at him with a closed expression.

'No connection between him and Damon?'

'Nothing known.'

'Maybe just not known, then. On Supertram, Damon was bitter about someone he used to think was his "soul mate".'

'Amy Roecastle?'

'No. He was looking at her photo but he wasn't talking about her. Someone from further back, I think. Someone he'd relied on, someone he thought was solid. Until they had a bust-up.'

Garvie looked at Watkins' photograph, met his fixed gaze. He was certainly solid. Heavy-lidded eyes, impassive. A man you couldn't stare down.

'Did Watkins have any convictions?'

'None.'

'Trouble with the police?'

'Nothing in his records.'

'What records? Adult records?'

'Yes.'

'What about when he was young?'

Singh looked at him. 'Release of that sort of information requires a formal legal procedure. We haven't made a request.' He paused. 'You're thinking they may have been on the youth offence programme together?'

'People bond in dark times. People like Damon need someone to rely on.'

'I will initiate the process,' Singh said. 'But it takes time.'

'Isn't there someone you can ask? Not Dowell.'

Singh thought. 'Actually, there is. He might remember. But, of course,' he added, 'the main thing is to find Damon.'

'Waste of time.'

Singh looked at Garvie suspiciously.

'Do you know where he is?'

'Lying low, getting high. Listening to the air.'

'Really?'

'That's what he told me. I believe him.'

'You think he can't be found?'

'I don't think *you* can find him.'

Singh pondered this. 'Listening to the air? He said that?'

'His words.'

'Somewhere quiet then. The countryside. Up at Froggett, or in Halton Woods. Somewhere where he can hide his van.'

Garvie shrugged.

Singh said, 'I think, in fact, he will be in touch again.'

'Why?'

'Because he needs it to be over, he's anxious, he wants the anxiety to end.'

'Anxiety's his old friend. Besides, he's smoking the pipe of peace.'

Singh frowned. 'I also give weight to what Amy says about Damon. It's hard to think of him as a murderer.'

'You think nervous people can't be murderers?'

Singh pondered that. 'It's true he has a temper. I was told that, and the record confirms it.' He got to his feet. 'Anyway, I must go now. There's much to do.'

'By the way,' Garvie said, 'who's running this investigation?'

Singh gave him a stiff look. 'Detective Inspector Dowell. I am his deputy.'

'Awks. He hates your guts.'

Singh ignored him. 'One final thing,' he said. 'Amy Roecastle is a material witness in the investigation and may yet be charged. It's essential you avoid making contact with her from this point on. Understood?'

'Fine. No problem.'

'OK then. Good. I'll be in touch.'

He crossed the room and left the flat, and Garvie called Amy. 'Listen, I need to talk to you about this whole thing. We mustn't tell Singh, though. He's got to work with Dowell now, and I don't trust Dowell. Can we meet? Corner of Pollard Way and Town Road at eight. Yeah, see you there.'

He rang off and sat in his shorts and T-shirt, thinking. At first he thought about Damon Walsh, which was straightforward. Then he thought about Amy Roecastle, which wasn't. His thinking about her didn't happen in his mind, as normal thinking did, but somehow in his body. It had started the day before, outside Red 'n' Black. Whenever he thought about her now he felt it in the pit of his stomach, the hairs along his arms. As if his fingertips were thinking about her, and the back of his neck, his internal organs, his heart, liver and kidneys, all of them thinking, everywhere together, about her smile, her eyes, the touch of her hands, the shape of her breasts, the tone of her voice.

Shifting in his seat, he pulled himself out of his daydream.

He could think about her endlessly. But he asked himself if he could trust her.

And he told himself that he trusted no one.

So he prepared to act accordingly.

33

She waited for him on the corner as arranged. Five Mile wasn't a part of town she'd been to before. From where she stood she could see a laundromat, a barber's and a shop selling second-hand electrical goods. Small gangs of people were standing eating on the pavement as the traffic went by noisily – vans, pick-ups and cabs. The odour of the warm air was part kebab, part petrol. Occasionally the people looked at her. She was dressed in the black trousers and tight top that her mother said made her look like a waitress from Bucharest, and her hair was done in a plait, which hung roughly against one side of her face, covering her ear. It made her other ear feel naked, and she kept touching it with her fingers as if she were trying to soothe it.

With her AirPods in, she was listening intently to the news, hoping to hear something about the Watkins murder investigation, but when she saw Garvie sauntering down Pollard Way, she quietly removed them and pushed them into her pocket, watching him nervously as he approached. It was surprising to see how many friends he had in the neighbourhood; they called out to him as he passed and he lifted a hand and strolled on, and came up to her at last, and, nodding, said affably,

'I'm not going to look for him, by the way. Just in case you were about to ask me to.'

It had been the first thing she wanted to say to him. She said crossly, 'So what are you getting involved for?'

'Stop you getting hurt.'

She paused. 'Why would I get hurt? I haven't got the gun any more.'

'It's not what you've got, it's what you know.'

'What do I know?'

'I don't know, you haven't told me yet.'

She watched him light up, cupping his hands, squinting against the smoke, flipping the match. He infuriated her, an unreadable boy who said the unexpected, who didn't seem to want anything from her but the truth. Then why did she have this odd feeling, half-irritated, half-excited when she was with him?

'You scared?' he asked suddenly.

'Yes,' she replied.

'That's good.'

He stood smoking calmly, looking as if there was nothing else to say.

'Listen to me now,' she said. She talked to him about Damon, how nervous he was, how needy; she explained his unfortunate tendency to get mixed up in things he didn't understand. Now he was a suspect in a murder enquiry, the subject of a nationwide manhunt. His picture was everywhere. He was alone, frightened of the police arresting him, disbelieving him, finding him guilty of something he hadn't done, sending him back to prison, that place of private nightmares.

Garvie nodded. 'None of which rules him out as a murderer.'

'Aren't you listening? We have to find him before the police do.'

'They're not going to find him. Neither are we.'

For a while they stood there in silence.

'Course,' he said, 'he might find us.'

'What do you mean?'

'Maybe he already did. At Red 'n' Black.'

'That wasn't Damon chasing us.'

'Are you sure? He knew you were there, of course.'

For a moment she just stared at him. 'Jesus, don't you miss anything?'

'Not the obvious stuff. *I worked it out, babe, I know what you got to do.* That's what he said to you at Sophie's party in front of everyone. He might as well have taken out an ad. He needed the gun back and he told you to go back to Red 'n' Black and get it.'

'It's like what you said before about dangerous things,' she said sadly. 'You can't ever really get rid of them. It's not his gun, though, I know it's not. Someone's taking advantage of him.'

'Who?'

'I don't know. So-called friends of his.'

'Bazza?'

'I don't know.'

He considered that. He said, 'Was Joel his friend?'

'I don't believe he knew Joel at all.'

Garvie smoked on for a minute or two. 'Big guy,' he said after a while. 'Dead eyes. Shoulders like a gorilla. I don't think people messed with Joel much.' He blew out smoke. 'But,' he added, 'someone did.'

'The police said it was accidental.'

'So far as I'm aware they haven't eliminated the other possibility that someone took that gun to Market Square, and deliberately got up close and personal with Joel, and fired three bullets into him and walked away and left him on the ground to bleed out. Someone mean and tough. Or someone desperate. Or maybe someone with a temper problem frightened enough to lose it and lash out.'

She was silent. Garvie finished his cigarette.

'What are we doing here, by the way?' she said at last.

'Waiting.'

'Waiting for what?'

'Transport.'

'Why?'

'We're going somewhere.'

Perhaps he would have said more, but his phone rang, and he stepped away to answer it.

Lights had come on in the shops, illuminating red and yellow signs for *Kebabs*, *Tyres and Exhausts*, *Mobile Accessories*, shops she'd never visited, never thought of. His shops, not hers; his litter-strewn pavement, his fluorescent strip lighting. Standing there by *We Fix and Trade*, he seemed more of a stranger than ever. As he talked, he glanced across and met her eyes, and she felt again a buzz of alarm, as if just by looking at her he could read her mind.

When he came back, he said, 'That was Singh. Turns out Damon knew Watkins on the youth offender programme.'

He said no more but left it hanging there between them.

She said at last, 'How does he know?'

'He's in touch with a guy who used to help out on the programme. He remembers both of them, Damon and Joel. Joel was an arm-round-the-shoulder kind of guy; Damon used to look up to him.'

She said nothing.

He went on, 'Thing is, we're not looking for Damon. But we are looking for his soul mate.'

'You're forgetting,' she said quietly. '*I'm* Damon's soul mate.'

He looked at her sadly. 'Sorry.' He seemed sorry too.

'Are you always this rude?'

He went silent, as if scanning his memories. 'No,' he said at last. 'I can be ruder. What you need to see is that rudeness isn't the point. Listen. On Supertram, Damon was talking about someone he'd trusted, someone he looked up to, someone he thought was always looking out for him – until they let him down, blamed him for something, turned on him. Not you. You helped him out big-time.'

She thought about that. 'OK. But it was years ago Damon and Joel were on the Y.O. They might not have even seen each other since then.'

He nodded. 'That's what we have to find out now.' Looking along the road, he said, 'And here comes our transport.'

The van drew up. It was a Ford Transit Custom with rear air suspension, adaptive cruise control, parking distance sensors and auto high beam. And of course sixteen-inch Michelin Agilis radials, Alpin model, front and rear.

The driver's window shunted down slickly, and Smudge stuck out his face. 'Lap it up, boys and girls,' he said. 'I've got it till ten, my brother said. Wild times. Let's go.'

'He's excitable around vans,' Garvie said to Amy as they got in. 'But what you have to keep in mind is: he's a genius.'

34

They drove up to Froggett, past Amy's house, towards Pike Pond. After a few miles the lanes narrowed and finally came to a stop at the edge of the woods. They went through an old wooden gate onto a dirt track. By now it was dark. The track – brilliantly and jaggedly lit by auto high beam – was a waterlogged sequence of holes and roots leading them, jouncing and thumping behind their crazy headlight beams, deeper among the black and dripping trees, to Smudge's evident glee. He was the Van Meister, Lord of Custom.

Amy said, 'I've never liked this place. Why are we here?'

Garvie did not answer. He seemed lost in thought. Smudge was too busy grinning to say anything.

At last they came to a small dirt clearing. In front of them were three concrete buildings and a melted pile of canvases. PJ's old used-to-be-white Ford Transit sat lopsidedly next to it.

Smudge pulled his brother's van alongside and turned off the engine.

'Pile of junk,' he said affably as he looked out of the window.

Garvie spoke to Amy at last. 'Does he tell the truth?'

'PJ? Why do you think he doesn't?'

'When Smudge went to distract him that night at Red 'n' Black he wasn't at the front desk where he should have been.'

'So?'

'So he could have been chasing us up on level three.'

'You don't know anything about PJ. When I needed him he was there for me, no questions asked. He didn't even ask me what was in the box. He's a friend. He loves peace.'

'OK.'

'OK what?'

'Let's go in and say hello.'

He helped her down out the van old-style, and she smiled at him.

He didn't smile back. 'It's muddy. Watch your step.'

They went cautiously through the mud, and they were halfway to the door of the garage when they heard the scream. It came from just behind the building, electrifyingly harsh, erupting in the quiet of the wood, ending as abruptly as it began, leaving behind a prickle of horror and hairs up on the back of the neck.

After a moment Smudge said, 'Maybe he's busy and we should come back later.'

But they went together round the corner of the

garage, and there found PJ stooped over a trap. He turned and looked at them, and dropped the twisted animal onto the ground. For a moment his face was distorted, then it settled again into peace-loving calm.

'Foxes,' he said casually. 'Vermin really. Though they too,' he added, 'are part of the great cycle of life and death.'

He straightened slowly, wiping his hands on his army jacket. 'Amy,' he said. 'And Amy's friends.' He showed his teeth. 'Welcome.'

Inside, they could still feel the woods around them, blackness and silence pressing against the thin walls of the garage, as they sat on the rugs passing round the spliff that Garvie had thoughtfully supplied. There was the same smell as before, of kerosene and old smoke and the perfume Amy was wearing. She sat with her back against the tatty sofa, glancing at Garvie from time to time as they listened to PJ, who sat facing them, cross-legged and bare-footed like a philosopher of old. There was a new spirit of love among young people, he was saying. Meditating briefly on the glowing end of the spliff, he drew deeply on it, and squinted sideways at Garvie. Some young people, he corrected himself. Some, he said, were bastards.

He scraped something, perhaps fox blood, from his fingers.

'Peace in the world,' he said, 'comes from within. All know. Few learn how not to forget.' The dope made his voice soft and harsh. The eye-patch made him look cunning. His horse-toothed smile was grey and big. His hands were big too, raw-boned and knuckly, as he passed the spliff.

Garvie looked beyond him, down the garage, past the garden chairs and folding table, to the far end, where the orange curtain was drawn back to reveal the mattress on the concrete floor still piled with charred mess, exactly as Singh and he had found it before. They had been wrong to make the assumption that it was the scene of a violent struggle. This was just the way PJ lived: a free spirit. Free of hygiene, anyway.

'How are you, PJ?' Amy said. 'How's your eye?'

'Healing itself.' He gave a slow, grey smile, somehow saintly. 'My karma will be slower to heal.'

'Got it in your karmas as well, did you?' Smudge asked, wincing.

PJ ignored him, went on: 'First there was the business with the men angry about your disappearance. Then there was my manager at the storage facility.'

'What do you mean?'

'He has insisted we part company.'

'You've been sacked? Why?'

'He objected to my preferred means of relaxation during the long watches of the night.' He held up the spliff to illustrate his meaning. He told her how, after he'd directed her to her locker that night, he'd gone into the back room to 'relax' for a moment.

'Perhaps I lost track of time,' he admitted. 'Though,' he added musingly, 'what *is* time?'

He'd been surprised by the unexpected appearance of his manager a little while later.

He shook his head sadly. 'Another man lost to his anger. I couldn't help him. It was better we parted.'

Amy said, 'Oh God, all this is my fault.' She gave Garvie a bitter glance.

PJ waved away her guilt. 'No such thing as fault,' he said soothingly. 'That's what you don't yet understand.' He fixed her with his one good eye. 'But,' he added in a low voice, 'you've had your own sorrow. I can tell just by looking at you. What is it? Someone has been breaking your heart. Am I right?'

Amy flushed.

Smudge said, 'Yeah, well. Don't look at me. Or Garv. It's that other guy.'

PJ, who had not looked at Smudge, in fact seemed barely aware of his presence, kept his eye on Amy.

'His name's Damon Walsh,' Amy said. 'I don't think you know him.'

'But I know that sort of boy, Amy. He had your heart and he's thrown it away.'

'Well, actually—'

'A boy with no understanding of himself. Lost to himself. I feel his pain, poor lad. He doesn't know the way. But you must protect yourself, Amy. I've told you this, many times.' He finished the spliff, looked regretful, and Garvie passed him a fresh one. PJ showed his teeth again. 'Now,' he said to Amy. 'Tell me why you've come to see me.'

She flushed again. 'You'd better ask him.'

The three of them turned to look at Garvie, who all this time had been sitting watching in silence. For a few moments more he just looked at PJ. Then he said, 'Tell us about Joel.'

Frowning, Amy said to PJ, 'I'd better explain. There's this guy Joel Watkins, who—'

Garvie said, 'No need to explain. PJ knows all about Joel. Don't you, PJ?'

He and PJ locked eyes.

At last the older man smiled. 'Of course.'

Amy said, 'Really? How?'

Garvie said, 'They drove together at One Shot, the dispatch company.'

PJ blew smoke and nodded thoughtfully. 'Joel Watkins. Van work, mainly. Sometimes bike. Yes. Another lost child. Very lost, that one. Drove a different car every week, if you know what I mean, all of them junk.' He gave a wink.

'Tell us more.'

It was a clear case of bad karma, as PJ explained. Like too many others, Joel Watkins was a child lost to himself, shut up in bad ways, locked away from true understanding, enlightenment ignored, disparaged even, though so badly needed.

'Besides,' PJ said, 'he pilfered. That's why he got sacked.'

Garvie leaned forward. 'That's interesting. His record doesn't say anything about any sacking.'

'Wouldn't do. Manager hushed it up. Don't want customers to know there's pilfering going on.'

'When did it happen?'

'The sacking? The Friday before he was killed. Sad, very sad.'

PJ elaborated. He had tried all he could to help Joel connect with his inner spirituality, had given him advice, most of it unsought, not so much in the way of instruction as out of love, from someone who knew for himself the darkness of a world without it. An arm round the shoulder, a word in the ear. Joel had responded with insults and threats, and for a while had led a vendetta against the peace-loving ex-Marine.

'But, yeah,' PJ said with obvious satisfaction. 'Bastard got caught skimming.' For months Joel had been knocking off goods from the loads he delivered, taking the odd box here, the odd package there, keeping it nice and unobtrusive. Then one day the manager found a load of stuff in his locker, and he was caught, fair and square.

'Joel didn't see it that way,' PJ said.

'What do you mean?'

'Anger was Joel's constant companion.' PJ smiled a long, wide smile. 'He went around telling everyone how someone had got him the rubber elbow.'

'He blamed someone else?'

'That's it. Went on and on about it. Someone had set him up. Deliberately done him over. He wasn't going to make his rent, he said.'

'What else did he say?'

'Impossible to make it out. Sound and fury. But

he was definitely pointing the finger at someone. He was going to make them pay.'

'Who?'

PJ gestured Pope-like with his upturned hands. 'There was no one to blame but himself.' Blaming was in the lost child's nature. 'Thing is,' he added, 'some lost children you can help. Others, sad to say, are beyond it. You have to move on, let them awaken on their own.' Wreathed in the sweet-bitter smoke of the spliff, PJ contemplated the grey cladding of the garage ceiling.

Smudge caught up with the conversation at last. 'Yeah, but. What we wanted to know is, had this Watkins fellow been hooking up with our man Damon in some way?'

Garvie nodded. 'To the point as usual, Smudge.'

PJ raised his upturned hands again as if to show there was nothing in them. 'No idea. I don't recall Joel ever mentioning a Damon. But who knows? What I do know is, they were both lost boys – lost to themselves. If you ever find your friend Damon, send him to me. I think I could help him.'

He closed his eyes and seemed to drift off, and after another ten minutes or so they quietly left him there, serene in his squalor, at peace with his karma, and went out again into the night.

They stood for a moment by their van, Smudge admiring it in the moonlight. Occasionally touching it. Near them were the grave-like trenches and piles

241

of earth where the police diggers had searched for Amy's body. The fine silhouettes of treetops around the clearing swayed faintly against the cloud-hazed sky. Once, far off, a fox barked, cold and sharp. Mist stood among the trees, as if the earth were letting out its breath.

Amy said, 'How did you know PJ and Joel both worked for One Shot?'

Garvie grunted. 'It got mentioned.'

'Ah yes. The boy who doesn't forget. But it doesn't look like Joel and Damon were still in touch. PJ was close to Joel. He would have known.'

Smudge opened the door, closed it for the pleasure of hearing it shut, and opened it again. He got in at last and settled himself behind the wheel.

'Fact is,' he said, 'we only learned a couple of things. First one: this PJ's a bit nuts. I got friends at One Shot. None of them are as out of it as he is.'

'Very good point, Smudge.'

'Second one: this Joel's got a temper.'

'Put your finger on it, again.' Garvie said. 'Quiet Man turns out to be Mr Angry. That's interesting.'

'Angry with whoever he thought got him the sack,' Amy said. 'Not Damon. Damon had absolutely nothing to do with him being sacked. It would be better if we could find Damon before the police do.'

Smudge agreed. He had mates on the alert all over the city. Sooner or later they'd turn something up.

Garvie sighed, shook his head.

'Well, what do you think we should do?' Amy asked him.

But for the next half an hour he said nothing, staring out of the window as they went back along the potholed track, around the lanes, and down at last into town, where Smudge pulled up again at the corner of Pollard Way and Town Road.

'Think I might go back to Pirrip Street tomorrow,' Garvie said at last.

Amy frowned. 'What for? Damon left there ages ago.'

'I told you, I'm not interested in where Damon is.'

'If you go then,' Smudge said, 'mind the dog.'

'It's OK. It's not his landlady I want to see.'

He said no more, just got out and without saying goodbye strolled away in the direction of Eastwick Gardens.

'Is he always like this?' Amy asked Smudge.

'Not really,' Smudge said. 'He can be much worse. Personally, I think it's why he doesn't get the girls.'

35

Morning sunlight showed Pirrip Street to itself through a fine screen of dust. The sunshine was warm, the dusty air smelled of hot broken glass, the true smell of the city, which lay all around, haphazard, ugly and reassuringly vast.

At number 8b Garvie leaned against the house wall, waiting. From inside the house he heard occasional chaotic dog noise, but he comforted himself, eyes half-closed, with Benson & Hedges. He didn't know how long he would have to wait. He reckoned maybe three cigarettes. But he was only halfway through the second when he heard the cough nearby.

He glanced round.

'No thanks,' he said. 'Not today.'

'You said that last time,' the kid said, his fists still up.

'I meant it for today.'

The kid appeared exactly as before, the same saggy short trousers, the same middle-aged man's face, the same bland determination to take the world for granted. Clearly, he would be like that till the day he died.

'Give us a cigarette then,' he said. 'Or I'll batter you.' A cunning look came across his face, making him look half-witted. 'I know you've got them because I can see one of them in your mouth.'

'Sharp today,' Garvie said. 'And looking good, by the way. But I can't give you one.'

'Why?'

''Cause I don't want to.'

The kid examined that thought from a number of angles and gave up. He was obviously used to giving up, and he did it with a sort of forlorn dignity.

'Anyway,' Garvie added, 'they're bad for you.'

This seemed no surprise to the kid, who nodded as if to say that bad things were his familiar friends.

'Well, Brainstorm,' Garvie said. 'Anything else to say?'

The kid thought about that. Nodded. 'Something to ask you.'

'Go ahead with your question. In your own time.'

'Is he dead?'

Garvie looked at him with new interest. 'Who?'

'Damon.'

'Why do you ask that?'

'The police been round. They do that when someone's dead. They did it with my dad,' the kid said.

'Well,' Garvie said after a moment. 'You got me. I don't know if he's dead.'

The kid nodded as if that settled it. 'I liked Damon,' he said. 'He said he thought he was going to die,' he added after a moment.

'Did he now?'

The kid nodded.

'You're full of interesting things today. You must have had a good breakfast.'

'Monster Munch.'

'What did Damon say exactly?'

'Dunno.'

'Come on. You are a bright and thoughtful boy. Don't give up now. Keep it going.'

But the kid became shy; he put his thumb in his mouth and refused to say any more.

'Did he say someone was going to kill him? Did he say he was going to die because he was sick? Did he say he was going to kill himself?'

The kid just stared at Garvie expressionlessly. After a while he took his thumb out of his mouth, and said, 'Wait here,' and disappeared down the alley at the side of the house.

Garvie waited. It was even quieter in the street now. He sucked on a Benson & Hedges, lifted his face to the sun and thought about Damon thinking he was going to die.

'Here.' The kid held out an envelope.

'What's this?'

'From Damon.'

Garvie opened the envelope. Inside was a plain piece of paper with a message written on it in capital letters in black felt-tip. Very low-tech: typical Damon. The message said: *LEAVE ME ALONE. IM WARNING YOU DONT PUSH ME MAN. ITS NOT MY FAULT.*

Garvie and the kid stared at each other for a bit.

Garvie said, 'Damon left this note with you?'

The kid nodded.

'When?'

Time seemed to be a conceptual problem for the kid. He shook his head.

'He left it with you to give to someone?'

The kid nodded.

'For me?'

The kid shook his head.

'For someone else who was going to turn up looking for him?'

The kid nodded again.

'Did Damon tell you who the guy was, who was going to show up?'

The kid shook his head. Looked inscrutable.

Garvie thought for a while. 'Do you *know* who it was?'

The kid nodded. Same blank expression.

Garvie said, 'You are polite and highly intelligent. How do you know who it was?'

The kid briefly took his thumb out of his mouth and said, 'He came before. Damon said he was going to come back.'

'I see. But he never did?'

The kid shook his head. Silently, without his expression changing, he began to cry.

'What now?'

'Didn't like him.'

'The guy who came? Did he frighten you? Was he nasty?'

The kid swallowed and nodded and wiped his eyes as the memory faded.

'Don't suppose you know this guy's name?'

Another shake of the head.

'Never mind. You are a clever and interesting boy with a brilliant future.'

The thumb came out for a moment. 'Why?

'Because you are going to answer my next question. What did this guy look like?'

For a long time the kid thought hard, then he said fluently, 'Big, tall, dark hair.'

Garvie thought about that. 'How short was his hair?'

The kid put the tips of his index finger and thumb very close together.

'What about here?' Garvie touched his upper lip.

'Lots.'

'This is the man Damon left his note for?'

The kid nodded.

'Final question. Was this man angry with Damon?'

The kid nodded energetically.

'I think you must be the most brilliant child of your generation. What's your name?'

'Smith.'

'Good. A good name. My name's Smith too.'

The kid smiled. It might have been the first time he'd ever done it. He didn't do it very well, but it looked like he enjoyed it. Then he closed his mouth and stared at Garvie impassively again. He stood there looking like the poorest person Garvie had ever seen.

Garvie said, 'You're such a good kid, I'm going to give you something.'

The kid nodded. 'A cigarette.'

'No. Something else.'

'What else?'

Garvie put his hand in his pocket and took out his wallet. He removed from it a thin thread of silver chain still scented, very faintly, with 'Alien' by Mugler, which he put back in his pocket.

'Here,' he said, holding out the wallet. 'You can have this. As it happens, due to an unforeseen development in my career, I don't really need it at the moment.'

The kid's expression didn't change. He stared at the wallet, as if confronted with something utterly beyond his comprehension.

'It's a wallet,' Garvie said. 'The person who gave it to me . . . well, let's just say she means a lot to me.'

'Is it full of money?' the kid asked at last.

'You get to take care of that bit yourself,' Garvie said. 'But that's not the point.'

'What's the point?'

'The point is that everyone needs to be given something once in a while.'

The kid fixed his unvarying stare on Garvie. 'Why?' he asked at last.

'You really are sharp today,' Garvie said. ''Cause that's a question I just can't answer. I just know it's true.'

For a minute or more the kid struggled to fit the

wallet into the pocket of his saggy shorts, and after a while gave up and stood there with it clenched in his fist, gazing at Garvie.

Garvie began to grin. It must have been catching because the kid began to grin as well, and they stood there grinning at each other.

36

In the café area near Communications and Records the TV was showing breaking lunchtime news. One or two men in uniform glanced at Garvie as he sauntered by, a boy in a scuffed black leather jacket, out of place among the back-room offices; but he soon turned away, slipping up the stairs, past Senior Management, to the floor above. He'd left Smudge in Reception causing a diversion, and was keen to put space between himself and the disturbance.

Upstairs, he strolled along another corridor between post rooms and storage facilities until he came to a windowless door featuring a temporary cardboard sign: DI SINGH. Not bothering to knock, he went inside. And found Detective Inspector Dowell behind the desk.

A moment of disquiet for both of them.

Neither spoke for a moment. Dowell shut the desk drawers with his good hand and leaned forward in the chair, propping his sling on the desktop. His piggy eyes shrank.

'Well, well,' he said at last. 'Garvie Smith. Come in to have a cosy chat with your man?'

'Looking for my uncle. I was told he was here.'

'Your uncle, yes. Mr Spots and Stains. Certainly he's friendly with young Raminder.'

They silently looked at each other for a while longer.

'Here's the thing,' Dowell said, all soft menace. 'We're all looking for this lad Walsh.'

Garvie nodded. 'And you want me to tell you where he is?' He lowered his voice and Dowell instinctively leaned forward. Garvie said, 'Somewhere you won't find him. Thing is,' he added, 'you're working at a disadvantage.'

Dowell's expression didn't change.

'Being stupid,' Garvie said. 'Makes everything harder. I think Smudge'll find him first.'

Now the policeman's expression changed; it got thicker, bigger, it filled his face. He shifted his eyes slightly downwards.

'What's in your pockets, son?'

'Nothing much.'

'Why don't you put it on the desk for me?'

Garvie hesitated. 'Don't you have to have a warrant to search my pockets?'

Dowell stood up. He was not a big man but he was big enough.

Garvie put the contents of his pockets on the desk.

Cheap disposable lighter. Pack of Benson & Hedges. A fine and faintly scented silver chain. Piece of paper folded in two with a note on the inside reading *LEAVE ME ALONE. IM WARNING YOU DONT PUSH ME MAN. ITS NOT MY FAULT.*

Dowell said nothing. He reached across and took the note and put it, unread, into his top jacket pocket. A ghost of a smile passed across his lips. He lowered his face with a bull-like movement, and stared at Garvie for a moment. Then left the room.

One floor below, in the chief's office, Singh stood in silence.

'It's about using the proper channels,' the chief said at last.

'Yes, sir. Though the information has now been formally disclosed.'

'The rules are there for a purpose,' the chief said, ignoring him. 'A good defence lawyer will have a case thrown out if information is shown to have been obtained first unofficially.' He looked at Singh with his usual lidless disapproval. 'Wasting months of expensive police work.'

'I understand, sir.'

The silence went on even longer than usual.

The chief said quietly, 'We don't rely on unofficial sources. And we don't, ever,' he said in an even quieter voice, 'share our information with third parties.'

Singh hesitated. 'No, sir.'

The chief fixed him with his gaze. 'At one time, Inspector, you were a' – he sought the right word – 'stickler for the rules. It was the secret of your success, some would say. Which has been sadly lacking lately.' The chief considered for a moment longer, then nodded and bent to his desk, as if Singh had already left his office.

Going across the open-plan to the staircase and up to the floor above, Singh reflected. The chief's warning had been clear: he knew about Singh's conversations with Paul Tanner; much worse, he may have heard something about his unorthodox dealings with Garvie Smith. This thought filled him with foreboding. He'd become careless; he needed to be more disciplined again. No one must suspect anything about his relationship with Garvie. It must be kept absolutely secret.

He went into his office and there found Garvie lounging in his chair with his feet up on his desk, fingering a cigarette.

'Do you think I'm good with people?' Garvie asked. 'Be honest.'

Singh found his voice, a hoarse whisper. 'What the hell are you doing here?' He hastily shut the door behind him.

'Helping out. Thought that's what you wanted me to do.'

'I mean, what are you doing *in my office*? People will see you.'

'Like Dowell, you mean? Yeah, I was chatting to him just now. I think I must have got on the wrong side of him somehow. Smudge is right, you know, I need to improve my people skills.'

'Chatting? To Dowell? *Here?* Oh my God.' Singh went briefly pop-eyed and let out a groan of dismay.

'I mean, I know we're never going to be close – but I really hated it when he took Damon's note off me.'

Singh's expression stopped in the middle of another contortion. 'What are you talking about, "Damon's note"?'

'Brought specially for you. A present. But Dowell took it. And the weird thing is,' he paused thoughtfully, 'he seemed to know I had it.' He got up and walked around thoughtfully.

Singh was struggling to control himself. 'None of this is good, Garvie.'

'I know. Least of all my people skills.'

'OK, OK. Let's be calm.' Singh made calming gestures with his arms, at odds with Garvie's extreme calmness.

Some moments passed.

'OK,' Singh said in his normal voice. 'Tell me, slowly, what is this note?'

Garvie told him.

Singh was silent for a while. 'And you think Damon left it for Joel Watkins?'

'The kid described Joel to a tee. Mr Frightening.'

'So. Joel was after Damon. It sounds like he was blaming him for something. And Damon wrote Joel a note telling him it wasn't his fault, and to back off – or else.'

'That's it.'

Singh sat down at the desk and folded his hands together. 'I've done some more work on Joel. I went to his flat in Tick Hill. It's a strange place. There's hardly any furniture in it. But a lot of weightlifting equipment. And it has a very expensive security system.'

Garvie said, 'Interesting. Joel moved jobs all the time but never missed his rent.'

Singh nodded. 'His outgoings frequently exceeded his income. We're on it: our Finance guys are looking into it now. My assumption is, he had accounts we don't know about yet.'

They were silent, thinking.

Garvie said, 'You're sure about Joel and Damon being together on the Y.O.? Who's this guy who told you?'

'His name's Paul Tanner, lives out at Childswell. He used to work on the programme and knew both Damon and Joel. He didn't want to tell me, in fact; he's protective of Damon. He may well still be in touch with him. He didn't like Joel. But, anyway, just now it was confirmed through the official channels.'

After a moment, Singh continued reflectively, 'Joel and Damon. Once they were close. "Soul mates", Damon thought. Then they fell out. The question is, why.'

'But the real question,' Garvie said, 'is *why so angry*? Joel scared the kid to death when he showed up looking for Damon. He was absolutely furious with him.'

Singh nodded. 'Joel blamed Damon for something. About getting the sack from One Shot?'

'No, Damon didn't have anything to do with—'
He fell silent.

'Garvie?'

The boy threw him a distracted look. 'Got to go.'
He paused. 'Funny, isn't it, how easy it is to miss the
obvious.'

'What are you talking about?'

'Sequences. Same numbers keep coming up. You
know, Pascal's triangle. Problem is, you think they
mean the same thing. But they don't. Same number,
different value.' At the door he turned and said, 'By the
way, last thing. Remember: you can't trust Dowell.'

'I know that. You don't have to worry.'

'It's you who should be worrying. He was going
through your desk drawers: did I say that?'

Singh frowned.

Garvie said, 'And when I say you can't trust him,
I don't mean anything trivial. I mean, watch your
back. Seriously.'

'It would help,' Singh called, 'if you didn't come in
here and chat to him.'

But Garvie was already in the corridor outside. As
he went he dialled.

She answered on the first ring, as if she'd been
waiting for him.

He said, 'Can you get hold of some posh clothes?'

'Don't understand.'

'Not your usual goth-punk rebel stuff.'

'I mean, I don't understand why I would need
some posh clothes.'

''Cause the place we're going won't let you in unless you're wearing them.'

'Which is where?'

'Meet you at ten outside the bowling alley in The Wicker.'

'I don't need posh clothes at the bowling alley.'

'Who says we're going to the bowling alley?'

She was halfway through asking him again where they were going when she realized he'd already rung off, and she sat there with the phone in her hand, sighing.

Singh sat in his office, sighing too. He thought about Joel Watkins getting angry, and about Damon Walsh getting frightened. And he thought again about what else Paul Tanner might know.

He picked up the phone.

'Detective Inspector Singh here. I would like to come and talk to you again.'

There was a pause. Tanner said, in an unsteady voice, 'Yeah. Actually, I was going to call you.'

'About what?'

Another pause. 'Something's happened.'

'What has happened?'

'I guess I should've told you sooner,' Tanner said. 'You'd better come round. But you have to be quick.'

37

Singh sat opposite Paul Tanner in his brightly lit living room.

'Why didn't you tell me this before?'

Tanner looked shifty.

Singh said, 'I asked you to contact me immediately if Damon got in touch.'

Tanner rubbed his face. 'I'll be honest with you, I wasn't going to tell you at all. There's a reason Damon doesn't trust the police. Last time you threw the book at him, he ended up inside, and it was hell for him, nearly destroyed him.'

'I understand,' Singh said. 'But the way for Damon to avoid that now is to come forward and talk to us. Anyway, tell me now what has happened.'

Tanner began to explain. The day before, he'd got a call from Damon. The usual story: he needed money.

'What for?'

'A phone,' he said. 'Didn't believe him at first. Thought he was after something to calm him down, weed or whatever. But when I said all right, no money, but I'll buy you the phone, he said yeah, cheers.'

'So you're going to buy him a phone. What then?'

Tanner swallowed. 'Well, I already bought it.'

'What?'

He'd bought the phone and left it, as Damon had asked, at a storage point near the station.

'So he might have picked it up already?'

'No, I just called the place. The package is still there. But, yeah, Damon's got the code, he might turn up at any time.'

Singh was already on his feet. 'OK. Give me the details.'

Tanner was on his feet too. 'All right. But listen. I don't want anything happening to Damon.'

Singh said angrily, 'You've just admitted aiding and abetting a suspect. You're lucky not to be charged with obstruction of justice.'

Tanner's face hardened. 'I'm looking out for Damon, right? He's got no one else to do it for him. I'm holding you responsible for his safety.'

Singh almost lost his patience. Not quite. 'The details,' he said. 'Quickly, please.'

The souvenirs kiosk sat in a long strip of stores between a halal restaurant and a tanning shop, opposite the pedestrian entrance to the station. By now it was the middle of the afternoon, the street was busy, pavements packed with people, the road clogged with slow-moving cars, taxis, buses and trucks, all shimmering in the sun. It was the public heart of the city, the habitat of travellers and hustlers, of brisk young tourists with backpacks and idling men in sunglasses and the cross-legged destitute with their thin voices and cardboard signs. The air was hazed with the noise of traffic and chatter. Everything moved, slowly but ceaselessly.

Dressed in black jeans and zip-up fleece and black silk headscarf knotted on the top, Singh moved too, shifting his position every few minutes, always staying on the station side. He had arrived at 14:00; now it was 15:30. Damon had not yet appeared.

At 16:00 he stood with a magazine among smokers at the station entrance.

At 17:00 he moved further along the street, methodically working the windows of shops selling bagels, insurance, postcards, chicken, money, wigs and novelties.

At 18:00, as the crowds thinned out, he sat in the corner window of a coffee shop.

Twice he called Paul Tanner. Damon had not been in touch again. The package was still in place.

At last the afternoon dimmed to evening, the shop lights came on, and at 21:30 the sky was dark above the little glitter of the street.

Singh called Tanner again.

'Perhaps he's seen you,' Tanner said.

'No,' Singh said evenly. 'He has not seen me.'

He rang off, and the second he put his phone away, he saw him, Damon Walsh the flaky boy, slipping like an eel through passers-by towards the souvenir shop. He was wearing the maroon hoodie he'd worn when Singh interviewed him, walking head down, moving quick and stiff-legged, pushing open the shop door and disappearing inside.

Singh left the station entrance and crossed the road, and positioned himself outside the halal restaurant, waiting.

A few minutes passed, and he prepared himself.

A few more minutes passed.

Peering through the souvenir-shop window, he found his view blocked by racks of badges and bumper stickers. He made a sudden decision. Moving quickly, he went inside.

The first thing he saw was the feet of the prone body of the shopkeeper lying next to the counter. Cursing himself, he leaped forward, over the man and down the aisle to a door at the end, and through the door into a dogleg corridor piled with cardboard boxes. At the corner, another shorter corridor led to a door. The door was open. In it stood Damon, fiddling with a package.

'Damon!'

Without turning, Damon bolted. He took off, all jerky arms and legs, across a yard and over a wire fence, and swerved away into the streets, scattering pedestrians. Singh leaped after him.

'Damon!' he called again.

In the street, he saw him dash across the road, careless of traffic, running manically, like a man animated by terror, towards the station entrance. A bus slid in front of Singh and for several seconds he lost sight of him. By the time he'd crossed the road,

Damon was nowhere to be seen. Singh ran down the short sloping entrance to the station and stopped, panting, as he scanned the concourse in front of him. Even so late it was crowded, a herd of people doing nothing very much with the stoical concentration common to commuters and livestock. A scene without anything out of the ordinary.

Then, briefly, a blur of maroon passing between the corner of a kiosk and the front end of a train idling at a far-off platform.

Singh set off.

He danced his way through the stationary crowd, running on his toes onto the platform just in time to see Damon turn the top of stairs at the other end and disappear onto the bridge across the tracks. As he ran he concentrated. He put himself wholly into his effort, as the Sikh masters taught. He *became* his running.

Going up the steps three at a time, he sprinted along the bridge, vaulted the ticket barrier at the end, ran across the walkway and taxi rank, and out again onto the streets, looking round.

But Damon had gone.

Singh turned in every direction but there was no sign of a maroon hoodie. He stood alone, hands on knees, gulping air, while travellers went past him without a glance; and gradually as the minutes passed he got back his breath. It was 22:00. At last, he turned and began to walk back, grimly, to the souvenir shop.

Which was when he saw Damon creeping round the corner back into the station.

He flung himself forward once more, went round the corner, and tackled him with explosive force high round the waist just before the ticket barrier. They rolled together on the concrete as travellers jumped screaming out of the way, crashed against a low wall, and Singh pressed his forearm across Damon's throat as his hood fell back, and he saw, to his confusion and horror, that it was not Damon at all.

38

At ten o'clock, half a mile from the station, Garvie and Amy stood in front of the bowling alley across the road from the Imperium casino.

He'd told her about the note Damon left for Joel. But he hadn't told her why they were there.

The Wicker was getting lively, noisy parties of men and women milling up and down the street in an air of edgy celebration, clubbers and drinkers, hen-night girls, sports boys, bar hoppers, dance freaks and fancy-dress brigades, all staking their territorial claims on the clubs and bars along the strip.

Garvie was wearing the all-black outfit of the Imperium male staff: black trousers, black shirt and waistcoat, black bow tie.

Amy stood poised and elegant on grey suede heels with tasselled, lace-up straps, wearing a one-shoulder, knee-length bodycon dress in grey stretch fabric, with a small clutch bag to match. Her hair was up, revealing the long nape of her neck and ears. To call the dress curve-hugging would be a laughable understatement, like calling a major explosion uncomfortable. It seemed to have been sprayed on.

They stood looking at each other.

'Simone Rocha,' she said. 'If you're interested.'

Garvie could feel himself beginning to sweat. 'I wasn't going to ask who you'd borrowed it off. I was going to ask if it was legal.'

'Will it do?' she asked.

'Oh yeah.' He swallowed. 'It'll do.'

'Good. Then maybe you can explain. Finally.'

He explained. It was quite simple. To recap. Joel Watkins was Mr Angry. He was angry because someone had got him the sack.

Amy said, 'But no one got him the sack. PJ told us. It was just Joel blowing off. He was caught stealing.'

'Right. No one got him the sack *from One Shot*.'

He watched her thinking about that.

'You mean someone got him the sack from some-where else?'

'He usually worked more than one job. Couple of days before he was sacked from One Shot he was sacked from Imperium. Singh mentioned it. Joel was constantly being moved on; it's like the same number recurring in a sequence. PJ heard him ranting about someone getting him the sack and naturally assumed he was talking about One Shot. But maybe he was blowing off about someone getting him the sack *at Imperium*.'

She looked over at the casino. 'So we're going over there to find out what happened.'

'That's it.'

'But what's this got to do with Damon?'

'Don't know yet. But Damon used to come here sometimes, play the slots. He told me that himself.'

'OK,' she said at last. 'But how do you explain your kit?' She put out a hand and straightened his collar, and ran her finger down the line of buttons on his shirt.

'Borrowed it from a friend. He's temping in the back office. Helps me blend in. I've got previous with the casino. It'll keep their attention off me. Though I don't know if I really need it now.'

'Why?'

'No one's going to be looking at me.' He paused, glanced at her. 'They're all going to be looking at you.' A look passed between them, interrupted by Garvie's phone ringing. He put it to his ear without looking at it, said, 'What?' and stepped away from her.

She looked over at the casino lit up soft blue and green, like an aquarium. Fake columns flanked the entrance, and in front of the columns stood two outsized doormen wearing dinner jackets and black bow ties and the blank expressions of the thoughtlessly violent. A large sign of unusual brilliance read *LIFE'S A GAMBLE ROLL THE DICE*. A much smaller sign, in the same perky style, read *Never Bet More than You can Afford to Lose*.

Garvie returned to Amy, looking more inscrutable than ever.

'What's up?'

He told her what Singh had told him, the trap laid

for Damon, the chase and its failure. Damon was still at large.

Amy said, 'He'll be panicking, desperate.'

'Yeah. And maybe in danger of losing it.'

They both thought about that.

'I wonder what he wanted a new phone for?' Garvie said.

Amy shrugged. She said, 'Did Singh say anything else?'

Singh's team had found a hidden account belonging to Joel Watkins. Nothing special, but full of irregular mid-sized payments, about one a month.

'Unexpected.'

'Not really. Singh just needs a friend in the team that handles vehicle theft. They'll work it out. The important thing for us is to find out what went down when Joel got the sack at the casino. By the way, before we go, there's this guy.'

'What guy?'

'Sort of bandy-legged, crazy-eyed, wet-faced sort of guy. Owner's son and manager. Darren Winder. You'll recognize him when you see him. Be good if we didn't bump into him.'

'Dangerous?'

'Just a bit irritating. Are you still up for this?'

'Wouldn't miss it.'

'OK, you go first.'

'Did you have a plan, or shall I blag it?'

'Why not just see what happens?'

'Always the most interesting thing to do, right?'

They looked at each other a moment, a little crackle of emotion passed between them, and she smiled at him. Then she stepped lightly across the road towards the mock-Roman frontage of Imperium, its fluted columns and thick-set doormen.

Garvie waited, watching her go. He counted down from 4,181 in the Fibonacci sequence, not particularly slowly – 4,181, 2,584, 1,597, 987, 610, 377, 233, 144, 89, 55, 34, 21, 13, 8, 5, 3, 2, 1, 1, 0 – and set off after her at a trot. By the time he reached the entrance she was already talking to one of the doormen. Pop-eyed with fascination, he seemed to be trying to lip-read her whole body. Distracted by Garvie's approach, he put out a traffic-warden-like hand.

'Been out to get Mr Winder's pills from the all-night pharmacy,' Garvie said. Glancing at Amy, he did a double-take, whispered to the doorman, 'Simone Rocha – from the TV,' and went past him.

A few moments later Amy joined him inside. 'I was doing all right on my own,' she said crossly.

'I could see that. But if you'd gone all the way and turned him completely to stone there would have been a fuss.'

'What now?'

The lobby where they stood was a sunken circle decorated like a tiny amphitheatre with nude statuettes in alcoves hung with ivy in stucco and a mosaic on the floor showing Neptune, god of the sea, demonstrating wrestling moves to a couple of only slightly unwilling nymphs. From the depths of a badly lit corridor came the noise of slots. Beyond, in tastefully dimmed lighting, they could see a corner of the cocktail bar and the entrance to the restaurant and, beyond those, the gaming tables surrounded by small crowds of people self-consciously wearing posh clothes.

'Good luck,' Garvie said.

'Where are you going?'

'Back office.'

'Doing what?'

'Finding out stuff.'

'OK. I'll do the same out here.'

He nodded. 'Best not stay long, though. See you in the car park at the back in half an hour?'

'Done.'

He stepped away and disappeared through a STAFF ONLY door she hadn't noticed, and she went forward among the other people, looking about her and listening. There was piped lyre music, very ancient Rome, and the clanking chug of the slots, and the murmur of voices from the restaurant and bar, and the periodic hush round the roulette table as if everyone watching was holding their breath. All the female croupiers and waitresses wore short white togas with their ancient Roman names on urn-shaped badges: 'Olivia', 'Fulvia', 'Messalina'.

'Livia Drusilla' offered Amy a glass of champagne. She was a bright-eyed girl with a crooked nose and friendly smile.

'Thanks. What games do you recommend?'

'Depends what you like. Haven't you been before?'

'Never. One of my cousins used to work here. Not a nice man. To be honest, it put me off.'

'Who was that then?'

'His name was Joel Watkins.'

Livia Drusilla nearly lost control of her tray. 'You're his cousin?'

'Practically grew up with him.'

'Really? Everyone's still talking about him here. You know, ever since the . . . No one knows what happened. But he was . . .'

Amy nodded. 'Don't worry. I know what he was like.'

Livia Drusilla had by now lost all interest in her tray of drinks. She would have been surprised to see it still there in her hand. Her eyes were fixed shining on Amy.

'Honestly,' Amy said, 'The things I could tell you about him. If we had time.'

'I'm on my break in fifteen,' Livia Drusilla said promptly. 'I could meet you at the back of the restaurant. Get you another free drink?'

Amy nodded. 'All right. We can swap stories about Joel, and then you can tell me which game to play.'

Elsewhere, Garvie went down the corridor that ran alongside the perimeter of the public rooms. It was quiet and plain and bare. No Roman theme. He'd been here once before. The only touch of opulence was the shag-pile carpeted staircase that he knew went up to the Winders' private suite. He walked past it, checking names on the doors that appeared regularly on his right-hand side – ACCOUNTS, MEETING ROOM, MEMBER SERVICES, LICENSING. Some of the doors he tried. They were locked. The work that went on in them was daytime work, obviously. But whenever the casino was open there had to be a back office servicing it. Somewhere. Eventually he came to a small lounge filled with sofas and plants, and sat down to have a rest and a think.

When he heard footsteps, he stubbed out his cigarette in a plant pot, and went along the corridor until he met a stern-looking middle-aged woman in a black dress suit coming the other way.

'Scuse me,' he said.

'Yes.' She peered at him through spectacles.

'I'm looking for the office. Mr Winder's asked me to fetch something from it.'

She looked at him. 'Don't you know where it is?'

'My first night. I'm from the temp agency.'

'What temp agency?'

'Office Angels. Dani Middleton's cover. He's not well.'

'Again! That boy!' She turned and pointed behind her. 'The evening office is through Cage Operations.' She sniffed and looked about her.

Garvie said promptly, 'I thought I smelled cigarette smoke. Back there.'

'Back where?'

'By the staircase.'

'Mr Winder's staircase?' She clicked her tongue. 'He told me he'd given up. I shall have to mention it again,' she said, half to herself. She peered at Garvie. 'What does Mr Winder want from the office?'

'Employee file.'

'You need to ask Janet. She'll help you.'

'Thanks.'

'Tuck your shirt in. And hurry along. You don't want to keep him waiting.'

Cage Operations was a dim space of desk silhouettes. At the far end of it a door with NIGHT OFFICE on it was framed by a fringe of leaky yellow light.

Garvie knocked and entered.

It was a windowless square room containing three desks loaded with the usual equipment and about twenty old-fashioned filing cabinets lined up like slot machines against the walls. Two women occupying the nearest desks turned to look at Garvie with interest. One had a grey bob, the other wore a brown cardigan.

'Janet?' Garvie said.

Grey Bob said to Brown Cardigan, 'They get younger, don't they?'

'Prettier too,' Brown Cardigan said.

They leered at him pleasantly while he looked from one to the other.

'Why don't you guess, love?' Brown Cardigan said. 'Which of us is Janet?'

Garvie pointed at Grey Bob, who smiled slyly. 'Why's that then?'

Garvie shrugged. 'Just got that look about you. Sort of Janet-ish.'

'Oh yes?'

'Yeah. Sharp. Stylish. Good-looking.'

She blushed.

'Besides,' Garvie said, 'your name's on the email on your screen.'

She laughed. 'All right, what do you want?'

'Mr Winder sent me to get an employee file.'

'Whose file?'

He took a piece of paper out of his pocket, and read from it. 'Joel Watkiss. Watkins. Don't think he works here any more.'

'Doesn't work anywhere,' Janet said. 'And no one's crying about it.' She nodded at Brown Cardigan, who opened the filing cabinet next to her desk and took out a brown manila file, very old-style, and passed it to Janet.

'Here you are,' she said to Garvie. 'All part of the great Joel Watkins saga, no doubt. Mr Winder must have had that file a dozen times in the last week.'

'Really?' Garvie said. 'Why?'

Janet gave him a long, cool look. 'What you don't know can't hurt you,' she said. 'Well, you've got your file. You better get back to Mr Winder. Tuck your shirt in.'

He went down the corridor, head down, still reading, flipping the pages. After a moment, he ripped out a few and put them in his pocket; the rest of the file he binned in the lounge area as he passed through.

The coast was clear – for about twenty seconds. Somewhere ahead of him there was a thumping noise and a moment later a man came abruptly down the staircase into the corridor. He was bandy-legged, his eyes were crazy, his face wet, and he stood there a moment looking about him in apparent outrage, then came directly towards Garvie with a strenuous inefficient movement as if somehow walking with his shoulders.

Garvie kept his head down and Darren Winder thumped past him without comment. As Garvie watched him disappear round a corner, he heard him call out to Janet, who had evidently left her office. Walking softly, Garvie retraced his steps as far as a door marked LAUNDRY near the corner of the corridor, and reached it just in time to hear their conversation.

He heard Janet say, 'Did you get the file?'

There was a random noise from Winder suggesting incomprehension.

'God, they get younger, don't they?' Janet's voice said, conversationally.

Winder's voice discovered language. It said, 'What?'

'The lad from the temp agency.'

'Lad from the temp agency?'

'Just now. Dark hair, slim. Got to say, very good-looking. Came for the file you were asking for.'

There was a slight pause, then Winder's voice suddenly found its natural level. '*What the fuck are you talking about?*' he said loudly.

There was a confused interchange of bewildered murmuring and alarmed bellowing, brought to a sudden halt by Winder: 'I'm telling you, I didn't ask for a file!' After a brief, fraught silence, he added menacingly: 'What file was it?'

Janet's reply was a very small murmur indeed. The momentary silence that followed was like an intake of breath, then there was the sudden noise of running footsteps, and Garvie stepped sideways into LAUNDRY where he could listen in peace to Winder's noisy stampede along the corridor outside; then he stepped out and went in the opposite direction down the now-deserted corridor, following signs to FIRE EXIT – as demonstrated before, nearly always the fastest way to reach the outside world, particularly in a casino, specially designed, labyrinth-like, to keep the punters inside, and even more particularly when the doormen at the entrance, if you ever get there, are likely to use all their charm to persuade you not to leave.

He walked past kitchen doors with round glass windows in them, and someone stuck his head out and called after him, and he went on, a little faster. Behind him and ahead of him he heard doors banging. Then an emergency alarm went off, a noise so powerful the walls of the narrow corridor seemed to throb. Security had been called. Through the explosive din Garvie walked on steadily past toilets and janitors' cupboards, went down a few steps and came at last to the fire escape. Running footsteps drummed in the corridor behind him as he leaned on the panic bar. Just in time. He allowed himself a smile of relief.

The bar didn't budge.

He leaned on it harder. It was stuck fast.

He rattled it with both hands. In vain.

Above the steps behind him a door crashed open, and a doorman filled the doorway instead.

Garvie glanced back. The doorman was big and angry, and he didn't want to be introduced to him. Leaning backwards, he kicked the bar so hard he wasn't sure for a second whether the blur of sudden squawking movement was the fire escape flying open or his foot flying off. Then he was jumping the metal railing outside, and running across the car park. Amy was waiting for him by the side of the near wall.

She didn't speak. She was busy watching the doorman and his two colleagues as they barged their way like log flumes through the flapping doors, closely followed by a bandy-legged man with a face apparently about to catch fire.

'Looks like you've got everything under control,' she said.

Garvie limp-jogged up to her. 'They don't like me,' he said sadly.

'I can see that. Suggestions?'

'Improve my people skills.'

'And?'

'All things considered,' he said, 'I think we should run again.'

He had just enough time to admire her fence-vaulting skills again as she went over the wall, then he joined her, and they ran together down the alley into the shadows.

39

They went along the darkened bin-crowded backs of bars and clubs, over a brick wall greasy with moss into another car park, through a gap in a tatty mesh fence, and slithered down the bank to the towpath. Amy took off her heels, and they ran under cover of the trees as far as the old gas pipe raised over the canal, which they crossed, high-wire-style, one after the other, to the station side, and picked their way across the tracks to emerge by the corner of the shopping mall.

There were people here. Amy put her shoes on and they got their breath back.

'That was fun,' she said after a while. 'I don't usually get so much exercise when I come down to The Wicker. Usually it's just boys and drinks. Never run-for-your-life.'

Garvie said nothing. He lit up and they drifted towards the station, mingling with the other people. As they went, Amy glanced at him sideways out of the corner of her eye. Hands in pockets, head down, cigarette in mouth. Shirt tails out, bow tie undone. Hair falling over his forehead. Expression gloomy.

They walked on again in silence for several

minutes. At the far end of the station concourse Amy turned towards Market Square and Garvie went with her, still brooding.

'Never mind,' she said at last. 'It was worth a try, even if you didn't get hold of anything.'

They went on again, and they were halfway down Charlotte Way before Garvie handed her the pages from the Watkins file, which she looked at in surprise.

'What are these?'

'Came into my possession. Just before the run-for-your-life bit.'

'*Joel Watkins*,' she read out loud. '*Personnel file, private and confidential*. It's his employment record at Imperium!'

'Just the disciplinary bit. The rest of it was pretty boring, to be honest.'

'How the hell did you get it?'

He looked surprised. 'They gave it to me.'

She was duly bewildered. 'Have you read it?'

He shrugged. 'Gave it a quick glance.'

'And why aren't you happy?'

He didn't answer and she began to read, fast. 'There's a lot here. *Verbal warning, 6th of February. Inappropriate comments, female staff.* Then it gives her Roman name.'

'Messalina, yeah. I remember her. More verbals later, if you read on. *Olivia, 17th of February. Fulvia, 3rd of March. Julia Agrippina, 14th of March.*'

She flipped pages. 'Lots of other black marks

and warnings. Playing slots on company time. Poor timekeeping. Abusive attitude, obviously. He really wasn't very pleasant, was he?'

'Keep going,' Garvie said. 'Fifth entry from the bottom.'

'Which one's that?'

Garvie recited: '*Written warning, 31st of March.*'

'Thought you'd only given it a glance,' she said.

'Stuck in my mind. Have you got it?'

'Yeah. *Unauthorized visit to Accounts.*' She looked at him. 'Snooping in Accounts?'

'Yeah. Interesting.'

'Hoping to get his hands on some petty cash. Thieving slimeball. But you're not happy.'

'No.'

She nodded. 'I know why. There's nothing here saying why he was finally sacked.'

He sighed. 'All the other stuff's just incidental. No payoff. We might have well not bothered dressing up. Although . . .' He glanced at her. 'No, I take that back.'

Amy stopped in front of the McDonald's at the edge of the square. At that time of night it was almost deserted. Two or three people sat alone with their coffees as if dazed by the glare of the lighting.

'I think you're being unduly pessimistic,' she said.

'You think?'

'I know.'

She pushed open the door into McDonald's.

'Come and meet Livia Drusilla. She's going to tell us exactly why Joel was sacked.'

They sat upstairs, away from the windows. No longer in her toga, Livia Drusilla was tall and neat and normal, and she sat with her toffee latte, smiling at Garvie.

'This is pretty exciting.'

'What is?'

'You being questioned for murder.'

Garvie glanced at Amy, who said to Livia smoothly, 'Obviously it was just routine. Just because they'd driven dispatch together.'

'Yeah. I'd love to be a dispatch driver. What do you drive?'

Garvie cleared his throat. 'A van,' he said.

'Yeah. What sort?'

'White. White-ish.'

'Yeah. And now you work at Imperium?'

'Last day today.'

'Oh. That's a shame. Now you won't be able to sneak your girlfriend in without paying.'

Garvie looked at Amy again.

'Don't worry,' Livia said. 'I'm not going to tell anyone.'

'So anyway,' Garvie said, 'you saw what happened when Joel got the boot?'

'Ringside seat. I was in the lobby and I heard it all kicking off.'

'What happened?'

It had been a warm night and the place was crowded. Livia had just finished serving drinks and was about to head back to the restaurant when she heard the shouting, and she put down the empty tray and ran outside with a few others. The two men were in the alley that runs alongside Imperium, Joel and a punter, struggling together. At first she thought that Joel must have been ejecting the punter for something, being drunk maybe or bad behaviour, but Joel was way too angry, shaking him and yelling at him. It was a personal argument. Joel'd got the guy in a throat-lock, as if he was going to twist his head off. Then the other guy got loose and started battering Joel. He slammed him into the wall, and he'd started throwing punches when Darren Winder and some of the other security boys ran out and pulled them apart. Everyone was ushered inside then so she didn't see what happened afterwards, but Joel was sacked on the spot, she knew that, paid off and told never to come back.

'When was this?' Amy asked.

'Beginning of August, I don't remember the date. My late shift. A Wednesday.'

'The first then,' Garvie said. 'Two days before he was sacked from One Shot. A week before he was killed.'

'And what happened to the punter?' Amy asked.

Livia shook her head. 'I suppose they gave him something, hushed him up.'

'But you don't think he was being ejected.'

'No. Didn't make sense. Joel was too angry. Like I say, it seemed personal.'

'What did the punter look like?' Garvie asked.

'Didn't get a good look at him, to be honest. Not dressed up, I noticed that. Some of the punters like to dress up, play the tables, sip their complimentary drinks, but some just come in to play the slots. They don't stay that long and they don't bother dressing up. Yeah, just some ordinary-looking guy in jeans and a purplish hoodie and a beanie.'

'Purplish – like maroon?'

'Yeah, that's it.'

'Tallish, black hair? Sort of wiry?'

'Yeah, that's it. Do you know him?'

'Don't know yet. What did they say?'

'Say?'

'You said there was shouting.'

'Right. Well, Joel was all *Bastard* and *Fuck* and, you know, *I'm Going to Lamp Your Head off.* I'm not sure about the punter.'

'He didn't say anything?'

'Let me think.'

They waited.

'Well. He kept telling Joel to back off. *I'm warning you!* Like if Joel didn't stop he was really going to lose it with him.'

'Anything else?'

She thought again. 'There was something, I can't remember what though.'

Garvie said, '*It's not my fault.*'

She looked at him, surprised. 'Yeah. Yeah, that was it. Funny you knew.'

Amy looked again at Garvie, who sat expressionless, looking at Livia.

'Interesting,' he said at last.

'Yeah. Weird too.' She smiled. 'You know what, we should go out some time, on a double date. My boyfriend's big into crime, he's always reading those books. He'd love it that you were, like, a real suspect.'

'That would be great,' Garvie said, getting up. Amy and Livia exchanged numbers, and they said goodbye and went out into the night.

It was nearly one o'clock, still warm. The sky was clear, stars visible through the finely shimmering city glare, and Amy and Garvie walked slowly back towards the station without speaking. There were fewer people about now. The night hush of cities had settled over the streets, a dull, low-level hum complicated by distant echoes of traffic.

'It was Damon,' Amy said at last.

'Sounds like it.'

'He had a fight with Joel, and Joel got the sack and blamed Damon for it.'

They walked a little further and she spoke again.

'OK. This is what we know. Damon and Joel met on the youth offender programme. They were close, Damon looked up to Joel, trusted him. Then they fell out, don't know why exactly, but Joel was mad at Damon. They had a fight at Imperium, Joel was sacked as a result and blamed Damon. So then Joel was really wild. And then . . .'

'Then what?'

'I don't know. Maybe nothing.'

'Then Damon showed up at your house with the murder weapon.'

They walked on in silence. They passed in front of the station, where a few people lingered, as if stuck at the end of their journey, sitting on the steps. They looked up at Amy as she went by. She was worth looking at. She'd taken off her heels and carried them, moving with gymnastic grace, smooth and compact in her outrageously tight dress.

She said, 'I still don't think he killed Joel. I mean, we don't even know where he got the gun from.'

'We know he had it.'

'We don't know he met Joel that night.'

'We know he was in Market Square when Joel was killed.'

'But we don't know what happened.'

'That's why we're thinking about it now. That's why we're keeping an open mind and not just defending him as usual.'

Their eyes met, and she nodded, and they walked on as far as the depot next to the shopping mall, where they paused. A truck was waiting to go in; there was a little sucking sound, then the gates shunted open with a metallic rattle like convict chains and closed again with a slow, sad sigh. It left behind the empty street, its shadow and a whiff of garbage.

Garvie took out his Benson & Hedges, tapped one out and tossed it absent-mindedly into the corner of his mouth. He held out the pack to Amy.

'Are you stupid? They kill you.'

'So does breathing, eventually.'

'You really are weird, aren't you?'

They moved on again, along the bland, shiny façade of the shopping mall.

'OK,' Amy said. 'Help me out. What am I missing?'

'Joel's finances.'

'What about them?'

'He lost jobs but never missed rent.'

She thought about that. She said, 'You were talking to Singh on the phone earlier. A hidden account. Something to do with vehicle theft.'

'Remember what PJ told us? Joel drove a different car every week, all of them crap.' He looked at her. 'Something you don't know is that Joel was on the Y.O. for car theft.'

'So he was buying and selling stolen cars on the side.'

'Singh's checking. It's a question of dates and dealers. But I think Singh's going to find something interesting.'

'What?'

Garvie said nothing. They went round the end of the shopping mall and turned into the alley that ran alongside the old railway track.

'Damon's van, of course,' Amy said quietly. 'Joel sold him his van.' She began to speak quickly as they walked. '*That's* why they fell out in the first place. Damon couldn't get the money together, you told me that. So Joel went after him for it. Mr Angry. And Damon couldn't believe it, his friend turning on him. He did what he always does. Said it wasn't his fault he couldn't pay. Dodged. Got frightened. Got out of Pirrip Street and left that note for the kid to give to Joel when he came round. But then,' she said in sudden distress, 'and this is typical of Damon, absolutely typical, he's such an innocent, he must have gone round to Imperium thinking he could sweet-talk Joel, start over, buy himself more time or whatever. And Joel got aggy, and got himself sacked into the bargain. Which only made Joel madder. And Damon even more bewildered and frightened.'

They turned out of the alley into the long street of small stores and petrol stations that would eventually lead them to Strawberry Hill. The ring road was not far away. Late-night trucks passing along it left a murmur in the air. They walked on in silence. Ten minutes passed.

'So,' Garvie said at last, 'we're back again with the most important question. What happened that night?'

She looked at him. 'We still don't know.'

'What if Joel got ugly? Threatened to tip off the police about the van. What was Damon frightened of the most?'

They stopped walking and looked at each other. Amy thought, but only for a moment. 'Prison.'

He looked at her, and her face was somehow fragile as if it might crack and break apart.

'What would he do then?' Garvie said quietly.

She stood on the dirty, cracked pavement, gorgeous and vulnerable, her bare shoulder trembling. 'Almost anything,' she whispered.

Her face shone with misery, beautiful and comfortless. They were in Cobham Road, ahead of them the shops, a few panels of dim light in the receding darkness, and the junction with Town Road. There was weak orangey lamplight on her bare shoulder and in her hair, and she lifted her face towards him, so beautiful and unruly and blurred around the edges by her distress.

'I don't know what to think any more,' she murmured.

She stood there, helpless.

Her mouth fell open and without thinking he stepped forward and kissed it.

Everything disappeared except what they could feel. She kissed him back. Her hands were round the back of his head, his hands were in the small of her back, on the back of her neck, in her hair. Her lips burned his. Through the thinness of her dress he could feel her belly against his. He was kissing her throat. The air turned to perfume. Cobham Road had vanished, the shops, the whole city had gone, and there was nothing but touch and scent and the pounding of hearts.

Then a passing car honked, and it all came back. They parted and stood there, panting slightly.

She wiped her face and smiled, and stood looking at him with misty eyes. 'You're still weird,' she said. 'And a part of me hates you for what you make me think about Damon. But . . .' She looked round. 'I have to get home. I can't walk all the way. I'll get a cab in Town Road.'

He nodded. 'I'll call you,' he said.

Their eyes met. 'I'd like that,' she said almost in a whisper.

She crossed the street and walked down Town Road, and he watched her until she disappeared. He shivered, though the night was still warm, and began to walk along Cobham Road towards Five Mile.

40

Fixing his eyes on the three tower blocks in the Plain beyond the shops, he walked down Strawberry Hill's main drag. It wasn't real walking. It was floating. To his right were small modern flats and maisonettes, to his left older brick terrace houses three storeys tall, sub-divided now into apartments. They were there, but he didn't really see them. Somehow his sense of time had gone to hell. It was nearly two o'clock in the morning. Light dampness cooling the air. Peaceful. There was a hush cushioned on the soft buzz from the nearby ring road, and Garvie drifted past the shut-up shops, the steepling outline of the *Polski* church, the launderettes and nails-and-beauty salons, smoking thoughtfully. He was no longer thinking about Damon or Joel Watkins. He was thinking only about Amy Roecastle.

He felt wildly distracted and at the same time, impossibly, deeply at peace.

In a daze he walked half a mile without realizing it, and when his phone buzzed he was surprised to find himself in Five Mile already, at the corner of Pollard Way and Bulwarks Lane.

He looked at his phone. Amy. Perhaps, like him,

she couldn't stop thinking about what had just happened.

'Hey,' he said softly.

There was a silence, then he heard her scream his name at the top of her lungs. It nearly broke his eardrum. 'He's here!' she screamed. 'He's after me!'

There was the brief harsh sound of ragged panting, then the phone went dead.

41

Electrified into horror, he ran. He dialled as he went.

A voice confused with sleep answered. 'Yes, hello, what is it?'

Garvie panted loudly: 'Town Road, where the taxis are!'

Singh said, '*What?* Garvie, is that you? What are you—'

'Just get there! It's Amy. Bring an ambulance!'

Garvie ran back down Pollard Way. He crossed the road, ran gasping down a long side street, and emerged at last on Town Road just beyond the medical centre. The road was empty and quiet, and he stood there panting, looking both ways. There was no one about, no cabs at the rank. He ran down the road, slowing at every side street, speeding up again when he saw it was deserted.

The sound of Amy's voice was still in his ears, unnaturally loud, panicked almost out of recognition. *He's after me!*

He'd been after her all the time. He must have followed them that evening. He must have seen them part on Cobham Road and followed her then, and found a place to attack her. Garvie cursed himself. As he ran, he looked up and down the street, at the shopfronts and forecourts.

Somewhere near but out of the way. Somewhere without lights, where noise would be quickly muffled. He scanned ahead as far as a driveway to an old furniture showroom, and speeded up again.

The showroom had been unoccupied for months. The driveway, full of weeds, doglegged round the side of the darkened building to a car park at the back, and Garvie ran down it, shouting Amy's name, and came to a stop in the middle of the concrete lot, turning and looking, the sudden quietness reverberating round him in waves. There was a shallow-sided yellow skip in one corner, a pile of corrugated roofing panels in another, weeds everywhere. Apart from that, nothing.

'Amy?' he shouted again.

Silence.

He'd been mistaken.

Then, as he turned, he caught sight of a scrap of something cool and grey and out of place by the kerb. One of her shoes.

He ran towards the skip.

She was sprawled inside it, legs twisted underneath her, her blank, bleeding face lifted to the night sky.

He jumped into the skip and felt her pulse, checked her injuries. He took out his phone. 'Where are you now?'

Singh's voice said, 'Coming into Town Road. Where are you?'

'Back of the empty furniture place, in the car park. Where's the ambulance?'

'Coming.' Singh paused. 'Is it needed?'

'Yeah, it's needed.'

As Garvie switched off his phone he heard the sirens in the distance. He sat with Amy in the skip, holding her limp hand. He did not think of the pages from Joel's personnel file that were no longer in her clutch bag. He did not think of a man desperate enough to risk killing her to get them. There would be time for that later. He thought of Amy, her expression as he kissed her, the feel of her lips on his, the sight now of her battered face.

42

They sat in Singh's Skoda Fabia in the car park outside Accident and Emergency. Although it was the middle of the night there was still a little low-grade activity around the entrance, doctors in green scrubs sweeping in and out periodically, ambulance drivers mumbling together over cartons of coffee, the usual sleepless smokers in wheelchairs hooked up to their mobile drips. Above them, ten storeys of dimly lit windows. Below them, in darkness, the ring road murmuring in its insomnia.

They hadn't spoken in ten minutes.

'You don't need to tell me,' Garvie said at last.

'I'm not telling you anything,' Singh said. He continued patiently to read messages on his phone.

'I know what it is to let someone down. I know what it feels like, to be let down. Someone explained it to me once.'

'Who?' Singh said.

'Damon.'

Singh grunted.

Garvie went on: 'You told me not to involve her. I put her in danger. You know that. She knows that. Her mother definitely knows it – I thought she was going to put me in hospital too when she showed up.'

Arriving half an hour earlier, Dr Roecastle had made her fury plain, and only her anxiety to be with her daughter, inside A and E, had prevented her from shouting at Garvie for longer.

'I was distracted, blindsided. I forgot she still had the pages from Joel's file. I should never have let her go off with them. I'm an idiot. She could have been . . .' His voice trailed away as he looked out of the window, up at the tall, dim façade of the hospital building. 'Let's get it all out,' he said angrily. 'You trusted me, and I let you down. She trusted me, and I let her down – big-time. That's the truth. I can't be trusted.'

Singh looked at him curiously. 'Listen,' he said. 'The first Sikh guru, Guru Nanak, said: "Let self-control be the furnace and patience the goldsmith." You are yourself. You are your own responsibility, not mine. Perhaps I can't trust you. Perhaps Amy can't. But that's not the main point. The main point is: you have to learn how to trust yourself.'

Garvie said nothing to that, and Singh went on.

'Amy is OK. Concussion only. She'll be monitored overnight and tomorrow, probably, she'll be dis charged. We're fortunate. We should both be thankful.'

'Believe me, I am.'

'Good, that's a start. Now, there has been a development.'

'Car theft-wise?'

'Yes. We mapped the dates of those one-off payments in Joel's hidden account with the records in the car theft database, and pulled a couple of guys in.'

'And you found Joel'd been moving on knock-offs.'

'Correct. One of the guys will testify to save himself a custodial sentence. Joel was his fence. But that's not the most interesting thing. There was one particular vehicle that caught our eye.'

'Ford Courier, white with rust markings, technically categorizable as "a piece of shit".'

'OK. You guessed. Yes, it passed through Joel's hands a couple of months ago. It looks like he sold it to Damon, who couldn't pay, and Joel went after him. And in those circumstances, as we know, Damon was liable to become desperate, to lash out.' He paused, pursed his lips. 'Which brings us to this evening. It was Damon who attacked Amy, wasn't it?'

'Don't know. Wasn't there. You'll have to ask her. But . . .'

'But it's likely. I know. You have your failures, I have mine.' He hesitated. 'I'm being formally reprimanded for assaulting a member of the public this evening, in fact. But, after my chase of him, Damon'll feel the net closing in, he'll be more desperate than ever. He would've been after Joel's file. He'd be worried that he could be identified from the account of Joel's fight with him at Imperium.'

'But the account wasn't in the file.'

'I know, you said. But Damon wasn't to know that.'

'How did he even know we were there?'

'I think he's been watching you all this time. At Red 'n' Black. At Imperium.' He leaned round to look Garvie in the eye. 'He's still watching you. We need to take steps now to protect both you and Amy.'

Garvie said nothing to that.

'Garvie? Are you listening to me?'

Garvie stirred. 'Not really. The real question is *why* there was nothing in Joel's file.'

More silence. The Fabia began to steam up. Singh rolled down a window and night air came in, cool now, and diesel niff from the idling ambulances.

Garvie opened the door.

'Where are you going now?'

'Home.'

'I'll take you there.'

'I'd rather walk.'

'What did I just say about safety?'

'Don't know. I'd stopped listening.'

'Garvie!'

'I'm young and semi-fit and unlike Amy I didn't get bashed on the head. Besides,' he added, 'and don't take this the wrong way, 'cause I know I have to spruce up my people skills, but I just don't want to talk to you any more. It's late. I'm a bit tired.'

'OK then.' Singh leaned over to the back seat and produced a police-issue padded coat and black beanie with the City Squad logo on it. 'At least take these. It's turned chilly and all you're wearing is that thin shirt from Imperium.'

Garvie ignored him.

'Here,' Singh said.

Garvie didn't move. Just stared at the beanie.

'Garvie?'

'What time is it now?'

'Nearly four. But—'

'He'll be asleep,' Garvie said, as if to himself. 'But that's all right. He never lets me down.' He turned to Singh. 'Think of that.'

'What are you talking about?'

'Trust.'

He didn't say goodbye. He just got out of the car and walked away down the hospital drive. Singh saw him light up at the turn of the drive before disappearing, hatless and coatless, into the dark.

Sighing and shaking his head, Singh took out his phone, and dialled.

'Hi,' he said. 'Yes, it's me. There's no need to worry. He's coming home now. It's OK, he'll be fine.'

For a while he continued to sit there, looking down the driveway into the darkness where Garvie had gone.

He didn't see Garvie take out his phone as he walked and make a call of his own.

After listening to the sleepy voice at the other end, he said, 'Listen, big man. Only you can save the world. No, I know you can. No, you're just being modest. All you have to do— Wait. Listen carefully. All you have to do, first thing tomorrow, right, is get yourself to the outhouse. Yeah you do, it's that funny little brick building by the pagoda. OK? I want you to go in there and find something for me. All this time I'd forgotten about it, but it's the really important thing. No, it's definitely in there. Yeah, I know it is. Someone went in looking for it a little while ago, but they couldn't find it 'cause it was too well-hidden, so it's still there. But you, you're definitely going to find it. Yes, you are. Because I trust you. Because you're a genius. OK, so we agree. Now I'm going to tell you what it is, and after that you can go back to sleep. Yes you will. You'll fall asleep straightaway. You'll sleep the deep, sweet sleep of all true heroes. Yeah. Because you deserve it. That's it, man. Simples. Oh, yeah, and give us a ding soon as you've got it. Now, this is what it is . . .'

43

Next day he was tired. The morning had gone, and half the afternoon, before he woke up. When his mother got home from her shift at seven thirty she found him still lying on his bed in T-shirt and shorts doing his old thing of staring at the ceiling. He turned his head towards her and they exchanged a brief look of unspoken difficulty before she went away.

He called Smudge again, and this time he answered.

'Did you find it?'

'Yeah. Eventually. Got to say, it wasn't easy. It was in this half empty tin of paint wrapped in a plastic bag. I wouldn't've ever found it if I hadn't been such a bloodhound. And my hands are all magnolia now.'

'Smudge, mate, you're a genius. I owe you big-time. I'll swing by and get it.'

'Yeah, all right. In the meantime . . .'

'Yeah?'

'Just wanted to ask. Something going on with you and this Amy chick?'

Garvie hesitated. 'Why?'

'Well, I've been picking up this vibe. I'm a martyr

to male intuition, mate. When we went out to see that bushman in the woods, for instance. And this afternoon she's been just sitting out on that patio at the back staring at everyone. Like she's got something on her mind or something.'

'How does she look?'

'Stunning, you know. I mean, talk about frontal—'

'I mean, her mood.'

'Oh.' He could hear Smudge thinking. 'Bit odd really.'

'What do you mean, "odd"?'

'It's the staring, Garv, it's weirding us all out. She's got this bruise on her face, but it's not that. It's, she looks like . . . she looks like she's got something on her mind, I can't put it more than that. Just wondered if it was you. But then I thought to myself, that'd be odd, wouldn't it, that'd be unprecedented, 'cause you never get the girl, do you, and you don't really know how to behave with them, and—'

'OK, thanks for that, Smudge. See you later.'

'Cheers then. Oh, bring some paint cleaner, will you?'

He called Amy.

For several moments after she picked up he listened to her breathing on the other end. 'Hi,' she said at last. Her voice a strained murmur.

'You all right?'

No answer.

'What did the hospital say?'

Long pause. 'They said . . . doesn't matter what they said.'

'Concussion is what I heard.'

She made a noise. 'Yeah, that'll do.'

'Listen, this is my fault. I should've taken those papers off you.'

He heard her sigh. 'I'm not your responsibility, Garvie.'

They listened to each other breathe.

'About what happened,' he said, 'I've had a thought. I don't know if you're up for it, but—'

In the same fragile undertone she interrupted him. 'Garvie, I can't see you just now.'

He thought about that. 'OK.'

'I've got some thinking to do.' Her voice was thin with pain.

He thought about that too. 'Understood,' he said at last. 'One question, though.'

'What?'

'Last night. Was it Damon?'

There was a long silence, unbroken.

'Doesn't matter then,' Garvie said at last. 'But listen. Promise me one thing. If he contacts you, be very careful, all right?'

'You really think he's going to want to talk to me?'

'Yeah, I think that's exactly what he'll want to do.'

He could hear her thinking about that. She said, 'You don't need to worry.'

'OK. Last thing.'

'What?'

'I'm thinking of you.'

She said nothing, and he hung up and lay on his bed unmoving for another half an hour. His mother came in again. She was dressed to go out in blue denim jeans, grey suede booties and flowing lilac top.

'You conscious?' she said.

He just blinked.

'You talking at all?'

'I can talk. I've been talking since I was two.'

She stepped into his room, looking around warily at the heaps of stuff everywhere.

'But maybe not right now,' he added.

She was looking at him with a troubled expression, challenging about the eyes, firm about the mouth. He knew that expression. That expression was his old friend.

'I been watching you, Garvie Smith,' she said. 'It's important we talk.'

He said, 'If it's about Amy, you're right, no need to say it.'

She narrowed her eyes. 'What do you mean?'

'I messed up. She got hurt. I know you've heard about it.' She said nothing, and he glanced at her. 'Aren't you going to bawl me out?'

'What am I, your conscience?' she said. 'You're going to have to get used to bawling yourself out. No. I wanted to talk to you about . . . well . . . about something else.'

Again she hesitated. Her manner was strangely

unsure; it made him nervous, and before she could speak again he said, 'OK, but I've got to shift now. Maybe later?' Getting off his bed, he started to get dressed.

'What do you mean? Where are you going?'

'Out. Like you,' he added.

'You're not going to see Amy Roecastle, are you?'

'What, are you my conscience? No, as it happens I'm going to see Smudge. He's got something for me.'

She was about to say something else, but her phone rang and she retreated into the living room, where he heard her talking in a murmur. She was still talking a few minutes later when he went past her on his way out. He said nothing, she said nothing either, though their eyes met; his last sight of her was a distracted gesture of goodbye as she stood by the kitchen window, lit up lilac and blue in the last of the sunlight, smiling into her phone.

Up at 'Four Winds' Amy Roecastle huddled under a blanket in the black-and-white living room, watching the news on television. On the side of her head was a glazed lozenge of black medical gauze where the stitches had been put in. The colours of the bruise under her left eye ran in blue and yellow streaks as far as her temple.

Ten o'clock. Her mother was out late at a committee meeting and she was alone in the house. Biting her lip, she fidgeted with her phone until she couldn't stand it any more and, for the twentieth time that day, speed-dialled the familiar number and listened again, stony-faced, to the voicemail message.

'Damon,' she said. 'Call me now. *Please*. We have to meet. Damon.'

She sat there, biting her lip, phone in her hand.

She tried to remember what had happened the night before. Her memory was confused and incomplete. As in a dream, she retained only a few disconnected images – the momentary impression of a man in a maroon hoodie glimpsed over her shoulder, a swirl of pavement under her feet as she ran. Apparently she'd called Garvie, though she had no memory of that.

She called Damon again, staring grimly at the phone as it went through to voicemail, and threw it onto the coffee table.

Sitting there with her fingers pressed into her eyes, she tried not to think about Garvie Smith, not to remember what they'd told her at the hospital, fixing her mind instead on what she needed to know.

Forty minutes later her phone buzzed, and she grabbed it and read the text.

NEW PHONE BABE BE OUTSIDE SAME PLACE IN TEN.

For a second she couldn't move. When she called the number it went straight through to voicemail, and she dialled again and the same thing happened. The third time she spoke:

'Damon, pick up. *Damon!* What's going on? Why have you got a new phone? I've been trying to call you all afternoon. I need to talk to you about last night.'

No answer.

Having stood up without realizing it, she found herself looking out of the window down the darkened driveway, peering from one side to another. It was a mild night. Any sort of movement made her head throb, but she got her jacket and went out of the house, wincing, walked down the drive and through the silently sweeping gates.

In the deserted turn outside she hesitated. It was still and very quiet. Dark. The tree-crowded side of the lane was solid darkness, the garden of her neighbour's house a confusion of mottled shadow. Beyond was the bus shelter. Her mouth was dry.

She was frightened, but also determined.

'Damon!' she called out. 'Stop playing games!'

There was no answer from the bus shelter.

Slowly she walked towards it, along the side of her neighbour's garden, past her neighbour's driveway.

'Damon!' she called again, more hesitantly, and there was a movement in the shadows inside the shelter, and she stopped as he came out quickly, and walked towards her in that jerky way of his, head down, hood hung over his face, fists clenched, moving fast and twitchy, and she gave a small cry as he tacked up close without a word and at last pulled the hood off his face.

She stared at him in horror.

'What have you done?' she whispered.

'It's not what I've done,' Garvie said to her. 'It's what you've done.'

She couldn't speak. He was wearing a yellow beanie with a HEAT logo. She couldn't take her eyes off it.

'Sorry to text you like that,' he said. 'But I had to see you. Listen, you don't have to tell me any of the emotional stuff. All that's your business.'

Something about the way he spoke told her that he knew everything at last, and she looked at him with sudden tenderness.

'Just tell me the facts,' he said. 'You've been in touch with Damon all this time, haven't you? That's how he knew where we were last night.'

She hesitated, frowned, finally nodded.

'Tell me.'

She began to explain. She'd been letting Damon know what had been going on, giving him the chance to stay a step ahead. First, at Red 'n' Black. After they'd been to PJ's, she'd called him to tell him what PJ had said about Joel. Later, when Garvie said he was going back to Pirrip Street, she'd called again to warn him in case he'd moved back there.

'And when we went to Imperium?'

Yes, she'd told him about their visit to Imperium too. Soon as she knew where they were going. 'I didn't know why we were going there.' She paused. 'But I think Damon did.'

There was a silence. A breeze passed through the trees at the side of the road.

'I'm sorry,' she said at last. Her eyes began to shine. 'Aren't you going to ask me why?'

He looked uncomfortable. 'I can work it out for myself.'

'Funny, isn't it,' she said, when she could, 'who you fall in love with?' She wiped her face. 'I had to try to protect him. But also, and you've got to believe me, I thought he was innocent. At first.'

'What do you think now?'

She bit her lip, glanced away. 'All the things you've found out. He couldn't explain them to me. And he's changed. These last few days he's been smoking that strong stuff. He's got paranoid, desperate.'

'And violent.'

'Yeah. And anyway' – she glanced up at the beanie he was wearing – 'now you've found that.'

He took it off and she shrank away a little. He said, 'He was wearing it that night, wasn't he? When he showed up here.'

She nodded. 'When he gave the gun to me.' She smiled. 'Gave me his hat too so I wouldn't get wet. He was sweet like that.'

'Smudge found the beanie where you hid it in the outhouse. You must have known straightaway what it meant.'

She bit her lip. 'I saw it on my newsfeed soon as Damon left. This guy in Market Square saying he'd seen the victim sitting outside the Ballyhoo with a guy wearing a HEAT beanie.'

'So it put Damon right there with Joel at the time

he was shot. They were having it out, a crisis meeting. I guess it didn't go too well.'

'No.'

'Mr Angry and Mr Frightened. Then the riot. And it kicked off between them.'

She made a noise. Garvie had never heard anything like it before. It sounded like crowd noise, a deep groan of indefinable emotion, and he caught her and held her while she wept.

At last she stepped away from him.

'It's over,' she said. 'Everything. I can't defend him any more. I don't want to. Not after last night. Not after everything else. But listen to me now.'

He said quickly, 'You don't have to explain what you did.'

'I want you to know. You're right: he was so frightened. Looking over his shoulder the whole time like he expected someone to come out of the shadows after him. He was saying stuff, gabbling. "It's mental down there." "I messed up, babe, messed up big-time." He was shivering like a dog he was so frightened. And then he said, and this is what I'll remember for the rest of my life, "I ain't got anyone else, babe, no one but you." And he looked at me, and I knew that it was true. Completely true. So I took the gun, and he told me he loved me, and he walked off down the lane.'

The darkness of the road under the trees seemed to surge a little about them and settle slowly again to stillness.

Garvie said nothing. There was nothing to say.

She said, 'So understand. It was a mistake to take the gun. But I took it because he needed me to. I'm not proud of it, but I'm not ashamed of it either.' She looked at him. 'Now do what you have to do, Garvie Smith. Tell Singh. But remember, please, remember how scared he'll be. And stop him from doing something stupid to himself.'

They parted at the gates. For a moment they stood there looking at each other.

As the gates began to close he said, 'You going to be all right?'

But there was no time for her to reply before the sweeping gates shut between them.

44

He walked home. Along the picturesque tree-shadowed Froggett lanes, past elegant villas tucked up behind their comfortable brick walls, down the long swoop of road from Battery Hill, by hedgerows increasingly tatty as he descended to the ring road, past the darkened hulk of the car plant moored in the middle of the deserted car park, through the overlit underpass autographed in graffiti, and finally into Five Mile, inert and dreamless under a scrappy night sky. He went through the gap in the mesh fence at the end of Driftway, and into Eastwick Gardens. Midnight. Scents of tarmac and privet.

He thought about the hat. His uncle would test it for signs that Damon had worn it, and possibly other things, nitrates maybe from the firing of the gun.

He thought about Singh and what he would say.

He thought about Damon, still at large, but now about to be the subject of a much bigger manhunt, increased news coverage, the whole circus.

And he thought about Amy and what she'd done, and how much she was still in love with Damon.

Hesitating at the lobby door, he wondered if he

should call Singh straightaway, but it was past midnight, so he put away his phone and let himself into the building, and went quietly up the dark stairway to his flat.

He set his alarm for early next morning so he could catch Singh at the beginning of the day and lay down on his bed in his clothes and listened to the night-time silence around him. He thought maybe he'd call Amy one last time but he didn't know what he'd say; besides, he was tired. The last image in his mind was her face, that last glimpse of her as the gates closed, and then he was asleep.

His phone woke him. He groped around and found it in the dark. Three o'clock. Unknown caller. For a second he was confused, then it fell into place, it was the most obvious thing that could happen, and he put the phone to his mouth and spoke.

'Where are you, Damon?' He heard a faint swirly noise, like a breeze, somewhere in the background. 'Don't think about it,' Garvie said. 'Just tell me where you are.'

Damon said, 'Can't, man.'

'Why?'

'I only got a minute.' There was crackle and interference, then Damon again, his voice harsh and slurry: 'This is proper fucked-up. You know what?'

'What?'

There was silence.

Garvie considered the silence.

Damon said, 'Got her text. It's over. Thing is, I messed up.'

'What did you do, Damon?'

'That night in Market Square. It all got out of hand.'

'What happened? We know you met Joel.'

There was more crackling, then Damon's voice came back. 'I lost my head, man. You know what?'

'What?'

There was a long pause again. And again the same sound of a breeze somewhere.

'Never trust no one,' Damon said at last.

'OK, Damon. Damon, listen to me. Before you go, just tell me this. Where are you?'

'It's my place. I'm going to miss it, man.'

Garvie could hear him choking up.

'Damon, stay calm.'

'It's no good any more. I can't take it. What I rang for is . . .'

'Is what?'

'Tell Amy. She's blocking me.'

'Tell Amy what?'

The soft, whooshing silence went on for several seconds this time.

'I don't know,' Damon said. And then, in a rush: 'You know what? Tell her goodbye. And tell her I'm sorry. Yeah. That's the truth. Oh God,' he said, 'here it comes!'

'Damon, wait!'

Very briefly, there was a different noise, a creeping metallic rattle, then the phone went dead.

Garvie was off his bed punching in another number as he put on his boots.

'Come on, Singh,' he muttered to himself. 'Come on, pick up.'

He froze with one of his boots still in his hand.

He could hear a phone ringing somewhere in the flat. Confused, he went out of his room into the living area, listening to the ringing getting louder. It was coming from his mother's room.

As he stood there numbly listening to it, the door of his mother's room opened and Singh came out dressed in shorts and T-shirt, holding his phone up to his ear. He stopped when he saw Garvie and they stared at each other.

His mother appeared behind Singh in her dressing gown and rested her hand on Singh's shoulder. 'Garvie,' she said in a low, troubled voice.

His adrenaline kicked in. 'No time,' he said. He couldn't look at her. He looked at Singh. 'Listen to me. Damon just called. He's about to do something stupid. We have to get there,' he said.

Singh didn't move.

'Now!' Garvie shouted. The anger in his voice surprised him. Singh began to move, boyish and oddly small in his over-sized T-shirt and baggy shorts.

'Garvie,' his mother said again, quietly.

'See you downstairs,' Garvie said curtly to Singh, and went quickly out of the flat.

He didn't realize how much he was shaking until

he reached the bottom of the stairwell; he had to hold onto the banister to keep himself from falling. His breathing was fast and he could feel his heart pulpy and horribly mobile in his chest. Then Singh was with him, and they ran together without speaking out to the small car park, towards the beige Skoda Fabia parked unobtrusively at the far end.

Singh was still buttoning his uniform as he got into the car. 'Garvie—' he began.

'Just drive,' Garvie said. 'That's what we've got into the car for, isn't it?'

'But we don't know where he is. You said yourself we couldn't find him.'

'I said *you* couldn't find him. I didn't say I couldn't.'

'Where then?'

'Town,' Garvie said; then they were pulling away down The Driftway, banging through the potholes.

45

Everything looks abandoned at three o'clock in the morning. The empty streets were silent. Not so the Fabia. With a wild noise it hurtled down Bulwarks Lane, swerved into Pollard Way and burst onto Town Road, the little car accelerating all the time.

'Where in town?' Singh asked, hunched over the wheel.

'Left here,' Garvie said.

The car fishtailed through ninety degrees, went through a red light, and headed towards the centre of town.

'Well? *Where?*'

'Thing about Damon, he's simpler than you think.'

'What do you mean?'

'Remember what he told me?'

'He likes to go somewhere he can get high. And hear the air. Which sounds to me like the country-side not downtown.'

'Damon didn't like trees much. City boy. In the city, if you want to listen to the air – you've got to get high. High up. Just like he said. His little joke.'

'So where—'

'He was telling me about it when I met him on Supertram. Smiling to himself as he stared out of the window; it was like he was dreaming about it. But he wasn't.'

'What do you mean?'

'He wasn't dreaming about it. He was *looking* at it. The multistorey car park. At the top. Good place to hide a van too, in a busy car park. When he called me I think he must have been out on the roof. I could hear the breeze, and something else too, a sort of metallic rattle. I've heard it before. It's the gates to the depot right there next to the multistorey.'

Singh said, 'Are you—'

'Let's suppose I am.'

Singh nodded. 'Five minutes. Ten at the most.'

Garvie stared out of the window at the city hurtling by, apartment blocks around the outskirts of the centre, offices and civic buildings.

Singh called Dowell and after that Paul Tanner.

'Damon trusts Tanner,' he said to Garvie. 'He may be able to talk to him.'

He floored the accelerator and the Fabia swerved left at the station, along the side of the rail track, accelerating towards the shopping mall which rose ahead of them black and blank against the ash-blue night sky. They turned sharply into a narrow alley that ran as far as the depot, and slithered violently to a halt.

They were out of the car before it had stopped rocking, running down the walkway to the depot, past the gates, shut now, round the corner to the multistorey beyond, and along its tall frontage, past the big, square entrance with its bollards and ramp and hanging boom, looking up at the roof as they ran.

'*Damon!*' Singh shouted once.

They ran round the far corner and stopped. And stood there together with the suddenly aimless look of people who have just failed to catch the bus.

Lying crumpled just ahead of them was the body of Damon Walsh, a broken shape as still as the ground he lay on. A homeless guy on his knees next to him turned to them, and said in horror, 'He jumped. He just dropped, easy like over the edge. Like he wanted it.' He lifted his hands, covered with blood, into the air and began to howl.

At the corner they waited in silence, occasionally glancing at the body, which Singh had covered with his jacket. The vagrant had fled.

'What did he say to you on the phone?' Singh asked quietly, at last.

'Stuff.'

'Did he sound suicidal?'

'Take a wild guess.'

'Did he say anything we need to know?'

Garvie looked at him impassively. 'Yeah.'

'What?'

'He said he lost it that night in Market Square.'

'OK.'

'That's what he said after I told him we knew he met Joel there.'

Singh took this in. 'You knew he met Joel in Market Square? You didn't tell me.'

Garvie looked at him briefly. 'Turns out there's stuff you haven't been telling me either.'

Singh looked away. From the direction of the business district they heard sirens getting louder.

Singh said, 'So it looks like the answer to the question "Did Damon kill Joel?" is yes. But the answer is too late.'

'Yeah. Things are moving on all the time. The question you're going to be asked now is why you didn't stop him chucking himself off the roof.'

Singh looked uncomfortable. 'What else did Damon say?'

'He said he was sorry. That was one thing.'

'And what else?'

'That he loved Amy for ever and ever.'

'He said that?'

'That's what I'm going to tell her.'

Singh nodded. 'I understand.' He moved away, scanning the multistorey roof.

Garvie lit up a Benson & Hedges. He sucked on it angrily and called to him, 'You know what? What he wanted, what he really wanted, probably the only thing he ever wanted in his whole life, was a place where he could go to forget it all. He told me he couldn't always get there. Well' – Garvie pointed his cigarette at the dark shape on the pavement

– 'he's there now.' He turned and walked away, then crouched down in the lee of the multistorey wall.

Blue lights were flashing in the alleyway; three policemen jogged into view, followed by Inspector Dowell. Ignoring Garvie, they went up to Singh and stood in a huddle, talking, none of them looking at the body.

For five minutes there was the scene familiar from a thousand cop shows, crackle and pop of police radios, the usual routines of useless orders, swivelling lights in cool misty darkness, blue and white barricade tape, crime scene bollards, as if the whole thing were turning into documentary. The first ambulance arrived. More swivelling lights, the unloading of more useless equipment, muted voices in the quietness, disconnected phrases like pieces of code. More documentary.

Paul Tanner arrived. He jumped out of his car, shoved aside the nearest policeman and went straight at Singh, and the policeman went down before Dowell and two others could get across to take control.

'This is on you!' Tanner shouted as he was dragged away. 'You let him die!'

He was hustled away to his car by Dowell.

Singh, bleeding from the nose, tried to go over to talk to him but Dowell kept him away, and at last he turned back, wiping his face.

Alone and miserable, he looked round for Garvie Smith, but the boy had gone; there was nothing in the shadow by the side of the car-park entrance except a couple of cigarette butts.

Half past four, almost dawn. Garvie found himself walking along the tracks of the old railway line that ran north from the canal. He seemed to have been doing it for some time.

It was surprisingly hard going, the sleepers were the wrong distance apart, but he made no attempt to get into a smoother rhythm. He welcomed the discomfort and difficulty. It distracted him. A layer of white mist floated above the ground ahead of him, spectral in the darkness. Overhead the sky showed phosphorescent green at the horizon, but he did not look up.

His body felt empty. He wished his mind was empty too, but it wasn't, it was over-populated with people he'd rather not think about – Damon, Amy, Singh. His mother.

In a while he found himself on the old country road that ran past the sewage works into Limekilns. The sky had changed to pink and gold but this was of no interest to him.

Then he was in Five Mile; it was fully dawn, grey and damp, and he went into Eastwick Gardens and up the stairs and let himself in.

His mother got to her feet, and Singh too, and they stood there looking at him.

'Where have you been?'

'Not here.' He looked past Singh's pinched, tired face to his mother. 'Does he live here now?'

'That's not the question, Garvie, and you know it.'

'What's the question?'

'We won't know that until we have chance to talk about it.'

'I'm too tired to talk about it,' he said.

Singh said to Garvie's mother, 'I'll go now. I just wanted to make sure he was safe. I'll . . .' He hesitated. 'I'll get my things.' He went past her into her room, and reappeared with his coat and briefcase.

'I'll call, Raminder,' she said.

Pausing on his way out, Singh said to Garvie, 'We will need to talk too, about Damon at least.'

'Amy knows everything,' Garvie said. 'You can talk to her.'

He heard the door close behind him. For a long moment he and his mother looked at each other.

'Get some sleep then,' she said. 'We can talk later.'

He turned and went into his room and lay down on his bed. After a moment he heard his mother's door close too. The pale light coming through the window was thin and cold like something deliberately intended to keep him awake, though in fact, despite walking half the night, he felt no tiredness as he lay there staring at the ceiling. Anyway, he still had something he had to do. He took out his phone and looked at it sadly before he called.

She answered at once, as if she hadn't been asleep.

'Hi,' he said.

'Hi.'

He hesitated. 'Has Singh called you?'

'No,' she said, puzzled. 'Why?'

For a moment he listened to her breathing, picturing her in that bedroom of hers, thinking to himself the unbearable thought that this was the last ever moment when she wouldn't know what had happened.

'Damon's dead,' he said.

She began to choke, a private noise he could hardly bear to listen to.

'Amy,' he said. 'Amy.'

She was crying, she couldn't speak, there was something in her mouth, her hand or knuckles perhaps, she was gasping for breath.

'Amy,' he said again uselessly.

She hung up.

46

August wound down, wet and windy, the chewed-up end of summer. Soon it would be the start of the new school year, light drizzle and dull skies, traffic piling up in the mornings, in the afternoons the streets crowded with kids in uniform.

Garvie lay on his bed, got up to eat occasionally, went back to bed.

Felix came round, trying to entice him out to the kiddies' playground at Old Ditch Road. Standing under his window, he good-naturedly flashed a half bottle of Glenn's at him, but Garvie just shook his head.

Even weed didn't help.

Smudge brought him his last pay packet from his brother, and the latest news. The job at 'Four Winds' was all done, including the pagoda, everything creosoted and painted, trim and smart and, according to Smudge, one of the wonders of modern fencing. Apparently Dr Roecastle was pleased; there was talk of a bonus. Amy Roecastle had not been seen for several days, however. She was, sensationally, still present in Smudge's memory, though he refrained from over-long descriptions. He was a boy of natural sensitivity.

On the Wednesday Smudge had a day off and they went together down to town, and by accident or subconscious intention found themselves outside the shopping mall, by the multistorey. The car park had re-opened after a few days of forensic investigation. Everything was normal again; no sign remained of what had happened there. For a while they loitered in the streets nearby. Garvie hadn't realized before what a big building the car park was, how tight a squeeze between the depot, the shopping mall and an office block. They walked all the way round it, along the stretch of road access at the front, the oil-stained delivery route to the depot, the paved walkway by the mall, and the narrow alley next to the office block, past all the entrances and fire-escape exits, and returned at last to the spot where Damon fell, and for a few moments stood gazing up at the concrete rim of the roof above.

Up there the air was different. You could hear it. Damon knew.

From his uncle, Garvie knew that the police had found Damon's den on the roof, a hidey-hole between ventilator shaft and generator housing. At some point in the previous fifty years the lock mechanism of the old access door on the top storey had jammed, leaving it shut but unlocked. Garvie could imagine Damon finding that it opened, cautiously going onto the roof and feeling the air on his face. He must have felt safe there, and free. There was no one to see him; the only CCTV camera at that level was pointed at a different part of the roof altogether; the access door to the car park below could be secured behind him with one of those good-value rubber wedges. He'd hauled a tarpaulin sheet up to the roof and hung it above the cubbyhole to keep the rain off. Underneath it the police had found a sleeping bag, some bottles of water, a bag of rubbish neatly tied. Also a baggie of weed, several packets of Rizla papers and the keys to his van, parked inconspicuously among other vehicles below.

In the meantime, the beanie with the HEAT logo had been positively tested by Forensics not only for Damon's hairs and other traces of DNA but residue of gunpowder nitrates. Garvie's final and awkward involvement had been to give an account to Inspector Dowell of his phone call with Damon. The investigation into the murder of Joel Watkins was closed.

At the same time, the internal enquiry into Damon's suicide, formally requested by Paul Tanner, had begun. Singh had already been called upon to answer questions.

Garvie would have liked to talk to Amy about all of this, but she wasn't answering his calls. He thought of her up at 'Four Winds', sitting alone in her room, thinking about Damon. He wanted to talk to her. But she did not want to talk to him.

Smudge put his arm round his shoulder. 'When's the funeral?'

'Saturday.'

'Going?'

'Don't know, Smudge, to be honest.'

'I'll come with. You know, if you need a bit of support.'

'Cheers.' They looked up together, one last time, at the multistorey roof. A little rain fell onto their faces, and they turned to go home.

At home everything was different now. Singh hadn't stayed the night again, but Garvie's mother met him regularly in the evenings. Garvie couldn't bring himself to talk to her about it. Just thinking about it filled him with a strange sensation like panic. As usual, his preferred form of communication was something close to silence.

His mother asked, 'Why don't you like him?'

'Just don't. Never have.'

'Try to like him for my sake.'

'Why?'

'Because you love me. Because we do things for people we love. Because I have the right to be happy, just like everyone else.'

There were no answers to these righteous philosophies. But they did not address the panic he felt; they only made him feel guilty as well.

'Listen, Garvie, I tried to tell you. I didn't want it to be a surprise.'

'What makes you think it was a surprise?'

She looked at him.

He said in a flat voice, 'Thursday the ninth of August: chat with Singh here. Friday the tenth:

calling him "Raminder", praising him to me before going out with your hair in a short, puffy bob. Monday the twentieth: dinner with him, you wearing leopard-print trousers and black top, with the big yellow bangles, him wearing his best brown suit and orange turban. Thursday the twenty-third: talking to him on your phone before going out to meet him, wearing new blue denims, lilac top and grey suede booties. I been around. I got eyes. I can see what's been going on.'

His mother looked at him, astonished. 'But,' she said. 'But then, if you noticed, why are you behaving like this?'

'Because I *didn't think it was serious*!'

And he went into his room and slammed the door.

Lying on his bed, he tried to order his thoughts. It was hard: they kept flying off.

He thought about sequences. Two of them. Joel, Damon, Amy. Garvie, Singh, his mother. Each sequence had its own rules; both had worked out to their logical conclusions. Questions had been given their correct answers. No mistakes.

He thought about questions. If Singh was the answer, what was it his mother had asked?

Then he thought about mistakes. Lots of them, in fact. Dr Roecastle thinking Amy had gone to a hotel. The police thinking Amy's body was buried in the woods. Damon losing it with Joel in Market Square. He himself forgetting that Amy was at risk. But it turns out life isn't all maths; there's a special category of mistakes that are the best, most beautiful, most brilliant things that anyone could have done. Into that category he put Amy taking the gun off Damon. 'I ain't got no one else,' he'd said. So she took it off him, because he needed her to, because she hoped to take away his pain and fear and give him love back instead. Who could call that a mistake?

He lay there for a while longer. Then he got out his phone and texted Amy to say he'd see her at the funeral.

47

The funeral was at the Catholic Church of Our Lady of Perpetual Help – the *Polski* church – in Strawberry Hill. Apparently Damon had been baptized a Catholic. No one was sure if he'd been aware of the fact. There was a brief ceremony in the Gothically darkened building, then the burial in the little cemetery outside. Damon's stepbrother, belatedly compassionate, had made available the family plot. It was five thirty in the afternoon, last service of the day.

Attendance was minimal. There were three guys who looked like they might have been Damon's friends from earlier days, two foster parents from Damon's childhood, Singh and Dowell representing the forces of law and order, and Paul Tanner, who left white-faced and angry shortly after the service inside, ignoring Singh. Smudge and Felix were there, in borrowed black suits. Garvie and Amy stood back from the grave on their own. Amy was wearing a severe black skirt and jacket, and a black hat; Garvie wore a button-down shirt and chinos. They kept their hands folded in front of them.

The priest recited a verse of scripture and said

a prayer, the undertakers worked the silk straps, a handful of soil cracked on the coffin lid. The Lord's Prayer was said. Then it was over, the priest moving back inside the church, taking the foster parents with him. A man manoeuvred a digger over and began to shovel earth into the grave.

Amy kept her eyes fixed on it. She'd hardly looked at Garvie throughout the entire service. When he asked if she was OK, she turned to him and he saw how pale she was, her lips almost white.

He said quietly, 'Tell me this. What happened at the hospital?'

She looked at him curiously. 'Why do you ask that?'

'Because when we talked about it on the phone, I said "Concussion?", and you said "That'll do". But it won't, will it? There's something you haven't told me.'

She turned away for a moment, and when she turned back her face was wet. 'When he attacked me, I miscarried. That's what they said to me at the hospital. Did you guess?'

'I suspected. I'm sorry,' he said. 'I'm very sorry.'

She put her hand out and squeezed his hand. 'Somehow I needed him. And, for a moment at least, he needed me too. It's enough. It'll have to be. There's nothing else.'

Without saying anything more, she walked away through the tombstones and out of the wicket gate.

Singh and Dowell had left. Smudge and Felix

came over and said a few words to Garvie, then they left too. Apart from one other guy sitting on a bench, Garvie was alone in the cemetery. He smoked a Benson & Hedges and did his best to think of nothing.

'Nice service, eh?'

He looked round. The guy from the bench stood there, offering him a cigarette.

'Wasn't going to come,' the guy said. 'Glad I did though. Music always gets me.' He was short, on the chunky side, with a smooth face and wiry brown hair, wearing a shiny blue suit, and he stood next to Garvie, looking at Damon's grave, smoking.

'Second funeral I been to in a month,' he said after a bit.

'Oh yeah?'

'Both young guys too. My age. First Joel, now Damon.'

Garvie turned to look at him. 'Joel Watkins?'

'Yeah. Met them both on a youth offender programme. You know, back in the day. Only heard about Damon yesterday. I been off radar.' He sucked in smoke. 'Typical. Always the same, Damon, getting mixed up in stuff that didn't have nothing to do with him. Know him well, did you?'

Garvie shook his head. 'Just through his girlfriend.'

'What about Joel?'

'Never even met him.'

'Joel was always a bit of a dickhead, to be honest. But Damon was sweet. I liked Damon.'

'I heard they were tight. Back then anyway.'

'Who?'

'Damon and Joel.'

The guy looked puzzled. 'Not really. Far as I remember, they never had nothing to do with each other.'

Garvie paused. 'So, what, they just hooked up this last month about the van?'

'What van?'

'The van Joel sold him.'

The guy frowned again. 'Bazza sold him his van. Joel didn't have anything to do with it. Told you, Joel and Damon didn't see each other.' He went on: 'Sad thing about the van was, Damon thought he was going to get a job with it.'

'I remember him mentioning it.'

'He was so happy, couldn't stop going on about it, it was going to turn his life round. Said he'd actually been offered a job soon as the van was up and running.'

Garvie thought to himself: *why is it that the obvious questions are the last ones to get asked?*

He asked: 'What job was that then?'

'Dispatch.'

'What company?'

'Same place Joel was working, as it happened. Wasn't Joel offered Damon the job, though. Like I say, they weren't close. And Joel got the sack there anyway just after. Did you hear about that?'

'Yeah. Caught skimming.'

The guy made a dismissive noise. 'Put-up job.'

'What do you mean?'

'Wasn't Joel skimming. It was this other guy – the one who offered Damon the job. He'd been skimming for years, they all knew it. When he was found out he threw the blame on Joel, got him sacked. That's why Joel went wild. Good job Damon never worked there, really.'

Garvie thought about this. Thought again about the obvious questions that don't get asked. He said, 'This dispatch driver who offered Damon the job. He knew Damon then?'

'Oh yeah, long time. Didn't I say? That's the point. Older guy. Damon looked up to him, took everything he said as gospel. I met him a couple of times, when we were on the Y.O. I think maybe he was Damon's sponsor. Can't remember. Everyone on the programme had a sponsor. Parent usually, but quite a lot of the kids didn't have parents so they got some sort of guardian type through the council.'

'And what was this guy's name?'

'My memory's all fucked-up. Had a nickname of some sort. Emdee. Veepee. I don't know.

'Doesn't matter.'

'Got a feeling he was ex-Services.'

Garvie nodded. 'Right.'

'OK then, got to go. Good to talk.' He held out his hand. 'See you around. Not at another funeral, I hope.'

Garvie watched him walk away. He phoned Smudge.

'Smudge, mate. You're friends with some of the drivers at One Shot, right?'

'Yeah.'

'Can you give them a bell and ask them a question?'

'What question?'

'Remember PJ telling us about Joel getting sacked.'

'Yeah. He was skimming.'

'But Joel blamed one of the other drivers. I'd like to know who.'

'All right. Give me five.'

Garvie stood at the side of Damon's grave. The freshly piled-up earth was tawny as oranges in the gathering shadows. Amy had added a bouquet; it lay against the small wooden cross as sad as an abandoned child's toy; there was no other decoration. Garvie stared for a moment, then turned and went down the path that led to the gate, and, as he left the cemetery, Smudge called back.

'Here's the news. And it's a weird one. Guy I talked to knew exactly who Joel pointed the finger at. Everyone was talking about it. And you'll never guess who it was.'

'I'm sure I won't.'

'Go on, have a go. Just for a laugh.'

'All right. I guess . . . PJ.'

There was a sad silence at the other end. 'You've gone and spoiled it. You're always doing that.'

'Sorry, Smudge. I'll make it up to you later.'

He looked at his watch. Seven thirty. He called Amy.

'Garvie,' she said, 'I can't do this any more. I'm sorry. I need some time not thinking about it.'

'Just a few quick questions then no more, I promise. Do you remember talking to PJ? He said he'd never heard of Damon. And when we left, do you remember what he said?'

There was a pause. She said, 'He said he was sorry he couldn't help us find him.'

'Yeah. But we never said we were looking for him, did we? So how did he know he was missing?'

She was silent.

'You said PJ was so loyal and trusting he never even asked what you had in the box. Suppose that was 'cause he already knew?'

She stayed silent.

'PJ told us he was stoned in the back room when we were at Red 'n' Black. Suppose he wasn't.'

'Garvie, what are you saying?'

'I'm saying we thought it was over, and it's not. Last question. This is important. Did you ever see Damon wear that HEAT beanie before?'

She thought about that. 'No. No, I never saw him wear it. That was the only time. Garvie—'

'Finished. But, listen now. Stay home tonight. Don't answer the door. Don't answer your phone, not even if it's me calling. Got it?'

'Yes, but—'

'Enough. I'll call you tomorrow.'

For a moment after he rang off he stood there motionless in the middle of Strawberry Hill shopping precinct. He called Abdul. No answer.

Sighing, he turned himself round and began to walk north, in the general direction of Tick Hill.

48

By the time he reached the track signposted *Childswell Garden Centre* it was nearly nine, and green and pink light was leaking fast from the deflated sky.

He was footsore but determined. He took out his phone and called his uncle.

'Garvie? Where are you? I've just had your mother on the phone, worried about you.'

Garvie turned away from the ring road onto the rutted earth road, and walked on between hawthorn hedges. 'Just out for a stroll,' he said. 'But I've got this question.'

'What question now?'

'The HEAT beanie. You found traces of Damon's DNA in it.'

'You know we did.'

'Anyone else's?'

His uncle hesitated, and Garvie heard noises of movement as if he was leaving one room and going into another. When he spoke again, his voice was lower and warier.

'Obviously this is confidential information, not the sort of thing I can talk about freely. But yes, we found traces of DNA from three other individuals, all unidentified.'

'Interesting. One of them will be Amy's. Damon gave it her to keep the rain off.'

'I see.'

'Another will be mine.'

'*What?*'

'Did I forget to mention it to Dowell? I had to put the hat on for a bit.'

'And what about the third one? Do you know that as well?'

'Not yet. But maybe soon.'

'Garvie—'

'Thanks then. Catch you later.'

He was properly in the countryside now. The ditches were full of nettles. The field on one side of the track was filled with shoulder-high rape seed, dried to a pink shade of beige. In the harvested meadow on the other an aftermath of bleached hay was strewn in small clumps like old wigs. Occasional noises broke through the stodgy hush: bird-gurgle in the hedgerows, the surf noise of traffic from the ring road and the occasional klaxon of a passing train. Far to his right were the houses of Tick Hill. To his left was the hospital where his mother worked, already silhouetted darkly against the sky. Ahead of him were more fields and woods.

He trudged on.

His phone rang. After a brief debate with himself, he answered it.

'Yeah?'

'Where are you, Garvie?'

'Here. Where are you? Eastwick Gardens?'

Singh hesitated. 'No. I'm still at work. Listen, I'm sorry I didn't have chance to talk to you at the funeral this afternoon. I think it would be a good idea if we talked.'

'I'm sure you do.' He said no more but walked on quietly listening to Singh breathing at the other end, low and regular.

'All right then,' Singh said at last. 'But, Garvie, you can call me at any time, about anything.'

'You're right, I can. In fact I got a question for you right now.'

'Yes?'

'Remind me. What's a smurf?'

There was a pause.

'A smurf's a runner,' Singh said slowly. 'A guy with dirty cash. Money from a criminal deal, say. He goes into a casino, buys gambling chips with it, plays the slots for an hour or two, and at the end of the evening changes the chips back for clean untraceable cash. Basic money-laundering.'

'It's what was going on at Imperium?'

'Among other things, yes. But why do you ask?'

'Doesn't matter. Catch you later.'

Singh was saying something else but Garvie put his phone back in his jacket pocket and walked on.

He was thinking of PJ. A peace-loving, weed-addled old hippy. An ex-Marine with traumatic combat experience. A quiet stealer of stuff at work, a persuasive blamer of other people. And for a while, the private chauffeur to the owner of Imperium casino.

Garvie thought about these things.

And then the most intriguing thing of all. Until his licence was withdrawn after a harassment charge, PJ had been official guardian to various young people, including, perhaps, Damon Walsh. Someone for Damon to trust.

Was it true? Had PJ been Damon's sponsor when he was on the Y.O.? Singh would be able to check. But Garvie wasn't inclined to ask him. He knew someone else he could ask.

He came to the end of the track and looked at the bungalow in front of him, a low, humped silhouette against the long, bland darkness of field behind. It was the only place out here so it must be the right one. Twilight had darkened to dusk; it was nearly night. Resting at the gate for a moment, Garvie looked back towards the city heaped up in the darkness like a smouldering pile of sparks. He listened to the breeze and insect-whine of traffic on the ring road below, and thought how the last thing Damon had listened to, up there on the multistorey roof, was breeze and distant traffic.

He turned and went across the lawn past a barbecue cabin and stack of weight-lifting kit to the door.

It was opened by a woman with a child on her hip, and she looked at Garvie, surprised, and the child on her hip stared at him too with the same surprise, and he nodded, to both of them, and said politely, 'Have I got the right place for Paul Tanner?'

'Yes.'

'Can I talk to him?'

'He's not here.'

'Will he be back soon?'

She looked past him, towards the track. 'Any minute now. I'm taking the kids to my mother's and I'm waiting for the car so I can get off.' Garvie saw bags in the hall behind her. Children's cries came from a room beyond. 'What's it about?' she asked.

'Kid called Damon. Just a quick question.'

She nodded. 'Paul's very upset about him. He went to his funeral today. He's angry with the police. He thinks they let Damon down.'

She looked at her watch and sighed, and the child sighed too, and Garvie felt he ought to sigh as well, just to keep his end up. From a room at the end of the hall another child began to scream, and, apologizing, she retreated, leaving Garvie alone for a moment at the door.

He stood there, thinking uncomfortably about PJ. He remembered his lantern jaw and tombstone teeth, his alarming smile, his frayed ponytail and big, knuckly hands. He remembered him twisting the fox's neck in the woods, the look on his face as he did it.

The child's crying continued. Garvie gazed down the hall littered with toys and discarded children's shoes. There were children's paintings Blu-tacked to the walls, and a bookcase with picture books on the shelves and a family photograph on top, and at the far end, just inside the kitchen door, an overflowing laundry basket. He frowned.

Slowly, not taking his eyes off it, he went down the hall and cautiously lifted the basket lid; and there lying on the top of the other laundry was a maroon hoodie.

His brain shifted a gear.

He saw three things very quickly one after another. Tanner's face in the photograph with his moustache and short cropped black hair – matching the Pirrip Street kid's description. The barbells he'd seen in the garden outside – equipment of a powerful man. Tanner helping out on the Y.O. – putting an arm round the young offenders. Three images falling into a row like cherries or bells in a fruit machine.

When Tanner's wife reappeared he was back at the front door.

'I'm sorry he's not here yet,' she said. 'I don't know what's keeping him.'

'Maybe he's popped into the casino,' Garvie said, keeping his eyes on her.

'More than likely,' she said. 'He's there most days. Have you seen him down there?'

'Yeah. Playing the slots.'

'Yeah, that's what he does.'

'Wearing that HEAT beanie of his.'

'His lucky hat, he says.' For a second she smiled

and showed her gums. 'He lost it, though. Just a couple of weeks back.'

Garvie nodded. 'Interesting,' he said. 'Do you know what?' he said, 'I probably don't need to talk to him any more, so—'

'Hang on,' she said. 'Here he is now.'

Headlights swivelled in front of the bungalow, and the shape of a Nissan Primera came jolting onto the gravel turnaround, and Paul Tanner got out and stood there in silhouette staring up at Garvie.

He rolled his shoulders a little, and came up the path.

49

Before Garvie could say anything Tanner's wife called to him, 'Lad here wants to talk to you about Damon. I was just saying you'll have been at the casino.'

Paul Tanner stood there, looking at Garvie. Garvie noticed things about him, how tall he was, slim like Damon but more powerfully built, pale with dark stubble – like Joel – on his jaw and upper lip.

'I can come back if you like,' Garvie said.

Tanner looked at him. 'No time like the present.'

He ushered Garvie down the hallway to a room at the back. It had glass-panelled French windows with views of the garden and countryside beyond, pitch-dark now. Toys of various kinds filled bright plastic cartons along the walls. There was an ironing board with a pile of clothes on it.

Garvie sat in a low easy chair and Tanner sat on a hard chair opposite. Tanner's wife put her head round to say she was leaving.

Tanner nodded. 'Stay out of trouble,' he said, and she blew him a kiss.

Then there was only the slam of the front door

and the grumble of car noise receding down the track before rural silence settled in.

Tanner looked at his watch. 'How long's this going to take?' he said.

Garvie watched him for a moment. 'How long will it take you to work out how dangerous I am?'

Tanner laughed. 'You're just a kid. You're not dangerous.'

Garvie ignored him. 'I think it'll be quick,' he said. 'Quick chat about Joel. How you killed him. After that, Damon. How you killed him too.'

There was a slow beat of silence in the room. Tanner screwed up his face, blew out his cheeks. He said, 'You must be out of your mind.'

'Let's pretend I'm not. It'll save time. So. You met Joel at the Ballyhoo that night, didn't you, and he lost it 'cause you hadn't brought the money.'

'I have literally no idea what you're talking about.'

'You're a smurf. Play the slots at Imperium every night, wearing your lucky HEAT beanie, laundering the Winders' dirty money. Problem was, when Joel started working there he must have recognized you from the Y.O. Hadn't trusted you then, didn't trust you now. So he did a bit of snooping in Accounts. And when he was sure, he named his price for looking the other way.'

Tanner gave a brief laugh, shook his head. 'Nonsense.'

'It was, yeah. And the next bit of nonsense was this. You didn't pay. Result: he laid into you outside the casino. Result: he got sacked. Result of that: Mr Angry. Mr Angry told you to meet him in Market Square. Nice quiet, public place where you could hand over the cash. The riot changed all that, didn't it? What happened? Did he go for you again? Things get out of hand in that alley? Fortunately, you'd taken protection.'

'All nonsense.'

'Yeah. Starring Damon, King of Nonsense. Flaky boy floating by, doing what he does best, getting mixed up in what he shouldn't. Perfect timing with all those police about, arresting everyone, and you with a murder weapon in your hand. Simple: you wrap it up in your beanie and hand it over, and stroll off without a care in the world.'

Tanner laughed. 'Why would he take it off me?'

''Cause he trusted you. 'Cause you needed him to. 'Cause on the Y.O. you were his mentor, weren't you, his hand-round-the-shoulder man, the man he looked up to, trusted, would have done anything for. His *soul mate.*'

There was a silence then. A flicker of something in Tanner's face.

Garvie said, 'Takes less than an instant to make up your mind to do something for someone you love, someone you trust. Damon took the gun from you, no questions asked. Just like Amy took it from him an hour later. Shows they're a thousand per cent better than you are.'

Tanner shook his head. But his eyes were hard.

Garvie said, 'It went wrong straightaway, though, didn't it? You hadn't expected Damon to pass the gun on to Amy, and by the time you caught up with him it was done. Suddenly, things were out of your control. You tried to get it back that night, in the woods, but you ran into Rex and Amy got away. You tried again at Red 'n' Black. And then in Town Road when you attacked Amy to get Joel's Imperium records.'

Tanner stood up. 'All right. You've had your say. Now you can fuck off.'

'Sure?'

'I told you. You're not dangerous at all. You've got nothing.'

Garvie considered this. He said, 'Couldn't find the beanie in the outhouse, could you? My mate found it. It's got your DNA on it. There's a croupier at Imperium will testify you were the man fighting with Joel, and a smart little kid in Pirrip Street who'll recognize you as the frightening guy Damon left a note for. There's a maroon hoodie out there in your laundry basket you wore when you pretended to be Damon picking up the phone in town, trying to throw Singh off the scent. Oh, and by the way, there's the CCTV footage from the roof of the multistorey.'

There was a pause.

Tanner shook his head. 'No camera,' he said.

'Not covering the roof where Damon was,' Garvie said. 'But round the other side, where that other roof door is. Oh, did you miss it?'

Tanner's face changed now, darkened.

'Thing is,' Garvie went on, 'I got to thinking of my last conversation with Damon, just a few minutes before he died. He said something odd at the end. "Here it comes." I thought he was talking about what he was going to do. But I think I misheard. What he said was: "Here *he* comes." He'd caught sight of you, coming across the multistorey roof towards him.'

Tanner stared at him for a long moment. He said quietly, 'You're not dangerous. You're stupid.'

Garvie shook his head. 'I'm *angry*.'

Tanner didn't take his eyes off him or change expression. 'Give me your phone.'

Garvie hesitated, then took it out and handed it to him.

Tanner scrolled through the call log, dropped it on the floor and trod on it. 'Who knows you're here?' he asked.

'Oh, lots of people. My mother, for instance. Damon's girlfriend, and her mother. Livia Drusilla at Imperium, her boyfriend, dozens of others, my mate Smudge, the man at the corner shop, why not. Oh, and the police of course. They'll be here any second. What do you think? Do I look like I'm good with people?'

Tanner said nothing. Turning, he walked out of the room and locked the door behind him.

At once Garvie got up and tried the French windows. They were locked. The other windows were locked too, and all the keys had been removed and put away somewhere, and after a few moments going round the room searching he went to the door and listened. Faintly, he heard the sound of Tanner speaking to someone on his phone. He went back to his chair and waited.

Several minutes went by. Tanner returned.

'I told work I'm going to be a bit late.'

He was wearing thicker boots, steel-capped, and gloves, and he stood there looking at Garvie.

He said, 'You think you're smart, but I'm smarter than you.'

'And much more violent, of course,' Garvie said. 'Been working out with those barbells. The way you came after us in Red 'n' Black. The way you attacked Amy. The way you pushed Damon off the roof.'

'I didn't push him,' Tanner said. 'He jumped. He couldn't face me.' He was breathing heavily now. 'Thing is,' he said, 'I didn't dislike Damon. He just wasn't smart enough to look after himself. And you know what? You're the same.'

'That's what they call in maths a false proposition.'

'No one knows you're here. My wife's got a terrible memory. You just got yourself into trouble.'

'One of us did for sure,' Garvie said. 'But not me.'

There was a sudden loud banging on the door at the front of the bungalow, and Singh's voice called out, 'Garvie!'

Tanner looked at him, bewildered, and Garvie took out a phone from his jacket pocket and showed it to him. 'Always check for the second phone,' he said. 'Do you want to have that conversation about stupidity now?'

Tanner lost it. He lunged for him, but Garvie got himself on the other side of the ironing board.

There was the sound of splintering wood down the hall.

''Cause you're so smart,' Garvie said, 'you'll know that the only result of chasing me round the ironing board is to give Singh enough time to get in here and make the arrest.'

Tanner shifted suddenly, and Garvie went the other way.

'Best thing you can do is get out of it, fast as you can. The French windows are locked, but the key's hidden under the plant pot on the windowsill over there. It's pitch-dark outside, and it's not far to the woods across the field, so there's a reasonable chance you could get there before Singh can catch up with you.'

Tanner grabbed hold of the ironing board, and Garvie grabbed hold of the other side of it.

'Course,' he said, 'it might be you're not so smart after all.'

Tanner's face twisted until it was unrecognizable. There was another crash from the front of the building, and staggering footsteps in the hall, and he spun away towards the windowsill.

By the time Singh had forced his way through the back-room door, Tanner had disappeared into the darkness of the garden outside. Singh ran panting over to Garvie, who stood by the French windows.

'Are you all right?'

'He broke my second-best phone,' Garvie said. 'I hope he falls and twists his ankle really badly.'

Singh moved towards the open French windows. 'Stay here.'

'Wait,' Garvie said, peering out into the darkness. 'Something's wrong.'

'What?'

'If he was making for the woods he would have gone *that* way.'

He found a light switch on the wall on the other side of the windows and the bungalow garden was instantly flooded with white light. Tanner stepped out from behind a water butt unwrapping something.

And faced them with a gun in his hand.

Singh shouted out, but Tanner sneered and turned away and took aim at Garvie.

'You fucking smart-arse,' he said in a hiss.

He fired.

It made a deafening noise like a slap on the ear with an agonizing echo and aftermath of crashing arms and legs as Singh flew sideways, in front of Garvie, and smashed into the ironing board.

A spray of blood spritzed across Garvie's shirt.

Clothes fell onto Singh's face, where he lay still.

Now there was only Tanner and Garvie.

They faced each other, the boy inside the window, the man in the garden outside pointing the gun towards him, suspended together in the moment before whatever moment was about to happen.

Then there was a small intrusion of movement in the opposite corner of the garden, and Dowell appeared, gun first.

'Throw it down,' he said to Tanner as he edged forward. He held his gun in front of him.

Tanner hesitated only an instant before spinning to face him, and Dowell came to a halt, and they stood there pointing their guns at each other, watched by Garvie.

'Gun down,' Dowell said softly in his Scots growl. 'Now.'

Tanner said nothing. It looked like he was shaking too badly to speak. All his composure was gone – his face was shockingly pale, a vein sticking out at the side of his head. But he made no move to give up his gun.

They stared at each other intently.

Dowell took another cautious step forward and Tanner jerked up his gun to point it at his face, and Dowell stopped again.

There was a moment of silence, then another moment.

Slowly Dowell bent down and placed his own gun on the grass.

'There,' he said quietly. 'Now give me your gun.'

Tanner said nothing. Jerked a little. Held the gun as steady as he could, pointing it at Dowell.

Dowell took a step towards him. 'I'm going to come over to you now,' he said, not moving his eyes from Tanner's, 'nice and slow, and you're going to give me the gun, and no one's going to get hurt.'

Tanner worked his mouth. His lips moved.

'Bob,' he croaked. 'Get back.'

Dowell came on slowly. One step. Then another.

'Back,' Tanner said more loudly.

'Easy,' Dowell said. 'Easy. No one gets hurt here.'

He was only a pace or two in front of Tanner now; he could have reached out and snatched the gun, but he took another step instead, and stood there with his chest against the muzzle of Tanner's gun, holding out his good hand. And as he lowered his gun Tanner began to cry.

'Thank you,' Dowell said softly.

Then something went wrong. It happened in a jerk, like a glitch in a video. Dowell shouted, 'No!' The gun was in Dowell's hand, then Tanner was grabbing at it, it squirmed up between them like a piece of wet soap and there was a shot, then another, and they fell squashed together onto the lawn, and struggled there a moment until Tanner stopped moving.

Dowell got to his feet, moving sluggishly as if underwater, already bleeding from a wound in his arm, and began to talk into a microphone on his collar. His eyes, full of pain and hostility, met Garvie's as he talked.

Garvie crouched by Singh who lay in the complicated mess of the ironing board, very still. His lips were slightly open, eyes closed. His uniform trousers were wet with blood from thigh to ankle. As Garvie watched, the eyelids fluttered once and he looked up, and when he tightened his grip Garvie realized that he was holding the policeman's hand.

Singh winced, moved his eyes slightly.

Garvie said, 'What the hell did you do that for? You could have been killed.'

Singh gave a faint smile. 'I promised your mother,' he whispered.

'Sounds like a strategic error to me.'

'We are our errors,' Singh said quietly and fainted again.

Dowell was talking outside, radio crackling. Sirens sounded, faraway. Garvie continued to hold Singh's hand.

50

In the living room of number 12 Eastwick Gardens Uncle Len put down the newspaper. On the front page was a picture of Detective Inspector Bob Dowell wearing two slings and a stiff-eyed expression. It was the second time in a month Dowell had received a wound in the line of duty, but it was his privilege, he said in an uplifting commentary, to serve the city in safeguarding it from violent criminals such as Paul Tanner, who had suffered a fatal wound as he resisted arrest.

It was the fifth day since Tanner's death and the papers had not yet tired of it.

'The situation was messy, I agree,' Singh said to Uncle Len, from where he lay on the sofa, leg up, 'but Dowell took great personal risk. He showed remarkable bravery. If he hadn't tackled Tanner it's probable the man would have done worse, and perhaps got away. He was desperate. He knew he was looking at a very severe sentence.'

'You took an extraordinary risk yourself,' Uncle Len said. 'You weren't even armed. You could have come away with much more than a flesh wound.' He turned to Garvie, sitting on the carpet with his back against the wall, and considered him for a while. 'And what sort of risk did you take?' he asked his nephew. 'Going on your own to his house.'

'Me? No risk at all. The man was a dunce.'

Garvie's mother said, 'Your smart-alec rudeness must have made him stupid.'

'I cannot agree with Garvie about the risk,' Singh said. 'But I will say this. It is because of Garvie that the truth about Tanner came out. Tanner had hidden himself well. He even fooled me into thinking he was Damon with that business of the phone being picked up from outside the station. And as for that final evening, Garvie texted me twice, once when he found the maroon hoodie, and again when Tanner left the room. And kept Tanner talking long enough for me to get there. I think we must acknowledge these things.'

Uncle Len said, 'What Garvie has to acknowledge is that you saved his life, Raminder.'

'Tanner wasn't a very good shot,' Garvie said. 'I expect he would have missed me altogether and no one need've got hurt.'

He avoided their looks.

Uncle Len said, 'What happens now, Raminder?'

Singh wasn't sure what posthumous verdicts would be handed down on Tanner. CCTV footage from the camera on the building adjacent to the multistorey had shown him arriving on the roof a few minutes before Damon fell to his death. Further forensic tests on the beanie revealed that the unidentified DNA on the HEAT beanie was indeed Tanner's. Livia Drusilla's testimony would be taken into account. So too Garvie's. Best of all, Garvie had recorded his conversation with Tanner on his second phone. But the investigations into the deaths of Watkins and Damon would now feed into the more wide-ranging investigation into the Winders' money-laundering at Imperium. It appeared already that Tanner had links to a criminal network who evidently had used him in their efforts to clean their dirty money.

'It will be a slow process,' Singh said. 'I'm not directly involved. Also I am invalided for the next month. And anyway,' he added, 'I am still facing a potential action for negligence over the failure to prevent the death of Damon Walsh.'

'What about that fellow PJ?'

One Shot had looked again into the pilfering and had belatedly concluded that PJ was responsible. But the man had disappeared. The police had visited PJ's garage in the woods and had found it boarded up.

'He's gone,' Singh said. 'I don't know where. Garvie?'

'Looking for himself, I expect. He's a bit of a lost child.'

They exchanged looks among themselves. Garvie's mother consulted her watch, and Singh and Uncle Len got to their feet. They were going to meet Aunt Maxie at a restaurant in Market Square. As Singh limped past Garvie on his crutches, Garvie held out his hand and Singh gripped it with his own, then went on.

After they had gone out, Garvie's mother stayed behind a moment, and exchanged a long look with her son.

'What?'

'At least you texted him,' she said.

Garvie shrugged. 'Tanner left me on my own, there was nothing else to do. I hate being bored.'

'I know that. I also know you'd rather step on a tack than admit to being in need of Raminder's help.'

'Yeah, well. On balance I thought I'd risk asking him anyway.'

She nodded.

'You look good, by the way,' he said.

She was wearing a blue short-sleeved wrap dress with red floral print design.

'It's a nice place we're going,' she said.

They were silent for a moment.

Garvie said, 'You know what? You can tell him to bring his toothbrush over if he wants.'

'Yes,' she said. 'I can. But I wasn't going to until you said it.'

'I'm saying it now.'

'Do you mean it?'

'Let's pretend I do; it'll save time. Anyway,' he added, 'I've been to his place. It's a dump. He'll be better off here.'

At the door she turned back. 'What are you doing tonight? Are you going out?'

He shrugged. 'Maybe. Got asked. Just thinking about it.'

'OK. See you later.'

'Yeah. Be good.'

He stayed where he was for half an hour or so staring at the carpet. Then he got up and went to look for his jacket.

51

The voice speaking out of the intercom said, 'Who is it?'

'Smith,' he said, and waited.

He realized, as the big wooden gates swung sedately apart, that he'd only ever been through them before in a van with Smudge. Those days seemed far off now. The driveway opened up in front of him, gracefully curved and smoothly lit, and he walked up it towards the house standing above, solid and confident on its rise against a tastefully twilit sky.

The door was opened by a bald, narrow man wearing a short red towelling dressing gown and flip-flops.

'Hello!' he said. 'You're Smith then.'

His teeth were too large for his mouth and when he smiled he seemed to be about to spill them down his front.

'Yeah.'

'Smith, the maths genius.' He continued to smile. It seemed to power his tufts of faded ginger hair which rose slightly as he spoke.

Garvie said, 'Your ex-wife'll remember me as the trespasser in her little art gallery.'

'Ah. You've worked out who I am.'

'It's not hard. You were described to me as a nut.'

Professor Roecastle's smile threatened to burst out of his mouth altogether. 'Excellent,' he said. 'Some people think logic's the thing but I prefer laughter and rudeness. You've left school, I hear. Why's that?'

'First reason is, I didn't get the grades to stay on. Second is, I didn't want to stay on.'

'Excellent reasons, both of them. You were up here doing the fence, I think?'

'Yeah.'

'Excellent thing, fencing. I bet you're pretty good at it.'

Amy came at speed into the hall behind her father and began to manoeuvre him out of the way.

'You said you'd change, Dad. Look at you.'

'Who cares about knees? I don't. I bet Smith doesn't.'

'I can live with your knees,' Garvie said. 'It's your smile that's so alarming.'

Professor Roecastle threw back his head and laughed hard at the innocent ceiling. 'He's as appalling as your mother told me,' he said, and went at last up the stairs to get dressed.

Garvie had remained all this time on the doorstep. He thought to himself, as before, that this was not his world, nor his people, nor his art, gabled house or tastefully twilit sky.

Not his Amy either.

She stood by the plinth of a late LeClerk looking

at him shyly. She was wearing blue jeans and the black vest he'd first seen in the photograph before he met her, and she'd put her hair up, leaving her shoulders and neck exposed, and for a moment he was hit all over again by her beauty.

'Hey, Sherlock,' she said softly.

'Hey.'

'Sorry about Dad.'

'Thought he didn't live with you.'

'He doesn't.'

'So what's he doing here in his dressing gown?'

'We just don't know. He arrived with a suitcase this morning, on his way to Perm in the Urals.'

'Course. Should have worked that out.'

They looked at each for a while.

'Aren't you going to come in?'

'Actually, I don't know what I'm doing here.'

'They want to thank you.'

'Can't they send me a card or something?'

But he stepped into the hall as Dr Roecastle appeared from the living room, a glass of white wine in her hand.

'So good of you to come,' she said. 'Please. This way. My . . . Professor Roecastle will be down in a minute. Dressed, I hope.'

They went into the living room and sat on different sofas, and Dr Roecastle put a glass of orange juice in Garvie's hand, and they all looked about them in different directions. Garvie remembered the way Dr Roecastle had sat there before, weeping, frightened, the way she had fixed him with her wet angry eyes. Now she was cool and brisk but strangely ill at ease. Soon Professor Roecastle reappeared, wearing a different dressing gown.

'Don't you want a beer?' he said to Garvie.

'I'm all right.'

'How about a smoke? An addict like you might develop a twitch.'

'I'll try to keep my shit together.'

No one seemed inclined to say anything useful. Garvie drained his glass.

'Well,' he said, getting to his feet, 'thanks for the orange juice.'

'Sit down, you fool,' Professor Roecastle said. 'Listen. I know my . . . Dr Roecastle here has had a tough time of it recently, and Amy too; it's been pretty extraordinary however you compute it, and I know you're just about the most difficult boy my . . . Dr Roecastle has had to deal with, although actually, that other one, the young man who died, sounds like a nightmare too, and before that there were some real—'

'For God's sake,' Amy said.

Dr Roecastle said abruptly to Garvie, 'I would like to apologize to you.' It sounded like the introduction to a much longer speech but, having said it, she fell silent.

'None of us knows how to behave,' Professor Roecastle said, smiling as if it was all a joke. 'That's the trouble. We're trying to thank you for what you did. Not that we like the way you did it. But frankly, Amy had got herself into danger, and no parent likes that, so we're grateful, very, very grateful, to you for helping her, and I for one believe your help was sincerely meant and not just, you know, arsing around, like my . . . like Dr Roecastle here thinks.' He cleared his throat nervously and put his teeth away for a moment. 'We were wondering if you could use some extra cash.'

Garvie stood up and looked at them all. 'My mother works hard all hours at the hospital and she's still waiting on a promotion that was promised months ago, and if she got it now it would be because it's well-deserved, not because it's a gift.'

Professor Roecastle nodded. 'Point taken. Dr Roecastle, take note. Well, good luck with the fencing.'

'Thanks.'

He went with Garvie as far as the living-room door. He had an envelope in his hand, Garvie noticed. 'By the way,' he said, 'I was meaning to have a little chat before you go about proofs for limits of sequences.'

'Why?'

'Well, they're interesting things. I'm a little surprised, that's all, that you'd already encountered them at school. I mean, usually that sort of thing is introduced at university, sometimes not until post-graduate study.'

Garvie said nothing.

He fixed Garvie with a stare almost as alarming as his smile. 'I saw Amy's book. No workings. Just the answer. That's interesting too.'

'Didn't have much time.'

'Sort of thing that's hard to do in your head, I'd have thought.'

'You'd know. You're the maths genius.'

Professor Roecastle nodded thoughtfully. 'Yes. Yes, I am. They even named a theorem after me, the fools. But what if ε were $\frac{1}{5000}$ and the common ratio were $\frac{1}{3}$,' he said. 'I wonder if I could work out what N would be then, in my head.'

Garvie stared at him evenly. 'Eight,' he said after a moment.

'Or $\frac{1}{2}$?'

'Thirteen.'

'Why?'

'Because the thirteenth term is $\frac{1}{8192}$.'

'And what else?'

Garvie hesitated. 'I don't know.'

'No, of course not. You wouldn't. You'd never even heard of this stuff, let alone been taught it. Yes, it's all very interesting.' His smile returned, all over his face. 'So. You're not going back to school.'

'Told you. Didn't get the grades.'

'That's right. Never mind, fencing's a great thing. As I say, you're probably pretty good at it. Well, anyway. Off you go then. Oh, one last thing.'

He held out the envelope.

Garvie looked at it. 'I told you already.'

'Don't worry, it's not money. Ever heard of the National Mathematics Foundation?'

'No.'

'Government thing. They're a bit dull, but well-meaning. Anyway, I seem to be their president. They give out bursaries – grants – for bright kids to study maths at a higher level. You know, special cases.'

'I just told you—'

'Of course. I only mention it in case for some reason the fencing doesn't work out. There's a letter in there you can give to the appropriate person at your school. At Marsh, that's Olivia.'

'Olivia?'

'You know her as Miss Perkins. She's special liaison with our committee. One of the best maths brains in schools education. She thinks you're a nightmare. I expect you are. But if you give her that letter, she'll make sure you get your place in the sixth form. The choice is entirely yours. You can throw the letter away if you feel like it. After all, there's nothing wrong with fencing. Perhaps it's your fate. Goodbye.'

Garvie was halfway down the drive before Amy caught up with him. She took hold of him and kissed him hard, her hands in his hair, her perfume all round him, and backed off a little, and they stood looking at each other in the moonlight.

'I'm sorry,' she said.

'Me too.'

'It was when they told me at the hospital that—'

'I know.'

'It all came clear then. How I felt.'

'Yeah.'

'I loved him, Garvie. I think I still do.'

'No need to go on.'

'What are you going to do now?'

'I'm thinking quite seriously of having a cigarette.'

'I mean, you know, the rest of your life.'

He shrugged. 'What about you?'

'Didn't I say? I'm going to San Francisco with my dad. He's doing research there after Perm. Just for a few months at first. But if I like it maybe I'll go to school there.'

He nodded and smiled.

'What?'

'Those American boys, they're going to have to watch out. You're a bit unpredictable.'

'That's me.' Her eyes shone as she smiled. 'Hey,' she said softly.

'What?'

'I'm going to miss you.'

'Good.'

He turned then before she could see the wetness on his cheek, and walked back down the drive. The gates were already open. He raised a hand without looking back, and then he was gone into the darkness of the lane beyond, and she turned and went back to the house.

*

He walked across the turnaround, past the bus shelter where he had hidden, through the unmoving shadows of the trees, onto the lane. It wasn't his world, nor would it ever be, and he was glad. He lit up, and began to walk down the hill towards the city.

After a while he remembered the envelope. Taking it out of his pocket, he was on the point of lobbing it over a fence into someone's garden when he stopped himself. He thought of people doing things for those they loved: Damon for Tanner, Amy for Damon. That saying of his mother's came into his head: *everyone needs to be given something once in a while*. He thought of the kid in Pirrip Street with the middle-aged man's face and an utter determination not to be taken advantage of, and he put the envelope back in his pocket and walked on.

Fencing wasn't to be his fate. He thought to himself that maybe he wouldn't bother with fate much at all.

When he was halfway down Battery Hill he got a call from Smudge asking him if he was coming out.

'Where to? Old Ditch Road?' He thought of the kiddies' playground, the cramped roundabout, the torture of the tiny swings. The drizzle.

'What?' Smudge said. 'The playground? Grow up, mate. No, it's like a bit of a celebration at ours.'

'What celebration?'

'Well, it's hard to say. I don't like to come out

with it all at once.' Garvie could hear the embarrassment in Smudge's voice. 'It's my brother, right? He's, well . . . he's lost his head and taken me on. You know, full-time. In the business. A proper apprenticeship like. With training and all that.'

'Course he has,' Garvie said. 'You're a fencing genius.'

'Yeah, well, you know, some people just take to it, I suppose. Best thing is, looks like I might be getting a van out of it.'

'Smudge,' Garvie said. 'That'll be one lucky van.'

'Thing is,' Smudge went on, 'some of the boys are coming round, you know, just to have a few drinks.'

'I'm on my way.'

'You'll come? My brother'll be there, though. I know you didn't hit it off.'

'No problem.'

'Really?'

'For you, mate, anything.'

He was smiling as he put his phone back in his pocket, zipped up his jacket, and walked on in darkness down the hill.

Acknowledgements

I'm enormously grateful for the help I received in writing this book. My editors at DFB – David Fickling, Bella Pearson and Anthony Hinton – provided bumper amounts of both criticism and encouragement through several drafts; and Christiane Steen at Rowohlt provided further decisive and valuable comments. Linda Sargent, DFB's outside reader, pointed out troublesome areas with her usual acuity and tact. Eleri Mason ripped the arse out of the first hundred pages of a late draft without any tact whatsoever, and more power to her. Alex Williams provided much-needed assistance on brands. Sue Cook's copyedit and Julia Bruce's proofread, as always, saved me embarrassment. Sam Hoggard checked the maths. Alison Gadsby masterminded the cover design supplied by Alice Todd. My thanks to all.

The point, as ever, is to make the book better, and I remain deeply grateful for all these interventions.

My friend Joe Nicholas died during the book's composition, and, in affectionate memory of our many conversations at that time, I dedicate it to Joe, and to my two children.